Frank Greene Bates

Rhode Island and the Formation of the Union

Frank Greene Bates

Rhode Island and the Formation of the Union

ISBN/EAN: 9783337378707

Printed in Europe, USA, Canada, Australia, Japan

Cover: Foto ©Andreas Hilbeck / pixelio.de

More available books at **www.hansebooks.com**

RHODE ISLAND

AND

THE FORMATION OF THE UNION

BY

FRANK GREENE BATES

Sometime Fellow in American History
Assistant Professor of History and Political Science, Alfred University

SUBMITTED IN PARTIAL FULFILMENT OF THE REQUIREMENTS
FOR THE DEGREE OF DOCTOR OF PHILOSOPHY
IN THE
FACULTY OF POLITICAL SCIENCE
COLUMBIA UNIVERSITY

New York
1898

PREFACE

THIS dissertation embodies the results of investigations begun in the American History Seminary of Cornell University, under the guidance of Professor Moses Coit Tyler, and completed in the School of Political Science of Columbia University, under Professor Herbert L. Osgood. The work was undertaken in order to ascertain the facts of Rhode Island's action from 1765 to 1790, and, if possible, to explain the fact that Rhode Island so long delayed her ratification of the Federal Constitution. The subject was suggested by reading an address by Mr. Justice Horatio Rogers of the Supreme Bench of Rhode Island, on "Rhode Island and the Federal Constitution."

The materials for such a study are in some directions scanty. The printed sources used were largely found in the libraries of Cornell and Columbia Universities. The manuscript sources were found in the archives of the State of Rhode Island, preserved in the State House at Providence, and in the collection of the Rhode Island Historical Society. Volumes of early laws were consulted at the Lenox Library, New York City. Newspaper files which were of constant assistance were found at the cabinet of the Rhode Island Historical Society, and at the rooms of the American Antiquarian Society, Worcester, Mass. Citations have been made of all authorities employed. Those to manuscripts are frequently unsatisfactory, as many, especially in the state archives, are imperfectly paged.

Many thanks are due to Professor Moses Coit Tyler for

123]

the careful training in historical method to which is due any scientific worth which this study may possess, and to Professor Herbert L. Osgood for advice and suggestions, and for assistance in reading manuscript and proof.

Acknowledgment should be made to Mr. Wilberforce Eames, Librarian of Lenox Library, New York; the Hon. Amos Perry, Secretary of the Rhode Island Historical Society; the Hon. Charles P. Bennett, Secretary of State of Rhode Island; Mr. E. M. Barton, Secretary of the American Antiquarian Society, and the officials of the libraries of Cornell and Columbia universities for their courtesy in giving access to the collections in their charge; also to Mr. Justice Horatio Rogers for suggestions given personally and in his printed address.

FRANK GREENE BATES.

SUMMIT, R. I., *July 12, 1898.*

CONTENTS

CHAPTER III

CHAPTER IV

CHAPTER V

Convention—Rhode Island refuses to appoint Delegates—
Newspaper Comments—Rhode Island in Disgrace—Work of
Convention reported to States—Eleven States Ratify—Con-
stitution referred to Freemen—Refusal to call a Convention
—Position of Parties—Anti-Federal Victory—Federalist
Rejoicing—Independence Day at Providence—Failure to
call Convention—Rhode Island alone—Tariff Debates affect
Rhode Island—Rhode Island lays a Tariff—Congress de-
bates Rhode Island Question—Anti-Federalists weaken—
Revenue Laws Suspended—Lack of Federalist Leaders—
North Carolina Ratifies—Situation grows Critical—Conven-
tion called—Struggle in Towns—First Session of Convention
—State election Anti-Federal—Hints of Coercion—Debates
in Congress—New Issues in Congress—Non-Intercourse
Threatened—Instructions of Towns—Second Session of Convention—Adoption—Bill of Rights, and Amendments Proposed—Rhode Island enters the Union.

CHAPTER VI

Bill of Rights Proposed—Amendments Proposed—Compar-
ison of Amendments of Different States—Amendments Pro-
posed by Virginia, North Carolina, and Rhode Island—
Amendments Proposed by New York and Rhode Island—
Amendments Proposed by Rhode Island Alone—Conclusions
from Amendments—Review of Colony's Growth—Formation
of Traits of Character—Colony's action in War—Causes of
Defection in 1781—Economic Conditions lead to Paper
Money—Causes of Opposition to Constitution—Coercion
Threatened—General Conclusions.

CHAPTER I

THE course pursued by the State of Rhode Island at the time of the formation of the Federal Union forms a distinct episode in the history of America. The fact that the people of a state should adhere tenaciously to their own opinions to the point of denying to themselves all participation in the framing of the constitution, and of refusing for a considerable period of time to accept the work of their neighbors, indicates that behind it all must have been most powerful and far-reaching causes. An historic view of the circumstances attending Rhode Island's adoption of the constitution, together with an examination of the causes of this event, is the purpose of this study. In a study of causes it is sometimes possible to distinguish between those immediate and those more remote. The line of demarkation, often difficult to determine, has been drawn in this instance at the point where Rhode Island first united with the other colonies in opposition to the British ministry. The immediate causes are found in the circumstances attending the Revolution, and in a train of events leading down to the Federal Convention. Among the remoter causes may be included a wide range of facts and tendencies which have gone to shape the political system, and the character of the people of Rhode Island.

The settlers of the four towns afterwards united as the colony of Rhode Island were refugees. Like the settlers of

Massachusetts and Connecticut, they had left the mother country to seek a home where they might be free from the restraints of the Acts of Uniformity. But the settlements on the shore of Massachusetts Bay did not prove to be a sanctuary for freedom of conscience, but rather a nursery for the particular form of belief held by the Puritan magistrates. The right of becoming a freeman was made dependent on membership in one of the churches. It was to this colony that Roger Williams came in February, 1631. Soon after his arrival the elders and magistrates of Boston, seeking to dictate to the church at Salem over which Williams had been settled as assistant pastor, met with stout resistance. In the controversy that followed, Williams asserted the doctrine of liberty of conscience. The result was a decree of banishment, on the charge that he had "broached * * divers new and dangerous opinions against the authority of magistrates; as also writ letters of defamation both of the magistrates and churches here, and that before any conviction, and yet maintaineth the same without any retraction."[1] After many weeks of wandering in the wilderness, and a brief stay at Seekonk, Williams with a few companions located at Moshassuck, which they named Providence.

The two settlements made on the island of Aquidneck in like manner owed their origin to the religious purgings of Massachusetts. These settlers were among the minority in the Antinomian controversy which raged in 1636 and 1637 Ten of the nineteen settlers, among them their leader Coddington, suffered banishment for their opinions. Seeking a place to found a colony where they might worship as they pleased, they decided to settle within Narragansett Bay. The prestige of Anne Hutchinson, and the asylum afforded in the new settlement, drew together there many of heterodox opinions.

[1] *Massachusetts Colonial Records*, i, 160.

A third asylum was that founded at Shawomet by Samuel Gorton. The spirit that had thrust out Williams and Mrs. Hutchinson could not tolerate the mystical views of Gorton, a bold and impolitic asserter of his opinions. At Aquidneck, where he stopped after his banishment from Plymouth, he found a home for but a brief season, but his restless soul could find no permanent abode there, and after a brief sojourn at Providence and at Pawtuxet, where his conduct provoked discord, he settled at Shawomet, afterwards called Warwick.

The people of these settlements, exiled from their fellow-countrymen, naturally would cultivate relations with their persecutors only in the direst necessity. Had they made the attempt they would have met with no response. They stood for soul liberty. That fact alone was enough to separate them from their neighbors. An early proof of the completeness of this separation is found in the instruction to the governor of Rhode Island to "treat with the governor of the Dutch to supply us with necessaries, and to take of our commodities at such rates as may be suitable."[1]

When rumors of Indian war led the people of Aquidneck to apply to Plymouth for a supply of powder, it was refused. This was deplored by Winthrop, for it would be, said he, "a great inconvenience to the English should they be forced to seek protection from the Dutch."[2] Danger from the Indians led to the contemplation of a union among the New England colonies. A petition from Plymouth, Connecticut, and the settlements on Narragansett Bay, to Massachusetts to unite in dealing with the Indians, while received favorably in regard to the two former, was spurned so far as the latter was concerned.[3]

---

[1] *Rhode Island Colonial Records*, i, 126.

[2] Winthrop, *Hist. of New England*, ii, 211.

[3] *Massachusetts Colonial Records*, i, 305.

In 1643 a union of the four colonies, Massachusetts, Connecticut, Plymouth, and New Haven, was formed with the express stipulation that no other colony should be admitted.[1] Neither Providence nor Rhode Island was invited to enter the union, nor was a direct request from them destined to receive a favorable reply.   On the eve of what might have proved a serious Indian war, the only concession to be gained was permission for Newport to buy one barrel of powder.   Even this was denied to Providence.   Indications that the United Colonies would soon substitute aggression for simple non-intercourse, was a potent factor in bringing about a union under a patent from the home government.

The band of settlers at Moshassuck had no intention of founding a state.   Their early organization was that of a town, composed of joint proprietors dwelling apart from any regularly constituted authority.   Their government was a pure democracy.   The householders met once a week to consult on the "common peace, watch and planting." "Mutual consent," says Williams, "have finished all matters with speed and peace."[2]   The first written compact entered into declared for government by the majority.[3]   When a modification was found necessary, the sparing hand with which power was delegated is remarkable.   Five "Disposers" were elected to have charge of the proprietary and governmental interests of the town.   These officers were elected for the term of three months, at the end of which time they were to give an account of their doings to the town.   Any one aggrieved by the action of the disposers might appeal to the town in town meeting.   Private disputes were settled by arbitration.[4]

[1] *Acts of the Commissioners of the United Colonies*, i, 3.

[2] *Narragansett Club Publications*, vi, 4.

[3] *Rhode Island Colonial Records*, i, 14.

[4] *Ibid.*, i, 27.

The settlers of Aquidneck, while yet at Providence, affixed their signatures to an agreement whereby they united themselves into a body politic to be governed by the laws of Holy Writ.[1] A "Judge" was chosen to preside in town meeting, where all political affairs were settled. Soon three "Elders" were chosen to assist the judge in his judicial duties, in framing laws, and in transacting public business; but all their acts were subject to revision by the quarterly meetings of the town.

On the removal of the government to Newport, those who remained at Pocasset organized similar forms there.[2] Becoming accustomed to representative government, the settlers soon expressly declared that the term of office among them should be one year.[3] In March, 1640, Newport and Portsmouth, or Pocasset, were united under a governor, deputy governor and four assistants.[4] Their government was declared, in March, 1641, to be a "Democracie or popular government."[5]

At Aquidneck, at Providence, and Pawtuxet, Samuel Gorton exhibited a contempt for the authority established there, prejudicial to good government and not to be tolerated in any well ordered community. Consistent with his denial of any authority not recognized by the home government, no organization was effected at Shawomet until the arrival of the Patent of 1643.

So loose was the political system of these settlements that dissensions were continually arising within them. It was feared that Massachusetts might at any moment begin an active policy of persecution on account of the degree of religious liberty there. In any case the lack of any legal status whatever as a part of the realm of England could but be fatal in an extremity. To procure recogniton from the

[1] *Rhode Island Colonial Records*, i, 52.   [2] *Ibid.*, i, 70.

[3] *Ibid.*, i, 70, 98.   *Ibid.*, i, 100.   [5] *Ibid.*, i, 112.

king, to secure stability at home, and to raise a bulwark
against the encroachments of her neighbors, Williams was
sent to England to secure a charter.   In 1644, Williams returned with a patent, obtained from the revolutionary government in England, for " The Incorporation of Providence
Plantations in the Narragansett Bay in New England."

This patent united the towns in an incorporation and gave
them jurisdiction over the territory bounded on the south by
the sea, on the west by the Pequod river and country, on the
east by Plymouth, and on the north by Massachusetts.   The
strength of the spirit of local independence on these communities, together with the fear of rousing Massachusetts to active
opposition, delayed organization under the patent until 1647.
The frame of government was constructed by the whole
people in general assembly.   Providence, on account of its re-
moteness, chose ten delegates to act for her; but though
represented by delegates, it is probable that a large number
of her freemen attended.   In consenting to unite her destiny
with that of the other towns, Providence retained for herself
full authority in town affairs, to elect and to empower officers
responsible to the town, to try all cases not reserved for a
general court of trials, and to enforce all executions.   Their
desire was to avoid all mingling of general and town functions.[1]   Neither at Portsmouth nor at Newport is there any
evidence that delegates were chosen.

By no patent in English colonial history were so few
restrictions imposed upon the grantees as by this.   Full governmental powers were granted, with the single restriction
that the " laws, constitutions and punishments" must con-
form to the laws of England, " so far as the nature and constitution of the place will admit."   Under this *carte blanche*
the assembly proceeded to institute a representative government consistent with the democratic precedents furnished

---

[1] Staples, *Annals of Providence*, 62.

by the towns. The general officers, a president, four assistants, a general recorder, and a treasurer were to be chosen annually at a "General Court of Election." All freemen were made electors. Such as could not attend should send their votes sealed to the assembly. Each town should present two candidates for assistant, and the one from each town having the highest number of votes was to be declared elected.

In the method prescribed for enacting laws both the popular initiative and the referendum were introduced. Any town might in town meeting propose a law, which must then be sent to the other towns for consideration. Next it was considered by a "General Court" of six members from each town. If a majority concurred, it was to stand until the next "General Assembly of all the People" for confirmation. The general court might propose measures which must be confirmed by the towns and by the assembly. Judicial power was vested in a "General Court of Trials" to be held twice annually, by the president and assistants. Town affairs were to be administered by six men called the "Town Council." Seldom has there been seen a more perfect embodiment of the principle which the founders had in mind when they declared their government to be "Democratical." [1]

But as is usually true in states in which the idea of popular government finds full development, internal dissensions were continually threatening the existence of the state itself. The submission of certain of the men of Pawtuxet to Massachusetts led to constant complications at Providence. At Rhode Island, Coddington and Nicholas Easton were at the head of two bitterly opposing parties. In September, 1648, Coddington presented to the United Colonies a request that the people of Rhode Island might be received into alliance,

[1] *Rhode Island Colonial Records*, i, 156.

offensive and defensive, with them.[1]   This petition, which
was presented without the knowledge of Providence, and
against the wishes of a large party on Rhode Island, had it
been successful, would have worked the destruction of the
colony.   Absorption would inevitably have followed alliance.   Fortunately for the future of the Rhode Island
colony, the petition was rejected by the commissioners.[2]

In August, 1651, Coddington returned from a visit to
England, bringing a commission creating him governor for
life of Rhode Island and Conanicut.[3]   The whole colony was
thrown into consternation.   Plymouth was advised to assert
her claim to Providence and Warwick.   These two towns,
however, thanks to their self-governing instincts, held fast to
the colonial organization, and together with the anti-Cod-
dington faction in Rhode Island, sent Roger Williams and
John Clarke to England to secure a revocation of Coddington's commission.[4]   In October, 1652, the desired revocation was issued from the office of the Secretary of State.[5]

Development in material prosperity and in population, as
well as experience in the past, gave rise to thoughts of a
more elaborate frame of government.   The restoration of
Charles II, moreover, made it necessary that the frame of
government should have royal confirmation.   The reception, in 1663, of a royal charter, placed the colony on a
more secure foundation.   The new government was organized on a plan only so much less democratic than before as
the growth of the colony demanded.   Power was given to

[1] Hazard, *State Papers*, ii, 99: *Acts of the Commissioners of the United Colonies*, i, 110.

[2] *Acts of the Commissioners of the United Colonies*, i, 110.

[3] *Rhode Island Historical Society's Collections*, iv, 99.

[4] *Narragansett Club Publications*, vii, 212, 228; 1 *Massachusetts Historical Society's Collections*, vii, 292; Hazard, *State Papers*, ii, 198; Backus, *Hist. of the
Baptists*, i, 269.

[5] *Narragansett Club Publications*, vi, 236.

elect officials and to make laws, with the restriction that the laws "be not contrary and repugnant unto, but as near as may be, agreeable to the laws of this our realm of England, considering the nature and constitution of the place and people there." The "general officers," consisting of a governor, deputy-governor, and ten assistants, together with a secretary and treasurer, were to be chosen annually "by such greater part of the freemen as are there assembled." It was the duty of the governor to call general assemblies, fill vacancies and see that the laws were executed. All general officers were liable to impeachment.

The legislative power was vested in a "General Assembly," to consist of the governor, deputy-governor, assistants, and deputies elected semi-annually by the towns. The assembly was empowered to fix the times and places of its meetings, admit persons as freemen of the colony, create offices and appoint officers of administration, make laws, establish courts, regulate the time and manner of holding elections, define the qualifications of electors, define the boundaries of towns, prescribe punishments, and grant pardons.

By act of May, 1666, judicial powers were vested in a general court of trials, to consist of the governor, deputy-governor and assistants.[1] This court was to sit twice a year to hear and to determine all causes. At the reorganization of the courts in 1729, this "Superior Court of Judicature, Court of Assize, and General Gaol Delivery" was given appellate powers only.[2]

The most remarkable feature of this charter is the preponderant influence given to the general assembly. It was the real source of all power. Not only did it exercise the usual legislative powers, but it assumed the functions of the executive in the appointment of all officers not directly

[1] *Acts and Laws of Rhode Island*, 1719, 15.   [2] *Ibid.*, 1730, 190.

elected by the people, and held the sole pardoning power. The assembly was in turn kept strictly in subordination to the popular will by frequent elections. To the governor remained only a few ministerial powers. He was not a branch of the legislature, but simply a member. No veto was given him. When, in 1731, the question was raised in connection with paper money legislation, the crown officers decided that the charter conferred on the governor no power of veto.[1]

It was quite in harmony with the ideas of the times that the supreme judiciary should consist of the chief executive officers. But in Rhode Island they were made so by the legislature, not by the charter. Both the manner of their appointment and the tenure of their office made them closely responsible to the representatives of the people. On the transfer of appellate jurisdiction to a chief judge and four associates, these officers were chosen annually by the legislature. From the close association of these departments was to evolve an assumption of authority by the assembly which was to endure longer than the charter itself.

When Roger Williams attempted to settle at Seekonk he was informed by Plymouth that, though he was then trespassing on the jurisdiction of that colony, if he would but remove across the river he would be upon free land. This advice having been followed, he supposed that no one but the king claimed jurisdiction over his lands at Moshassuck. Coddingon's company, learning that Sowams, where they first proposed to settle, was in the domain of Plymouth, selected the island of Aquidneck, which was then acknowledged to be beyond the boundaries of that colony. Only seven years later, however, a magistrate was sent to Rhode

---

[1] *Rhode Island Colonial Records*, iv, 458–461.

Island to forbid the existing government to exercise authority there.[1]

The sojourns of Gorton at Providence and Pawtuxet were
short and stormy. The conduct of this man, who was "be-
witching and bemaddening poor Providence,"[2] led four of
the inhabitants of Pawtuxet to place themselves under the
jurisdiction of Massachusetts, there to remain until 1658.
This action was followed by a formal announcement by
Massachusetts of her protectorate over the men of Pawtuxet,
and a general denial by Gorton of that colony's assumption.[3]
The protectorate of Massachusetts was based on a theory
that, whenever any person submitted to her jurisdiction, her
authority at once extended over the lands of that person,
though they lay outside her chartered limits. Gorton soon
removed to Shawomet, where his party purchased a tract
from Miantinomi, chief sachem of the Narragansetts.

The dissatisfaction of Pomham, a subordinate chieftain
who held Shawomet and who denied the sale to Gorton, led
to his submission of himself and his lands to Massachusetts.
That colony at once took up the cause of Pomham against
Gorton. A long controversy ensued. Shawomet was in-
vaded and Gorton and his followers were taken as captives
to Boston, where after imprisonment they were banished
and forbidden to return on pain of death.[4] On his return to
Shawomet, Gorton was chosen to carry to England the submission of the Narragansetts to the king, and at the same
time to prosecute the case against Massachusetts.[5] In the
meantime the general court of that colony granted ten

---

[1] Winthrop, *Hist. of New England*, ii, 270.

[2] *Narragansett Club Publications*, vi, 141.

[3] Force, *Tracts*, iv, 19.

[4] *Rhode Island Historical Society's Collections*, ii, 255; Hazard, *State Papers*,
ii, 10.

[5] *Rhode Island Colonial Records*, i, 134.

thousand acres of the Shawomet lands to settlers, but the claims now put forth by Plymouth to the same territory prevented a settlement.[1] The result of Gorton's mission was an order from the Commissioners of Plantations restoring to the Shawomet settlers their lands, and forbidding Massachusetts to assume authority over them.[2] Already Williams had returned with the patent of 1643, and the interests of all the towns were soon to be blended in a common cause.

On August twenty-seventh, Massachusetts announced that she had received a patent, under date of December tenth, 1643, granting to her all of Rhode Island west of Narragansett Bay, especially mentioning the Narragansett Country.[3] The origin of this document is obscure, and by the friends of Rhode Island has been declared to be a forgery. That Massachusetts was not certain of its legality is indicated by the fact that it was not produced until it appeared probable that the Rhode Island settlements were about to organize under their patent. Moreover, had the claim rested on a firm basis, a colony with the instincts of Massachusetts would have spared no effort to enforce it.

Thus it appears that, before any authorized government was instituted in the colony, its whole territory had been claimed by one or both of its eastern neighbors. Against these claims the towns struggled singly until 1647.

The claims of Connecticut and Massachusetts to the Pequod country were adjusted in 1658, by fixing the Mystic River as the boundary between the two colonies, completely

---

[1] *Massachusetts Colonial Records*, ii, 128; I *Massachusetts Hist. Soc. Collections*, i, 276.

[2] *Rhode Island Colonial Records*, i, 367; *Rhode Island Hist. Soc. Collections*, iv, 195; Winthrop, *Hist. of New England*, ii, 282.

[3] *Massachusetts Colonial Records*, iii, 49.

ignoring Rhode Island.[1]   In this tract, lands were granted to
settlers as early as 1649.   These were held by Rhode Island
to be within her territory.   In violation of Rhode Island law
Humphrey Atherton and others, not citizens of the colony,
bought large tracts at Quidnesett and Namcook in the
Narragansett country.[2]   This purchase, which depended for
its validity on the Narragansett Patent, led to a remonstrance
and preparations to contest the case before Parliament.   On
account of the injuries inflicted on the Mohegans, the United
Colonies condemned the Narragansetts to pay a fine.   Their
lands were pledged as security for payment.   This mortgage
having been assumed by Atherton, the lands were forfeited
to him in default of payment.   The occupation of the same
territory under the Pettiquamscut purchase by Rhode Island
authority led to conflicts in that region.   Certain persons
from Newport about the same time began a settlement at
Pawcatuck, and soon came in conflict with Massachusetts
authority established there.

The granting of the charters of Rhode Island and Connecticut gave a new aspect to the whole question.   Under
the terms of their charter, which granted to them the territory on the western side of Narragansett Bay, Connecticut
assumed jurisdiction over the whole territory.   The Rhode
Island charter, granted soon after, fixed the western boundary at the Pawcatuck River, with the express provision that
nothing in the Connecticut charter should be construed to
conflict with this later one.   The results of arbitration between the colonial agents embodied in the Rhode Island
charter were repudiated by Connecticut, paving the way to
a boundary dispute of two centuries in length.

Connecticut at once proceeded to extend her government
over the Narragansett Country and was vigorously opposed

[1] *Acts of the Commissioners of the United Colonies*, ii, 209.

[2] 3 *Mass. Hist. Soc. Collections*, i, 213.

by Rhode Island. In March, 1665, the royal commission headed by Col. Richard Nicolls, appointed to subjugate the Dutch settlements, and to settle all questions of appeal, jurisdiction, and boundary, after hearing the representations of the colonies interested, erected the Narragansett Country into a province called "King's Province," over which the governor and assistants of Rhode Island were made magistrates. This gave that colony for the time being jurisdiction over the disputed territory.[1] In October, 1664,[2] and again in 1670,[3] conferences were held on the subject between representatives of the two colonies, but without result. In the meantime, there was a continual struggle by Rhode Island to maintain her authority against the incursions of Connecticut. Violence was repeatedly resorted to on both sides. Such was the condition of affairs until King Philip's War engaged the attention of both parties.

At the close of the war the members of the Atherton Company who continued to incline to the side of Connecticut, opened the whole question again. A second royal commission, in its report of October, 1683, rejected the claim of Rhode Island, and recommended that the question be decided by the home government in favor of Connecticut.[4] Since the Privy Council took no action on the report, the work of the commission was of no effect. In 1699, at the command of Lord Bellomont, the dispute was submitted to the authorities in England, with recommendations from Bellomont highly adverse to Rhode Island. Nothing came of this attempt at settlement. During the whole period hostilities were carried on upon the disputed territory. Officers on both sides were arrested in the performance of their duties. Taxes laid by each side were resisted by the other.

[1] *Rhode Island Colonial Records*, ii, 93.

[2] *Ibid.*, ii, 50.   [3] *Ibid.*, ii, 3c6.   [4] *Ibid.*, iii, 140.

Becoming fearful that the reference of the dispute to England might result in the loss of both charters, commissioners
were appointed by both sides, in 1702, to settle the question.[1] Their conference resulted in the concession by Connecticut of all that was claimed by Rhode Island, fixing the
boundary substantially as later conferences have confirmed
it.[2] But though her commsssioners had reached an agreement, Connecticut delayed the execution of the agreement
until a movement was made to lay it before the king. The
case was laid before the Board of Trade in February, 1723,
and in February, 1727, the final decree came from the king.[3]

The eastern boundary, though never the subject of such
fierce contention as that on the west, was destined to wait
even longer for settlement. It has already been noted that
Plymouth, which at first made no claim to the islands in
Narragansett Bay, in 1644 laid claim to Aquidneck. In
1645 a magistrate of Plymouth laid claim to Shawomet. In
May, 1659, the assembly appointed commissioners to determine the eastern boundary, but without result.[4] By the
charter of 1663 the eastern limit of the colony was fixed at
three miles east of Narragansett Bay. An attempt to fix
this line failed owing to the refusal of Plymouth to participate.
In spite of the charter, in 1682, Plymouth laid claim to Hog
Island, and in 1684, extended the claim to the island of
Aquidneck.[5] The royal commission of 1664 gave Plymouth
jurisdiction to the bay, pending the decision of the king.
By the Massachusetts charter of 1691, Plymouth was an-
nexed to that colony, and the eastern boundary became the
concern of Massachusetts. In 1734 Rhode Island in a petition to the king asserted her right to the eastern shore of

[1] Arnold, *Hist. of Rhode Island*, ii, 10.

[2] *Rhode Island Colonial Records*, iii, 474.

[3] *Ibid.*, iv, 370.   [4] *Ibid.*, i, 409.

[5] Arnold, *Hist. of Rhode Island*, i, 477.

the bay. The case having gone through the regular process of investigation, an Order in Council in November, 1738, decreed that the commissioners should determine the line. The commission sat on April 7, 1741,[1] and decided in favor of Rhode Island, giving to her five towns on the eastern border. On appeal from both parties, the decision was confirmed by the king in council, in May, 1746.[2]

The same commission fixed the line on the north-east, which was more closely connected with the northern boundary question. This latter was opened by the town of Mendon when it was feared that under the original deed of Providence, Rhode Island might claim a part of that town. Ineffectual measures were taken to settle this question in 1705 and 1706.[3] About this time an armed force from Mendon entered Rhode Island and carried off several prisoners to Boston. Such acts of violence led to further attempts at settlement, but it was not until 1746 that this was decided by an Order in Council.[4]

These boundary disputes of Rhode Island, though seemingly petty and barren of interest, were a most potent factor in shaping the character of her people.

Were each state called upon to indicate its particular contribution to the institutions of America, Rhode Island would point unhesitatingly to the principle of liberty of conscience. Though the honor of the first enunciation of this principle is disputed by Maryland, Rhode Island has successfully maintained her position. Roger Williams found that in Massachusetts religious liberty was no more a fact than it was in England. The first charge made against him before the general court was that he held the doctrine

[1] *Rhode Island Colonial Records*, iv, 586-7.

[2] Arnold, *Hist. of Rhode Island*, ii, 134.

[3] *Rhode Island Colonial Records*, iii, 528.

[4] Arnold, *Hist. of Rhode Island*, ii, 134.

" that the magistrates ought not to punish the breach of the first table otherwise than in such cases as did disturb the civil peace." [1]   The settlement at Providence was an embodiment of Williams' idea.   In the first written compact remaining, that signed by the second comers, the agreement was to be governed by the majority " only in civil things." [2] In the form of government which succeeded the more primitive original organization in 1640, it was resolved " as formerly hath been the liberties of the town, so still to hold forth liberty of conscience." [3]   At Rhode Island, the same " General Court of Election " which declared the government to be a democracy, also declared that " none be accounted a delinquent for doctrine: provided it be not directly repugnant to the government or laws established." [4]

Under the patent of 1644, which was silent on the subject of religion, the declaration of religious liberty went hand in hand with that of political freedom.[5]   When in the absence of laws on the subject, complaints of Sabbath breaking were brought in, the assembly refused to make any law on the subject.[6]   An opportunity for putting into practice the principles so persistently maintained was offered on the arrival in Rhode Island of certain Quakers, fleeing from persecution in Massachusetts.   In reply to a letter from Massachusetts urging the banishment of the Quakers, Rhode Island said that no law existed in the colony under which persons could be molested in matters of religion.   Though the extravagant acts of the Quakers were obnoxious to the people of the colony, yet they resolved to adhere to their fundamental principle, so long as it did not jeopardize civil order.[7]

[1] Winthrop, *Hist. of New England*, i, 193.

[2] *Rhode Island Colonial Records*, i, 14.

[3] *Ibid*, i, 28.   [4] *Ibid.*, i, 113.

[5] *Ibid.*, i, 156.   [6] *Ibid.*, i, 279.

[7] *Rhode Island Colonial Records*, i, 376.

When, as on this occasion, the maintenance of soul liberty seemed to threaten the structure of civil society, the colony had for its guidance that letter of Williams to the town of Providence in which the state is likened to a ship which puts to sea bearing men of different faiths. He declared that, while these men might not be compelled to attend the ship's prayers or be restrained from offering their own, yet the commander must have authority, not only over the direction of the voyage, but over peace and justice among those on board. In such a case it could not be maintained that there should be no commander because all were not of the same faith.[1]

With this principle well established, the agent at the royal court was able to procure in the patent of 1663 a provision, "that no person within the said colony, at any time hereafter, shall be anywise molested, punished, disquieted, or called in question, for any difference in opinion in matters of religion, and do not actually disturb the civil peace of our said colony."[2] The marked contrast between this provision and the rights not only of the other colonies, but of Englishmen at home, makes this grant a notable one in the history of English imperial government.

The course of legislation during the first half of the eighteenth century indicates that the principle in question was held no less sacred in that day than it had been by the founders of the colony. Nothing was more in opposition to this idea than that any one sect should be favored above another. To guard against such a contingency, the assembly, in 1716, in an "Act for Perpetuating the Liberty of Conscience" granted by the charter, and for preventing any church "from endeavoring for preëminence or superiority of one over the other, by making use of the civil power for the

---

[1] *Narragansett Club Publications,* vi, 278.

[2] *Charter of Rhode Island.*

enforcing of a maintenance for their respective ministers," passed an act providing that whatever salaries any congregation might see fit to provide for their ministers, should " be raised by a free contribution, and no other way."[1]

The continued presence of the Quakers had made itself felt at different times in the political as well as in the religious life of the people, particularly at the time of King Philip's War. The militia laws consequent on the participation by the colony in the wars against Spain and France, imposed upon the people of that persuasion duties incompatible with their belief. To relieve them, an act was passed in June, 1730, " for the relief of tender consciences, and to prevent their being burdened with military duties."[2] The preamble of the act relates that, by the operation of the existing militia laws, certain persons " have suffered great damages, and excessive charges have accrued to them by having their goods distrained and publicly sold, contrary to that freedom and liberty of conscience by the charter granted to all persons of a peaceable and quiet behavior." Hence it was therein enacted " that no constraint shall be laid upon the conscience of any person whatsoever, by force of any act or law for the keeping up or regulating the militia within this colony, nor shall any person be compelled to bear arms, or learn or exercise himself in the art of war, whose principles are, that the same is inconsistent with the doctrine of the gospel." Six years later this law was repealed.[3]

Again, in an act " for more effectually putting the colony into a proper posture for defense," on the occasion of the outbreak of the war with Spain in 1740, it was provided that,

---

[1] *Rhode Island Colonial Records*, iv, 206; *Acts and Laws of Rhode Island*, 1719, 80.

[2] *Acts and Laws of Rhode Island, Supplement to Digest of 1730*, pt. i, 217.

[3] *Ibid.*, pt. ii, 277.

in case of an alarm, persons taking an oath that they could not conscientiously bear arms, might be excused. Such persons were, however, held liable to do service as aids, scouts and watches.[1] Again, in the year 1744, a law was passed for the relief of Quakers, similar in its provisions to that of 1730.[2]

But while the colony was thus reiterating the principle of religious freedom, there appeared upon the statute books a law totally inconsistent with her professions. The digest of laws printed in 1716 contains among those passed at the first session of the general assembly after the reception of the charter, an act that " all men *professing Christianity*, and of competent estates, and of civil conversation, who acknowledge and are obedient to the civil magistrates, though of different judgments in religious affairs, *Roman Catholics only excepted*, shall be admitted freemen, and shall have liberty to choose and be chosen officers in the colony, both military and civil."[3]

Investigation has proven that the expressions " professing Christianity," and " Roman Catholics only excepted," do not appear in the original act of 1663–4, nor does it in the manuscript digest of 1705. From this and other evidence it appears that these provisions never received legislative sanction until they were unintentionally accepted by a general act confirming the digest of 1730. Not a single instance appears of the provisions having been enforced. From this it must be concluded that, though on the statute book until 1783, in spirit this restriction never existed.[4]

The colony's favorable situation for trade by sea was appreciated by the first settlers. Commercial relations were

---

[1] *Acts and Laws of Rhode Island*, 1745, 234.

[2] *Ibid.*, 293.   [3] *Ibid.*, 1719, 3.

[4] *Acts and Laws of Rhode Island*, 1719, Introduction, 14; *Rhode Island Historical Tracts*, ser. 2, i. The act reappears in the digests of 1730 and 1767.

maintained during the seventeenth century, both with the
Dutch and with some of the English colonies. Commerce
did not rise to importance, however, until about the beginning of the next century, nor were vessels owned in the
colony to any extent before that time. A report to the
Board of Trade in 1680 shows that the entire shipping of the
colony then consisted of a few sloops.[1] There were no merchants worthy of the name, and the small trade which existed consisted of exports of horses and provisions. The
awakening of the spirit of commerce throughout the British
dominions became perceptible at the dawn of the eighteenth
century. During the years preceding 1708, the shipping of
the colony increased from four or five vessels to twenty-
seven, most of which hailed from Newport.[2] This increase
was ascribed both to the growing taste for the sea among
young men, and to the superior speed of the Rhode Island
vessels, which enabled them more easily to escape their
enemies. Shipbuilding became an important industry after
the revolution of 1688. Down to the year 1708 eighty-four
vessels were built in the colony. The English trade at that
time consisted of imports to the value of £2000 annually,
through the port of Boston. Direct trade was carried on
with the other colonies, the West Indies, Madeira, and
Surinam. To the tropical countries were exported lumber
and farm and dairy products, in return for sugar, molasses,
and dyestuffs. English goods were frequently obtained
through this channel. With specie, molasses, and sugar
brought from the south, and with rum distilled in the
colony, the Rhode Island trader carried on a thriving business with the other colonies, bringing back their products
for exportation. By the year 1731 direct trade was established with England, Holland, and the Mediterranean.[3] The

[1] Arnold, *Hist. of Rhode Island*, i, 448. [2] *Rhode Island Colonial Records*, iv, 57.
[3] Arnold, *Hist. of Rhode Island*, ii, 106.

profits of the carrying trade had by the year 1740 swelled the fleet trading to Europe, Africa, and the West Indies to one hundred and twenty sail.[1] Dye woods were now carried from the West Indies by the Rhode Island traders to England, where they were exchanged for English goods intended for colonial use. Some vessels had found a source of profit in the slave trade between Africa and the West Indies. As the years passed commerce grew apace. During the year 1763, one hundred and eighty-two vessels cleared from Newport for foreign voyages, while three hundred and fifty-two sailed in the coastwise trade. These, together with the fisheries, gave employment to two thousand men.

As the colony grew, Newport was no longer the sole seat of trade. From the year 1730 onward Providence claimed an increasing share of commerce. To such an extent did the shipping of that port increase, that between 1756 and 1764 the number of vessels belonging there which were lost, amounted to sixty-five. The town itself was building up. In 1751, a cargo of lumber sent to London direct was exchanged for dry goods which supplied three new stores in town. Intercourse with the country towns demanded better highways. Heretofore the post road from Pawtucket to Westerly was the only exception to the general neglect to which the highways were condemned. In 1734 a road to Plainfield was provided.[2] The next year provision was made for bridges in Scituate.[3] From that time on, there frequently appear appropriations for highway purposes in various parts of the colony.

It was near the close of the seventeenth century that the colonial manufactures became of sufficient importance to rouse the opposition of the manufacturers in the mother

---

[1] *Rhode Island Colonial Records*, v, 8.

[2] *Ibid.*, iv, 492.   [3] *Ibid.*, iv, 512.

country. The laws of 1699, 1732, and 1750, in restraint of
colonial manufactures, sought to crush the manufacture of
woollens, hats and iron, as well as to place heavy restrictions
on apprenticeship in those industries.   In spite of oppres-
sive legislation, various industries grew up in Rhode Island.
Iron-works were established with marked success at Potowomut.   The fisheries and the foreign trade led to extensive
manufactures at Newport.   At one time there were no less
than seventeen factories for the manufacture of sperm oil
and candles.   Five rope walks were in operation.   Three
sugar refineries handled the imports of that article from the
West Indies, while twenty-two distilleries contributed rum to
the return cargoes.[1]

The part taken by the colonies in the wars between England and France between 1690 and 1763, imposed upon them
a heavy debt.   In their efforts to relieve themselves of this
burden, recourse was had in many colonies to emissions of
paper money.   Massachusetts led the way in 1690, followed
in 1709 by New York and New Jersey.   Rhode Island followed in 1710, Pennsylvania in 1723, and Virginia in 1755.
During the years 1710 and 1711, Rhode Island issued
£13300.[2]   This was followed in the year 1715 by the issue
of a bank of £4000 in paper.[3]   The banks differed from the
other issues of paper in that they were for larger amounts
and were loaned to the people for a term of years on landed
security.   The ordinary issues were for small amounts and
were issued to meet the immediate demands on the treasury.
A second bank in 1721[4] was followed by a third in 1728.[5]
One emission created the demand for the next.   Thinking

[1] Arnold, *Hist. of Rhode Island*, ii, 300.

[2] *Rhode Island Colonial Records*, iv, 93, 102, 106, 123, 128; *Acts and Laws of Rhode Island*, 1719, 60-63.

[3] *Acts and Laws of Rhode Island*, 1719, 75-79.   [4] *Ibid.*, 1730, 115.

[5] *Ibid.*, 1730, 152.

men saw only disaster as the inevitable result of adherence to this course, but their efforts to stem the torrent were of no avail.   The issue of £60000 in 1731,[1] and the defeat of the sound money party were followed by other banks in 1733,[2] 1738,[3] 1740,[4] 1743-4,[5] and 1750.[6]   The total face value of the nine banks issued prior to 1760 was £465,000, though it must be remembered that some was issued when paper was much depreciated, and that many of the bills never circulated at their face value.   Throughout the period from 1710 to 1760, bills were frequently emitted for the immediate use of the treasury.   A report made in 1749 gives the amount of bills issued for that purpose at £312,300, of which there remained in circulation £135,335.[7]

The occasion for the issue of paper was first of all the expense of the French wars, both in contributing to the fitting out of expeditions, and in putting the colony in a state of defense.   To this was added the plea that there was an insufficient medium of exchange to meet the demands of trade, wherefore commerce was decaying and the farmers were discouraged.   Among the reasons assigned for the issue of the bank of 1731 was a desire to promote hemp raising, and the whale and cod fisheries, by a bounty.   The bank of 1733 had for its object the building of a pier at Block Island.

As the earlier banks became payable great difficulty was experienced in making collections.   The relief of debtors then became an avowed object of the paper issues.   But in spite of this, collections were made with the utmost difficulty.   In 1741, in Providence alone, five hundred and

[1] *Acts and Laws of Rhode Island, Supplement to Digest of 1730*, pt. i, 231.

[2] *Ibid., Supplement to Digest of 1730*, pt. ii, 252.   [3] *Ibid.*, 1744-45, 211.

[4] *Ibid.*, 1744-45, 229.   [5] *Ibid.*, 1744-45, 271.

[6] *Rhode Island Colonial Records*, v, 318.

[7] *Rhode Island Historical Tracts*, viii, 191.

thirty-nine suits of this nature were in progress. During
the following year one thousand and forty more were upon
the docket in the same county.[1]

The depreciation of the paper was uninterrupted, and became very great. The seventh bank, that of 1740, was in
" new tenor " bills, one of which was to equal four of the
old bills. Matters grew steadily worse until the issues
ceased. In 1763 an act was passed declaring that henceforth gold and silver coin only should be lawful money.[2]
The value of the Spanish dollar was fixed at six shillings
sterling. By that year the earlier bills had depreciated so
that one Spanish dollar equaled seven pounds in paper.
In 1764 the issue of 1750 was rated at five for two of specie.[3]

The blame for the depreciation was laid at the doors of
the importers of English goods, who, the balance of trade
being against the colony, were buying up gold and silver to
remit to England.[4] But the history of paper money in
Rhode Island does not differ greatly from that in the other
colonies. Depreciation and disorganization of business followed again and again. It would seem that not only to
those who perceived the true causes, but to those who
simply saw the disastrous effect, the warning would have
been sufficient to deter the people from ever again having
recourse to this financial expedient.

The organization of more elaborate government under the
charter of 1663 was followed by the consciousness of colonial unity. The advance of settlements into new country
contributed to the same end. This growth of a political
sense caused the squabbles which were continually arising
in the various towns to seem comparatively unimportant.

[1] *Rhode Island Historical Tracts*, viii, 56.

[2] *Acts and Laws of Rhode Island*, 1767, 165.

[3] *Rhode Island Historical Tracts*. viii, 208.

[4] *Ibid.*, viii, 161, 188.

Even the fiercest of these, the Harris land dispute, which raged in Providence for many years and reached its height in 1677–9, rose scarcely to the dignity of a colonial question.

In colonial politics there were for many years circumstances which prevented marked party divisions. The dangers of Indian war, the frequent interference of royal commissioners and governors in colonial affairs, and the perpetual warfare waged with Massachusetts and Connecticut checked internal dissension. But as these dangers were removed, the natural tendency to party division often asserted itself.

In the seventeenth century, as might be expected in a community devoted almost exclusively to agriculture, disputes arose, usually in regard to land. But with the development of commerce the situation was changed and a new element was brought into the field. Interests were then no longer identical for the colony as a whole. Economic conditions then decreed that what was for the interest of the rising trade was often detrimental to agriculture. On this foundation the building of parties was simple. No sooner did a debtor class arise in consequence of the second intercolonial war, than there appeared an element of discontent arrayed against conservative business interests. In Rhode Island this condition of things began to assert itself in the first quarter of the eighteenth century.

The efforts of the colony to aid the expeditions against the enemies of Great Britain led, as we have seen, to the issue of paper. The cause of paper at once commended itself to all discontented elements, and by the year 1731 they were in a majority in the general assembly. In that year a bill for the issue of a bank of £40,000 passed that body. The depreciation of the former issues and the consequent disorganization of business arrayed a strong party of the more substantial interests of the colony against the policy. After the bill passed the assembly the governor attempted to veto it. The assembly denied the power of the governor to veto a bill, and were supported in their position by the law officers of the crown.[1] The sound money party was at the next election completely defeated.

The rise of commerce tended to concentrate power at two centers, Newport and Providence. Newport had been both the capital and the metropolis of the colony. There centered the social, political, and commercial life. There assembled annually the "General Court of Election," which it was the privilege of all the freemen to attend. There, until 1747, were held the terms of the superior court. After 1732, the governor was always chosen from one of the leading families of the town or from the family of Greene of Warwick, which was closely connected with Newport by business and social ties.

Naturally the culture of the colony was to an extent centered at the capital. Among the intellectual lights of the town were numbered the two divines, Honeyman, and McSparran. The brief sojourn of Bishop Berkeley at Newport left its impress on the intellectual growth of the town. The names of Smibert and Gilbert Stuart are inseparably connected with the Newport of that time. The Wanton, Malbone, Redwood, and Whipple families were powers in the commercial world. Their ships were found in the ports of Europe and the West Indies, and on the coasts of Africa. Among the first families of the place were also to be found the names of Brenton, Bull, Coddington, Vernon, and Brinley.

Providence had begun to develop early in the century. An increasing commerce came to her wharves. A generation whose chief interests lay in that town were building up an extensive trade. Its position on the mainland at the

---

[1] *Rhode Island Colonial Records*, iv, 456–61.

head of Narragansett Bay gave it great advantages which were augmented by the improvement of means of communication by land. The marked growth of the town dates from 1730. About that time the town street was built up, new stores were opened, and the tonnage of the port largely increased. Among the families contributing most largely to this upbuilding, none was more prominent than the Browns. As the place grew in importance, her development was watched by Newport with a jealous eye. It was perceived that Providence would soon demand political recognition commensurate with its budding commercial strength, but the old metropolis would not yield without a struggle. Gradually Providence drew to herself the northern towns of the colony which were naturally tributary to her, and placed herself in open opposition to the dominant power of Newport. The latter found its strongest support in Newport and Kings counties and in a faction led by the Greenes of Potowomut. The election of Stephen Hopkins of Providence as governor in 1755 was the first political victory of the northern party. Again, in 1756, Hopkins was victorious. During his second term certain of his acts gave color to the charge that he had overridden an act of the general assembly,[1] that he had appointed to responsible positions incompetent members of his own family, that he had received unwarranted compensation for public services, and that the disposition of certain goods confiscated by the state had been made to the financial advantage of the governor.[2]

The leadership of the Newport party had fallen upon Samuel Ward, who came into the assembly in 1756 as a deputy from Westerly. The son of Richard Ward, a merchant of Newport, who was governor in 1741–3, he was fitted by birth and training to assume the leadership of his

---

[1] *Rhode Island Colonial Records*, v, 445.

[2] Gammell, *Life of Samuel Ward*, 260.

section of the state. His marriage into a prominent family of Block Island and his subsequent removal to Westerly tended to attach more firmly to his cause those portions of the state. Under his leadership the forces united against Hopkins and restored to the governorship William Greene of Warwick. A pamphlet by Hopkins, in which he charged the assembly with obstructing his administration, was met by a vindication by Ward. Smarting under defeat and the charges made by his opponents, Hopkins instituted a suit against Ward for libel. To remove the trial from the influences of party strife the case was taken to the courts of Worcester county, Massachusetts.[1] Here it lingered, to embitter political relations in Rhode Island, until 1760, when judgment was rendered for the defendant by default. Governor Greene having died before the expiration of his term of office, Hopkins was chosen by the assembly to complete the term. At the next annual election he was re-elected over Ward, who now became the opposing candidate. The line of cleavage had shifted from the horizontal to the vertical. Losing its nature as a war between classes, the strife became sectional, and the contest assumed all the vindictiveness of a personal rivalry. For ten years these two men continued to be the contestants at each annual election. Only thrice, in 1762, 1765, and 1766, was the Ward party able to overcome the increasing influence of Hopkins.

The pitch to which the passions of the two parties had been aroused became subversive of order and prosperity. As early as 1762 a proposal for a compromise was made by Ward, but was rejected by his opponent.[2] In February, 1764, the two chieftains simultaneously made proposals for reconciliation. Those of Ward were addressed to the gen-

[1] *Rhode Island Colonial Records,* vii, 68.

[2] Gammell, *Life of Samuel Ward,* 263.

eral assembly, proposing that both the contestants retire; that the governor be chosen from Newport, and the deputy-governor from Providence, and that the upper house be equally divided between the two parties. Hopkins in turn proposed that Ward accept the deputy-governorship, which had been made vacant by death. But the presence of growing anarchy could not overcome the lust for power, and so the fight went on.

Again, in the campaign of 1767, efforts were put forth to secure a compromsie. The deputy-governor and nine assistants, friends of Ward, proposed that they nominate a governor and that the Hopkins party name the deputy-governor and half of the assistants.[1] To this proposition Hopkins, who was now out of office, agreed, provided that Ward would retire from the field. This concession was refused and both parties stripped for the fight. The overtures of the Hopkins party being scorned they took an aggressive attitude, and at the annual election won by a larger majority than ever before. Governor Hopkins could afford to be magnanimous. The Ward party was crushed by defeat. In the following October, Hopkins proposed a compromise. He suggested that Ward choose a governor from the Hopkins party, that Hopkins choose a deputy governor from the Ward party, and that the assistants be chosen alternately in like manner. The result of this effort was the choice of Josias Lyndon of Newport as governor, and Nicholas Cooke as deputy governor.[2] Thus closed perhaps the bitterest political struggle in the history of the colony and state. The way had been prepared so that, long after the principals in this affair had been removed by death, new conditions might revive the spirit of this old struggle to embitter a new conflict between the forces of order and of anarchy.

[1] *Rhode Island Colonial Records*, vi, 551.
[2] *Ibid.*, vi, 550.

In this earlier period of the colony's history one glimpse is afforded us of its attitude toward colonial union. Here too we see Stephen Hopkins, the leader of the colony in the coming contest with the British ministry, before his excursions along the by-ways of partisan politics. The prospect of further hostilities with France, as well as indications that the Six Nations were falling away from their allegiance, made desirable some union between the colonies. Exhortations to the colonies to maintain friendly correspondence with each other, and to be prepared to aid in repelling attacks on any one of their number, were followed by directions to appoint commissioners to attend a "general interview" between the various governments at Albany.[1] Following their appointment as delegates by the assembly, commissions were issued to Stephen Hopkins and Martin Howard, empowering them to take such measures as would be most effectual in maintaining a permanent friendship with the Six Nations, to inquire into what forts were building on the frontier, and by whom, to announce the readiness of Rhode Island to do her part toward the protection of the Indians against their enemies, and "in general, as far as the abilities of this government will permit, to act in conjunction with the said commissioners in everything necessary for the good of his majesty's subjects in those parts."[2] This did not contemplate a delegation of power to any central organ of government outside the colony.

Under date of August twentieth, the commissioners presented a report containing a statement of the condition of the colonies in relation to the Indians and the French, and the plan of union agreed upon by the convention. The plan was held for further consideration.[3] Before it came up the Ward-Hopkins fight had begun, distorting facts by charge

[1] *Rhode Island Colonial Records*, v, 397; *New York Colonial Documents*, vi, 802.
[2] *Rhode Island Historical Tracts*, ix, 4.   [3] *Ibid.*, ix, 4.

and refutation. Hopkins, attacked by his opponents, issued his " True Representation " as a political tract in his own defense.[1] This was met by " Philolethes " in "A Short Reply." [2] In December of the same year news came from the colony's agent in England that action was likely to be soon taken on the Albany plan of union. This was unnoticed until the following March, when " Philolethes " avers that the governor and upper house sent to the lower house a resolve that on examination they find the plan " to be a scheme which, if carried into execution, will virtually deprive this government at least of some of its most valuable privileges, if not effectually overturn and destroy our present happy constitution." [3] Whether or not this be true, the assembly instructed the agent to be on the watch for anything respecting the Albany plan which might " have a tendency to infringe on our charter privileges," that he use his utmost endeavors to get it put off until such a time as the government is furnished with a copy and has an opportunity of making answer.[4] The attitude taken toward the plan on both sides of the Atlantic relieved the colony from any further consideration of the matter. On its revival in March, 1755, this question became the shuttlecock of politicians in the great contest just commencing. It is evident that in the heat of strife the facts were exaggerated, but it is equally certain that there was a strong sentiment against yielding control over the colony to any central colonial government.

Rhode Island's history as a colony thus reveals certain distinguishing characteristics, the product of conditions both external and internal. The very cause of its being, religious oppression, and the advanced views of Williams, decreed

[1] *Rhode Island Historical Tracts*, ix, 4.
[2] *Ibid.*, ix, 59.   [3] *Ibid.*, ix, 61.
[4] *Rhode Island Colonial Records*, v, 424.

that here should be perfect liberty of conscience. That succeeding generations appreciated the value of the principle, defending it against all attack, the records of later years attest.

In territory the colony was not rich. But that which it possessed became more highly prized with each struggle for its possession. Both the religious and territorial controversies developed a dislike and distrust of the surrounding colonies, which the adjustment of the troubles could not allay. The sense of isolation from the other colonies seemed to reflect itself in the people, and to develop the spirit of local independence to a high degree. The religious persuasions of the people, numbering among them so many shades of belief, tended toward individualism. There was little of that drawing together into towns centering about a church organization, elsewhere noticeable in New England. The people, on the contrary, lived apart, and little of public spirit was to be seen.

From the earliest settlement the government of the colony was in fact, as well as in theory, democratic. In the earlier years this did not present a strong contrast to the conditions existing in the other colonies, but on the conversion of many of the colonies into royal provinces the difference became more marked. Connecticut alone could then approach her in political freedom. Not only were these two colonies the envy of their neighbors, but it was only by the intervention of fortuitous circumstances that they were permitted by the home government to retain their charters of freedom. Sensible of the dangers through which they were passing, they were led the more to prize this boon of free government, and look askance at any movement to unite their fortunes with those of larger communities which were less free. Those financial experiments and disasters accompanying the economic development of the colony caused political lines to be drawn first between classes, and later between sections and men. Religious liberty, local independence, democracy, and individualism, these are the characteristics of her development. With such a history Rhode Island approached the Revolution.

CHAPTER II

ALMOST before the bells ceased ringing in celebration of the fall of Quebec, there came across the Atlantic rumors that England was to tighten the reins of her control over the colonies. The mercantile interests of England had for more than a century been laying restrictions on the foreign commerce of the colonies, and the year 1699 marked the first of a series of repressive measures designed to throttle American manufactures. But in spite of all this the colonies throve and grew rich, until England determined that the time had arrived to draw a direct revenue from America.

Lord Grenville, on March 9, 1764, took the first step in this direction by announcing the intention of the government to lay a stamp duty in America. The arrival of this news in the colonies found them already aroused to a sense of their former injuries, through the work of Otis and the other fathers of liberty. In Rhode Island their efforts had been seconded by Stephen Hopkins in the *Providence Gazette*, which was to be the organ of Americanism in that colony. The writings of Hopkins, particularly the " Essay upon Trade in the Northern Colonies," [1] prepared the way for Rhode Island's remonstrance to the " Lords of Trade," the first official remonstrance from America.[2] The essay entitled " The Rights of the Colonies Examined," which was prepared by order of the general assembly, exerted an influence be-

[1] *Providence Gazette*, Jan. 14 and 21, 1764.
[2] *Rhode Island Colonial Records*, vi, 378.

yond the colony where it was written.   When the call came
from Massachusetts for joint action on the proposed Stamp
Act, Rhode Island appointed a committee to join with those
of the other colonies in such measures as should seem advisable to secure the repeal of the Sugar and the Molasses
Acts, and prevent the passage of the proposed Stamp Act.[1]

News of the passage of the Stamp Act reaching America
in April, 1765,[2] first gained attention from the legislature of
Virginia in a set of resolutions declaring the rights of the
people.   This was followed by a circular letter from Massachusetts calling for a meeting of committees from all the
colonial assemblies to meet at New York on the first Tues-
day in October.   The town of Providence, in compliance
with this, adopted on August thirteenth a set of resolutions
embodying those proposed by Henry in Virginia, and recommended the appointment of delegates to the proposed meeting.[3]   The assembly acted promptly in appointing delegates,
who, while the sincerest loyalty and affection for his majesty
were expressed, were directed to unite with the commissioners from the other colonies in drawing up an address, and in
all measures for presenting the same.[4]   The agent in London was, at the same time, directed to support all "necessary measures in procuring relief in these important affairs."
The results of the congress were reported to the assembly
of Rhode Island at its October session.[6]   The sentiments of
the colony at this time may perhaps best be shown in the
language of Governor Ward, the only one of the colonial

[1] *Rhode Island Colonial Records*, vi, 404.

[2] *Providence Gazette*, Apr. 6, 1765.

[3] *Providence Town Meeting Records*, v, 122–3; *Providence Gazette*, Aug. 24, 1765.

[4] *Acts and Resolves of the General Assembly (MS.), 1762 5*, Sept. 11, 1765.

[5] *Ibid.*, Sept. 11, 1765.

[6] *Rhode Island Colonial Records*, vi, 465–71.

governors who refused to take the oath to support the Stamp
Act. In a letter to the agent in London, he said: "You
will consider, sir, that our all is at stake. . . . If the late
regulations are continued and enforced we shall be entirely
undone. . . . We unanimously esteem our relation to our
mother country as our greatest happiness, and are ever
ready, and at the hazard of our lives and fortunes to do
everything in our power for her interest, and all we desire in
return is the quiet enjoyment of the common rights and
privileges as Englishmen, which we imagine we have a natural and just right to."[1] The remonstrances of the colonies
were rewarded by the repeal of the Stamp Act.

The distinction made in the colonies between direct taxes
and commercial imposts pointed the way for a revenue act,
passed in June, 1767, imposing a duty on glass, paper,
paints, and tea, establishing revenue boards in America, and
proposing to make use of writs of assistance. The purpose
of the act was to raise a revenue to pay the salaries of the
civil officers, and thereby make them independent of the
people. Roused by this assault on the established order of
things, Boston led the way in a vote to forbear to use or to import the listed articles, and appointed a committee to secure
subscribers to a non-importation agreement and to communi-
cate with the other towns and colonies.

Providence was not slow in following the lead of Boston.
At a town meeting held November twenty-fifth, to consider
measures for promoting industry, economy, and manufactures, a strong sentiment in favor of non-importation prevailed.[2] A committee, appointed at this time reported in
December an agreement for non-importation, and a recommendation for the encouragement of the flax and wool industries. To secure the general enforcement of the agreement

[1] *Rhode Island Colonial Records*, vi, 474.

[2] *Providence Gazette*, Nov. 28, 1767.

it was voted to discountenance in every lawful manner all
who should not enter the agreement.[1]   Newport, on December fourth, voted unanimously for non-importation, and
discouraged the use of certain imported goods.[2]   This spirit
was not long in permeating the colony.   The subscription
lists swelled in numbers, the wearing of homespun was
adopted by all classes, and spinning became popular at
social gatherings.[3]

The Massachusetts assembly, in February, 1768, voted to
transmit to the other colonies a letter giving its sentiments
on the question of the hour and asking for an exchange of
views on matters of mutual interest.[4]   Though not complying until several months later, the Rhode Island assembly
at its next session referred the circular to a committee who
were also instructed to draw up an address to the king and
to the secretary of state.[5]   A report was made on September sixteenth containing an address to the king which declared the revenue act to be an infringement on the rights of
the colonists under the British constitution.[6]

With the whole force of parliamentary resentment turned
against Boston, Virginia came bravely to the front.   The
legislature of that colony, in informal assembly, drew up a
non-importation agreement, together with a circular letter to
the other colonies and a set of resolutions upon the rights
of the people.   The action of Virginia was laid before the
Rhode Island assembly at its June session 1769,[7] and in
October the Virginia resolutions were in substance adopted.

[1] *Providence Gazette*, Dec. 5, 1767.

[2] *Ibid.*, Dec. 12, 1767.

[3] *Ibid.*, Dec. 12 and 19, 1767.

[4] *Boston Gazette*, Mar. 14, 1768.

[5] *Acts and Resolves of the General Assembly* (*MS.*), *1766–9*, Mar. 2, 1768.

[6] *Rhode Island Colonial Records*, vi, 559.

[7] *Acts and Resolves of the General Assembly* (*MS.*), *1766–9*, June 13, 1769.

A committee was ordered to report an address to the king to the next session.[1]

The colonists found it much easier to pass resolutions of non-importation than to maintain them when adopted. A tendency to break the agreement was noticeable all along the line. The early action of Providence on the subject had not met with entire success. Infringements led to a call for the Sons of Liberty to meet at the dedication of a liberty tree in that town on July twenty-fifth, 1769, to agree on effectual measures to secure non-importation.[2] The effect was not satisfactory. Violations became so numerous that merchants in New York ceased to have any dealings with those of Rhode Island.[3] Providence, suffering from the conduct of those merchants whose avarice exceeded their patriotism, again adopted a non-importation agreement.[4] It being learned soon after that a cargo of the tabooed goods was daily expected by certain merchants, a town meeting was hurriedly called and the offending merchants were obliged to surrender the goods in question, to be held in bond until the revenue acts should be repealed.[5] Boston and New York having decided to extend the period of non-importation until the revenue act should be repealed, Providence emulated the example of those towns, and several merchants expecting consignments of the prohibited goods were compelled on their arrival to transfer them to the custody of a town committee.[6] Owing to this energetic action the feeling against Rhode Island subsided.

Rumors of the repeal of the revenue act furnished a pre-

[1] *Acts and Resolves of the General Assembly* (*M S.*), *1766–9*, June 13, 1769, Oct. 28, 1768.

[2] Staples, *Annals of Providence*, 223.

[3] *Boston Gazette*, Oct. 9, 1769.

[4] *Providence Gazette*, Oct. 14, 1769.   [5] *Ibid.*, Oct. 21, 1769.

[6] Staples, *Annals of Providence*, 223.

text of which the loyalists of Newport were quick to make the most, and the agreement was quickly set aside.[1]   In Providence a meeting of merchants had repealed the agreement except in respect to tea, but another meeting declaring this too precipitate, voted to continue the old arrangement. It was further resolved that, should any bring into the town any prohibited goods, his name should be published in the newspapers.   To set the position of Providence aright before the world, the proceedings of this meeting were widely published.[2]

Newport displayed a less patriotic spirit by freely breaking the agreement, regardless of the censure of Providence. Soon it was evidenced that Providence was still in bad repute in some quarters.   A spirited protest was entered against her by the town of Windham, Connecticut; Philadelphia refused to trade with a Providence vessel, and in New York prohibited goods brought from Rhode Island were seized.[3]   These circumstances led to another declaration from Providence that they had adhered strictly to non-importation, and that the wholesale discriminations made against the town by the southern and western colonies were unjust.[4]   The statement was accepted by Boston and trade resumed.[5]

With the continuance of the policy of taxation, committees of correspondence were appointed in many towns in Massachusetts.   The appointment of the Gaspee Commission was the more definite act needed to incite the other colonies to action.   This commission was created by royal instructions at the close of 1773 to investigate the burning of the Gas-

---

[1] *Providence Gazette*, May 26, 1770.

[2] *Providence Town Meeting Records*, v, 165; *Providence Gazette*, June 2, 1770.

[3] *Providence Gazette*, June 30 and July 7, 1770.

[4] Staples, *Annals of Providence*, 227.

[5] *Providence Gazette*, Sept. 15, 1770.

pee. Its object was to discover the offenders and turn them over to Admiral Montague to be taken to England for trial on charge of high treason. The military force of General Gage was placed at the disposal of the commission. These preparations kindled the smouldering flame. The civil authorities refused to give their assistance in any way. The chief justice declared that he would give no order for an arrest on the application of the commission, nor would he allow his officers to do so.[1] It speaks well for the fidelity of the colony that the royal commission, sitting in the midst of a community where the offenders were generally known, was unable to apprehend a single one of the participants. While the Gaspee affair was under discussion, Virginia resolved to appoint a committee of correspondence and to invite the other colonies to do likewise. In response the Providence *Gazette* said, "Embrace this plan of union as your life. It will work out your political salvation."[2] Forthwith the assembly appointed a standing committee of correspondence.[3] When the matter came before the other colonies, the action of Virginia and Rhode Island lay side by side. The failure of the Gaspee Commission put an end to royal instructions, but not until they had served to accustom the colonies to common thought and action through committees of correspondence.

In the Spring of 1773, it was learned that an attempt would be made to force taxed tea upon the colonies. Though intense excitement was created, no official utterance appeared from the Rhode Island assembly. Several of the towns took action, notably Providence and Newport, declaring it to be the duty of all to oppose the tea tax.[4] The

[1] Bancroft, *Hist. of the United States*, iii, 434.

[2] *Providence Gazette*, May 22, 1773.

[3] *Rhode Island Colonial Records*, vii, 227.

[4] *Ibid.*, 272; *Providence Gazette*, Jan. 22, 1773.

town of Bristol, in its resolves, went even further, saying that the charter having been broken, the people "may in time be provoked to renounce their allegiance and assert an independency."[1] By these resolves no practical result was produced beyond adding a link to the chain of sympathy which bound the colonies together.

On the recommendation of the king, Parliament, to punish Boston for indulging in the "Tea Party," enacted the Port Bill. But an attack on one was an attack on all. Salem and Marblehead offered to Boston the use of their wharves. Aid began to flow in on all sides. Providence, assuming Boston's cause as her own, instructed her deputies to secure aid from the assembly for the stricken town.[3] Resolutions were also adopted against making the town an asylum for persons whose interests and principles were inimical to the interests of America. The presence of any such persons was to be discouraged by every lawful means.[4] A broadside headed "Join or Die," which appeared in Newport, reveals the temper of the patriots there as well as did their votes in town meeting to join in any measures of relief.[5] Westerly, too, offered her sympathy.[6] Neither at the June nor at the August session did the assembly offer aid to Boston, though at the former a day of fasting and prayer was set apart.[7] At the August session it was voted to submit the

[1] *Rhode Island Colonial Records*, vii, 274.

[2] Action was also taken in Warren, Westerly, Little Compton, Middletown, South Kingstown, Jamestown, Hopkinton, Richmond, New Shoreham, Cumberland, and Barrington. *Rhode Island Colonial Records*, vii, 272, et seq.

[3] *Providence Town Meeting Records*, vi, 18; *Providence Gazette*, May 21 and Aug. 13, 1774.

[4] *Providence Town Meeting Records*, vi, 19; *Providence Gazette*, Sept. 3, 1774.

[5] *Rhode Island Colonial Records*, vii, 293; *Providence Gazette*, May 28, 1774; *Am. Archives*, i, 343.

[6] *Providence Gazette*, May 28, 1774.

[7] *Acts and Resolves of the General Assembly* (*MS.*), *1774-5*, June 14, 1774.

question of relief to the towns assembled for the election of
deputies, that these might be instructed on the subject.[1]
After the discussion of the matter in town meeting, sub-
scriptions came in from many towns accompanied by expressions of sympathy.   All expressed the conviction that
the cause of Boston was their own, and, rather than submit,
death in defense of their rights would be preferable.[2]   Scituate spoke in clear tones when she appointed a committee to
unite with the other towns in a plan that should "have a
tendency, under the blessing of Heaven, to insure us our in-
violate rights and privileges."[3]   Again in tones no less clear
did she speak when she thought her rights endanged in later
years by her sister states.   The material assistance furnished
by the towns was principally in money and cattle.[4]

For many months the idea of a general congress of the
colonies had been developing.   It found expression as early
as August, 1773, and was repeated unofficially at various
times before May, 1774.   The first call from any political
body was made when the town of Providence, on May 17,
1774, instructed her deputies to promote a movement for a
congress of representatives of the colonial assemblies.   The
purpose should be to form a firm union between the colonies.[5]   Following the instructions of Providence, the assembly, on June fifteenth, adopted resolutions declaring that "a
firm and inviolable union of all the colonies, in councils and

[1] *Rhode Island Colonial Records*, vii, 257.

[2] *Providence Gazette*, Sept. 3, 1774.

[3] *Rhode Island Colonial Records*, vii, 283.

[4] The correspondence of the towns with Boston is to be found in 4 *Mass.
Hist. Soc. Collections*, iv, 1-278.   Providence and North Providence contributed
money (*Providence Town Meeting Records*, vi, 20), seven towns sent sheep, and
two sent horned cattle.

[5] *Providence Town Meeting Records*, vi, 15.

measures, is absolutely necessary for the preservation of their rights and liberties," and favoring a congress.[1]

Two delegates, Stephen Hopkins and Samuel Ward, were chosen to attend such a gathering, with instructions to promote the sending of a remonstrance to the king, and to take any other "reasonable and lawful" measures for securing their liberties They were further to secure a regular annual meeting of delegates.[2] These were the first delegates to be chosen by any colony. Rhode Island was likewise the first colony to call for a convention, though it failed to fix a time and place of meeting. These were supplied by Massachusetts two days later. In giving Rhode Island credit for first calling for a convention, too much stress should not be laid on the fact, for the same force was at work in Massachusetts, though it did not find official utterance as soon. In Virginia too, before the action of Massachusetts and Rhode Island became known, a call had issued. So in at least three colonies the same conclusions were working out simultaneously.

On the eighth of December, the Rhode Island delegates made their report to the assembly. The work of the congress being approved, it was recommended that the towns appoint committees of inspection to carry into effect the Articles of Association.[3] Congress had recommended that, unless a redress of grievances was secured, it was expedient that a second congress should be held in May of the next year. In compliance, the assembly "determined to cooperate with the other colonies in every proper measure for obtaining a redress of the grievances and establishing the rights and liberties of all the colonies upon an equitable and

[1] *Acts and Resolves of the General Assembly* (MS.), 1774–5. June 15, 1774.

[2] *Ibid.*, June 15, 1774.

[3] *Ibid.*, Dec. 8, 1774.

permanent foundation."[1]   The delegates to the first congress
were reëlected, with authority to " consult and advise," and
to enter into and adopt all reasonable and lawful measures
" for the support, defense, protection, and security of the
rights, liberties and privileges, both civil and religious, of all
the said colonies or any of them."[2]

Providence had already set the example for the towns by
publishing the Articles of Association, and adopting measures to prevent the exportation of sheep.[3]   At a meeting a
month later that town appointed a special committee of
eighteen to see that the articles were enforced.[4]   A committee was also appointed in Newport for the same purpose.[5]
Newport's reputation for Toryism again gave rise to rumors
that her citizens were not observing the agreements of the
colonies, and that ships were fitting out there for trade in
defiance of the Articles of Association.   The committee of
correspondence promptly sent a letter to Philadelphia, where
the rumor originated, stating that all ships had been laid up
on December first, and all preparations for export had
ceased.[6]   Various notices in the papers show that in general
through the colony an effort was made to keep the agreement.[7]

The prelude to the drama was now ended.   At Lexington
and Concord the curtain had risen on a great tragedy.   As
the news of this event ran through the colonies they realized
that war was upon them.   In the emergency a special ses-

---

[1] *Rhode Island Colonial Records*, vii, 267.

[2] *Acts and Resolves of the General Assembly* (*M.S.*), *1774-5*, Dec. 9, 1774.

[3] *Providence Gazette*, Nov. 26, 1774.

[4] *Providence Town Meeting Records*, vi, 21.

[5] *Providence Gazette*, Dec. 24, 1774.

[6] *American Archives*, i, 1098.

[7] *Providence Gazette*, Mar. 11 and June 17, 1775; *American Archives*, iii, 661.

sion of the assembly was called to take measures of defense.[1]
It was voted to raise a force of fifteen hundred men to remain in the colony as an army of observation, to repel any
insult or violence that might be offered to the inhabitants.
If necessary for the protection of any other colony, it was to
join and coöperate with the forces of the neighboring colonies. Military preparations had been making for months.
The militia laws had been revised, military companies had
been formed and supplies collected.[2] A committee was to
consult with the authorities of Connecticut on measures of
defense for the New England colonies.[3] The speaker of the
House of Representatives, in announcing the action of the
assembly to Connecticut, remarked with evident satisfaction
that "greater unanimity was scarce ever found than was
manifested in the lower house on the great questions that
came before them."[4]

But in spite of the unanimity in the House of Representatives, the measures of the patriots were by no means unop-
posed by a portion of the citizens. The spirit of opposition
made itself manifest in the upper house of the assembly in
the form of a protest against the raising of an army of
observation.[5] This protest, signed by Governor Joseph
Wanton, Deputy Governor Darius Sessions, and two assistants, alleged as a motive the opinion that "such a measure will be attended with the most fatal consequences to our
charter privileges; involve the colony in all the horrors of a

[1] *American Archives*, ii, 362.

[2] The most important military measures may thus be stated chronologically:
June, 1774, Light Infantry chartered; Oct., Newport, Providence, Pawtuxet,
Gloucester, and Kentish companies chartered; Dec., Providence Train of Artillery,
Fusileers, and North Providence Rangers chartered; committees appointed to re-
vise the militia laws, and to procure arms and ammunition.

[3] *Acts and Resolves of the General Assembly (MS.), 1774-5,* Apr. 24, 1775.

[4] *American Archives*, ii, 389.

[5] *Acts and Resolves of the General Assembly (MS.), 1774-5,* Apr. 25, 1775.

civil war, and, as we conceive, is an open violation of the oath of allegiance which we have severally taken, on our admission into the respective offices we now hold in the colony." [1]

In the flush of triumph at the outcome of the Revolution, and burning under the recollections of that stormy period, it has been the custom to belittle the character, number and importance of the loyal element of the American people in that great struggle. A century's tranquillizing influence should enable us to realize what the leaders of the patriots were forced to admit to their own generation : that probably one-third of the people of America were opposed to the Revolution.[2] While these loyalists were from all ranks of society, it must be admitted that on an average the balance was in their favor as compared with their opponents, in respect to wealth, intelligence, and social position. In the opposition to the measures of the popular party in Rhode Island, two motives may be distinguished. There was a conservative spirit, ruling a class of men who, while they loved their country and stood firmly for its liberties during the intellectual period of the Revolution, shrank from armed opposition to constituted authority. Then there was a commercial spirit prevailing among a large class of influential merchants whose wealth had been gained mostly in trade. Though in the main patriotic, they were dominated by business instincts, and to them armed rebellion suggested all the horrors of civil war, the destruction of trade, and the sacrifice of accumulated wealth. These motives, mingled in every proportion, were to be found not only in Rhode Island, but with still other motives throughout all the colonies.

Both the conservative and the commercial spirit were

---

[1] *Rhode Island Colonial Records*, vii, 311.

[2] *Works of John Adams*, x, 63, 87, 110.

well exemplified in Governor Wanton, who signed the protest against the raising of troops. Sprung from a family of
colonial governors and bearing in his veins the best blood
of New England, he was alive to the wrongs of his country,
but he shrank from rebellion. He came into office just at
the time of the firing of the revenue vessel, Liberty. In
the correspondence which followed this act the governor
strongly supported the action of the colonial court, while
complaining loudly of the customs officers for abusing and
misrepresenting the colony.[1] On being apprised of the
depredations of the Gaspee in Narragansett Bay, Governor
Wanton sent the high sheriff of Newport to demand of her
commander his commission and the instructions bringing
him into the colony.[2]

In reply to a letter from Admiral Montague in which
that officer censured the colony severely, Governor Wanton
returned an answer worthy of the man and of the times.
Concerning his duty as governor he said: " Please to be informed that I do not receive instructions for the administra-
tration of the government, from the king's admiral stationed
in America."[3] While expressing a willingness to aid the
officers of the crown in the execution of their duty, he con-
tinues: " Please to know that I will send the sheriff of this
colony at any time, and to any place within the body of it,
as I shall think fit."[4] It was after such exhibitions of
patriotism that he entered his protest against the raising of
the army. When the time arrived for the annual inaugura
tion of the government, Governor Wanton transmitted to the
assembly a request to be excused from attendance at the
session on account of illness.[5] At the same time he recommended to their careful consideration the conciliatory letter

---

[1] *Rhode Island Colonial Records*, vii, 42.

[2] *Ibid.*, vii, 62.   [3] *Ibid.*, vii, 64.

[4] *Ibid.*, vii, 64.   [5] *Ibid.*, vii, 332.

from the Earl of Dartmouth, under date of March third, 1775, asking that it be treated "with that tender calmness and deliberation" which the importance of it demanded.[1] "The prosperity and happiness of this colony," continued he, "is founded in its connection with Great Britain—torn from the body to which we are united by our religion, liberty, laws, and commerce, we must bleed at every vein. Your charter privileges are of too much importance to be forfeited." After recommending the avoidance not only of every appearance of anger, but a respectful demeanor toward the king and parliament, he concluded: "I shall always be ready to join with you in every measure which will secure the full possession of our invaluable charter privileges to the latest posterity, and prevent the good people from that ruin and destruction which in my opinion some of the orders of the late Assembly must inevitably involve them in, if they are not speedily repealed."[2] A curt query whether he intended to accept his election, and if so would he give his attendance in the assembly, caused him to repeat his plea of illness.[3]

The attitude of the governor was by no means acceptable to the assembly. A resolution was passed in that body forbidding the deputy governor or the assistants, in direct contravention of the terms of the charter, to administer the oath of office to him except in open assembly, and, further, that until such oath was administered he should be suspended from his office.[4] The charges enumerated against him were, besides, that he had entered a protest reflecting on the assembly, and failed to qualify as governor; that he had refused to sign the commissions of the newly created officers of the army, and had neglected to proclaim a fast day decreed by the assembly. These resolutions brought out the state-

[1] *Rhode Island Colonial Records*, vii, 322.   [2] *Ibid.*, vii, 322.
[3] *Ibid.*, vii, 334.   [4] *Ibid.*, vii, 325.

ment that, had he not been suspended, the fast would have been proclaimed in ample time. The commissions he could not consistently sign after entering the protest.[1] The explanation being unsatisfactory to the assembly, at the October session, the office of governor was declared vacant.[2] Though not removing from the colony like so many of his party, his political sun had set, and the remainder of his life was passed in quiet retirement.

In other quarters the commercial motive was making itself felt in a way scarcely appealing to the finer sympathies. The love of gain had already brought some of the trading class into collision with the patriots for violations of the non-intercourse agreements. Some of the people of Newport persisted in gratifying at the same time their loyalty and their greed by supplying sheep, butter, eggs, and other provisions to the British army at Boston.[3] Writing to General Greene, Governor Cooke comments upon these acts thus: " I am sorry I have so much reason to tell you that there is such a strong party at Newport that countenances and joins with them, and gives them all the intelligence and supplies in their power. In short, I think there is great reason to fear they will soon be the strongest party in that town, if some method is not taken to prevent it." [4] To prevent such a result was the object of stringent laws passed by the assembly. It was enacted that any person acting as pilot on any armed vessel going in or out of the waters of Rhode Island, not in the service of one of the colonies, should be fined not to exceed £500, or imprisoned not to exceed twelve months.[5] The loyalists were, however, not to be deterred, and so at its next session the assembly declared

---

[1] *Rhode Island Colonial Records*, vii, 336.

[2] *Ibid.*, viii, 392.   [3] *Providence Gazette*, June 3, 1775.

[4] *Rhode Island Hist. Soc. Collections*, vi, 114.

[5] *Rhode Island Colonial Records*, vii, 364.

it traitorous correspondence, punishable with death and confiscation, to supply the British with provisions or pilot their
vessels.[1] The pitiable condition to which the people of Newport were reduced led to a provision in the act whereby they
were allowed to supply the British with provisions in return
for immunity from plunder granted to their boats.

To make more rigorous the lot of the detested Tories,
measures were instituted to confiscate their property. At
the October session, 1775, no less than fourteen acts of confiscation were passed.[2] It is of interest to note that the
greater part of the forfeited estates were those owned by
wealthy citizens of Boston, holding property in the Narragansett Country. Confiscation of property and the trans-
portation of suspected persons to the interior towns were resorted to constantly during the early years of the war. The
attitude of the colony toward the loyalists, as well as the
steps taken to assert their rights as Englishmen, indicates
the position of Rhode Island at the outbreak of hostilities.

To attempt to fix the first suggestion, by an individual, of
independence, would but prove vain. Imperceptibly it was
approaching. A few bold spirits like Hopkins and Samuel
Adams had long watched its progress with approving eyes,
but the popular mind was not, during the year 1775, prepared for such a measure. Even Congress repeatedly dis-
avowed any intention of separation. As early as June 9,
1775, that body advised Massachusetts to elect representatives to conduct the government until a governor of his
majesty's choosing should consent to govern according to
the terms of the charter.[3] Advice of a similar nature was
given to New Hampshire, South Carolina, and Virginia. The
growing sentiment of independence seized the masses,
powerfully moved by the forcible, plain English of Paine's

---

[1] *Rhode Island Colonial Records*, vii, 389.

[2] *Ibid.*, vii, 376–86.   [3] *Journals of Congress*, i, 80.

" Common Sense," which appeared in January, 1776. As early as November 27, 1775, a Rhode Island man wrote : " The die is cast. The union of the two colonies with Britain is at an end. It is as easy to bring two poles together as to bring about an accommodation. The great question between America and Great Britain is now reduced to a point; we must be independent or slaves. We must declare ourselves free. A federal, not an incorporating, union must be completed as soon as possible." [1] General Greene, who had repeatedly counseled united action, now boldly recommended independence. [2] To the delegates in Congress Rhode Island recommended that all measures of partial and colonial defense give way to the united exertion of all under a supreme, superintending power. [3] Through the columns of the colonial press may be traced a steady advance of opinion leading to an official utterance on May 4, 1776. As North Carolina was the first colony to declare independence, so was Rhode Island the first to renounce her allegiance to Great Britain. This step was taken May 4, 1776. It had been voted by the lower house of the assembly to call upon the towns at the spring election to vote on independence. But as there were several towns which it was feared would reject the proposition, the plan was not carried out, lest a divided vote might weaken the cause in Rhode Island.[4] On the inauguration of the government, no time was lost in approaching the cause which was uppermost in the minds of all. Under the title of " An Act Repealing an Act entitled An Act for the more effectually securing to His Majesty the allegiance of his subjects in the colony and dominion of Rhode Island and Providence Plantations, and altering the forms of all commissions,

[1] *Amer. Archives*, iii, 1686.

[2] *Ibid.*, iv, 571.   [3] *Rhode Island Colonial Records*, vii, 451.

[4] Staples, *Rhode Island in the Continental Congress*, 68.

of all writs and processes in the courts, and of the oaths prescribed by law," the assembly, with but six dissenting votes,
passed an act which placed the colony a step in advance of
her sister colonies.[1]

Regarding government as a contract, the preamble to this
act relates that protection and allegiance are reciprocal.
The king in violation of the compact had introduced fleets
and armies into the colony to force upon the people a de-
testable tyranny. As under such circumstances it becomes
the right and duty of a people to make use of the means at
hand for their preservation, therefore the act of allegiance
was repealed. It was further enacted that in all commissions, writs, and processes at law, wherever the name and
authority of the king had been employed, should be substituted " The Governor and Company of the English Colony
of Rhode Island and Providence Plantations." The courts
were no longer to be the king's courts, nor were written
instruments of any kind to bear the year of the king's reign.

Having thus practically cut the bond which held them to
the old country, it was appropriate that the next proceeding
should be directed toward closer union with the other
colonies. This idea was embodied in a letter of instructions
forwarded to the delegates in Congress. They were empowered to join in consulting and advising, " upon the most
proper measures for promoting and confirming the strictest
union and confederation between the said United Colonies,
for exerting their whole strength and force to annoy the
common enemy, and to secure to the said colonies their
rights and liberties, both civil and religious;" and further
they were empowered, in conjunction with the delegates of
the other colonies, " to enter into and adopt all such measures; taking the greatest care to secure to this colony, in
the strongest and most perfect manner, its present estab-

[1] *Acts and Resolves of the General Assembly* (*MS.*), *1776, Pt. I*, May 4, 1776.

lished form, and all the powers of government, so far as
relate to its internal police and conduct of our own affairs,
civil and religious." [1]   Though the instructions avoided, on
account of a lack of perfect unanimity among the towns,
any direct charge on the subject of independence, it was intended that the prevailing sentiment of the people should
not be mistaken. [2]   In regard to union there was no dissent,
and to that topic the instructions were confined. But not
more emphatic were the instructions on the side of union
than in preserving the peculiar liberties of the colony. The
simple direction to "secure to the said colonies their rights
and liberties, civil and religious," and to take care " to
secure to this colony in the strongest and most perfect manner, its present established form, and all the powers of government, so far as relates to its internal police and conduct
of our own affairs, civil and religious," bring vividly to mind
all those circumstances in her history which had blended to
form the character of the colony. The banishment from
Massachusetts; the struggling settlements dedicated to soul
liberty; the unequalled privileges of the charter, and the
century of conflict waged over every foot of the narrow
territory granted by that instrument, all these were present
before the colony when it prepared to step forth from the
tutelage of England, and join its fate with that of its sister
colonies. In these lines were summed up the history of the
past and the hopes for the future.

Sustained by such expressions of encouragment, Congress
proceeded on its way to a formal declaration of independence. On the receipt of the news of the declaration, the
assembly approved the action and did " most solemnly en-
gage, that we will support the said General Congress, with our

[1] *Rhode Island Colonial Records*, vii, 526.

[2] *Ibid.*, vii, 527; Staples, *Rhode Island in the Continental Congress*, 68.

lives and fortunes."[1]   Already, at the June session, it had
been enacted that all persons suspected of unfriendliness to
the United Colonies should take a test oath declaring their
belief in the justice and necessity of the resistance to Great
Britain; that they would in no way furnish aid or comfort to
the enemy, and that they would assist in the defense of the
United Colonies.[2]   Now on the receipt of the declaration, it
was added that no male under twenty-one years of age
should make appeal to the assembly, commence an action
in court, or have the right to vote or hold office until he had
subscribed to the test oath.[3]   The invocation "God save the
King," which had long closed the records of the sessions of
the assembly, in June, 1776, became "God save the United
Colonies," and at the July session, "God save the United
States."

After independence the next step was to formulate a system of government.   Under gradually broadening instructions the Continental Congress advanced beyond the exercise of simply recommendatory functions, to those of a truly
national character.   The instructions to the delegates to the
second Congress, particularly at its second session, show a
marked advance in the national spirit.   Massachusetts gave
her delegates authority to "direct and order."[4]   South
Carolina's delegates were to "concert, agree to, and effectually prosecute measures to secure a redress of grievances,"[5] while Maryland bound her citizens "to execute, to
the utmost of their powers, all resolutions, that the said Congress may adopt."[6]   North Carolina delegated such power
as would make their acts "obligatory, in honor, upon
every inhabitant thereof."[7]   Rhode Island's delegates were

---

[1] *Acts and Resolves of the General Assembly* (*MS.*), *1776, Pt. II,* July 19, 1776.
[2] *Acts and Resolves of the General Assembly* (*MS.*), *1776, Pt. I,* June 16, 1776.
[3] *Rhode Island Colonial Records,* vii, 588.   [4] *Journals of Congress,* i, 51.
[5] *Ibid.,* i, 54.   [6] *Ibid.,* i, 53.   [7] *Ibid.,* i, 53.

to join in "consulting upon proper measures to obtain a repeal of the several acts of the British Parliament, for levying
taxes upon his majesty's subjects in America, without their
consent ; and upon proper measures to establish the rights
and liberties of the colonies upon a just and solid foundation." [1]   The onward march of events led, during the Spring
of 1776, to further instructions.   Rhode Island then gave
power to " consult and advise " for the purpose of annoying
the enemy and securing the liberties of the colonies by
making treaties with foreign powers, or by any other prudent and effective means. [2]

During the earlier sessions of Congress the colonies, advancing from the bestowal of advisory powers, had gradually
bestowed authority, express or implied, even to the point of
declaring independence.   Congress in its acts had kept
somewhat in advance of its expressly delegated powers.
Foreign affairs it controlled entirely.   Military authority it
exercised as the only body competent to do so.   In civil
affairs Congress was not supreme.   To bring order out of
the chaos of powers it was necessary at once to adopt some
definite frame of government.

As early as June eleventh, 1776, a committee of Congress
was directed to present such a plan. [3]   They reported July
twelfth, [4] and the plan was taken up ten days later. [5]   After a
month's debate it was laid aside until well into the following
year.   During these days discussion centered about the
eleventh and seventeenth articles.   The former provided that
common charges should be met from a treasury supplied by
the states in proportion to the number of inhabitants, " of
every age, sex, and quality, excepting Indians not paying

[1] *Journals of Congress*, i, 70.

[2] *Acts and Resolves of the General Assembly (MS.), 1776, Pt. I,* May 4, 1776.

[3] *Journals of Congress,* i, 370.

[4] *Ibid.,* i, 408.   [5] *Ibid.,* i, 420.

taxes."[1]   Article seventeenth gave to each state one vote in
Congress.   This was the rock on which it was feared that
the confederacy would split.   It was a concession to the
small states.   This the delegates of the larger states naturally opposed, and for a time they refused to consider aught
but a proportional representation.   The small states were
even more loud in their demands.   Delaware's representatives came instructed to accept nothing but equal representation.[2]   New Jersey feared that otherwise the small states
would become the vassals of the larger.[3]   On behalf of
Rhode Island, Stephen Hopkins observed that there were
four large, four small, and four middle-sized colonies; that
the four largest contained a majority of the population, and
that, if proportional representation were given, these could
overrule the rest.   The Germanic, Helvetic and Belgic con-
federacies furnished him with instances of unions voting by
states.[4]   The draft of the articles which came from the committee of the whole contained no change in the disputed
points.[5]

The articles were debated at various times during the
summer of 1777, and at last, after a discussion lasting sixteen months, were argued in their final form on November
15, 1777.[6]   Marchant, one of the delegates, in person bore
the articles to Rhode Island, and at a special session of the
general assembly on December 19 laid them before that
body, with a personal recommendation that they be ratified.
According to custom, the final discussion was deferred until

[1] Gilpin, *Madison Papers*, i, 27; *Hist. of the Confederation. Secret Journals of Congress*, i, 294.

[2] Gilpin, *Madison Papers*, i, 34   [3] *Ibid.*, i, 35.

[4] *Ibid.*, i, 38; *Works of John Adams*, ii, 501.

[5] *Hist. of the Confederation, Secret Journals of Congress*, i, 304–15.

[6] *Ibid.*, i, 349.

the next session.[1]   On February 9, they were taken up, and
a committee directed to draw up instructions to the delegates
authorizing them to sign in behalf of the state.[2]   As reported
from the committee and adopted, the instructions embodied
three amendments.   These were: first, that in case of sick-
ness, death, or other unavoidable accident, a state might be
represented by one delegate; second, that an estimate of
valuation be provided every five years; third, that as the
unoccupied lands formerly held by the crown had been
taken by the common efforts of all the states, they should be
held as common property.   To that end all such lands should
be forfeited to the United States, jurisdiction remaining in
the states where they might lie.   The first two of these
amendments were prompted not only by economy, but by a
fear that an unjust burden might be thrown upon the state.
The third was the expression of Rhode Island's position on
that question of the public domain which was destined to
play so important a part in the history of the confederation.
The instructions then proceed in a high strain of patriotism
which cannot but be admired in contrast with the provincial
spirit which permeated the councils of the state a decade
later.   Said they: " Although this Assembly deem the
amendments and alterations, herein proposed, of very great
importance, yet the completion of the Union is so indispen-
sably necessary that you are instructed, after having used
your utmost influence to procure them to be made, in case
they should be rejected, not to decline acceding, on the
part of this state, to the Articles of Confederation; taking
care that these proposed amendments and alterations be
previously entered upon the records of the Congress, that it
may appear that they were made before the signing of the

---

[1] *Acts and Resolves of the General Assembly* (*MS.*), *1777, Pt. II*, Dec. 19, 1777.

[2] *Acts and Resolves of the General Assembly* (*MS.*), *1778*, Feb. 16, 1778.

confederation; and that this state intends hereafter to renew
the motion for them.   This Assembly trusting that Congress,
at some future time, convinced of their utility and justice,
will adopt them, and they will be confirmed by all the states." [1]
This was followed by a formal act empowering the delegates
to sign the articles in such form " as Congress shall think
best adapted to a transaction so important to the present
and future generations," [2] provided that eight states should
accede to the same.   Moreover, in case any alterations or
additions should be made by nine states in Congress, the
delegates were likewise to ratify them.   The assembly
pledged the faith of the state to hold the action of her delegates in signing the articles, binding on the state for all time.
In this action the state not only ratified the articles as proposed, but trusted to the judgment of nine states so far as to
ratify in advance whatever they might propose thereafter.

In the meantime other states were considering the same
subject, and by the end of July, 1778, the delegates from
ten states had affixed their signatures to the instrument.
The refusal of New Jersey, Delaware, and Maryland to do
likewise forced upon the young nation the question of a national domain.   The extension of the British claim to territory beyond the Alleghanies, and the extinguishment of that
of the French, had brought vast tracts of land under the control of the English government.   To whom would the Declaration of Independence, if sustained by the strong arm of
victory, transfer the title to this noble possession?   Did
the title pass to those states which by their charters were
granted jurisdiction in these western wilds, or was it to be
absorbed by the nation by whose united efforts it was
wrested from Britain?

The larger states, claiming title and jurisdiction under

[1] *Acts and Resolves of the General Assembly (MS.), 1778*, Feb. 16, 1778.
[2] *Rhode Island Colonial Records*, viii, 366; *Journals of Congress*, ii, 612.

charters, went on their way disturbed only by the disputes aroused by conflicting grants from the crown. To the smaller states, whose restricted limits gave them no hope of jurisdiction over lands in the west, it was left to make the creation of a national domain a vital issue. Six states laid no claim to western territory. These were New Hampshire, Rhode Island, New Jersey, Pennsylvania, Delaware, and Maryland. Of these, Rhode Island, Delaware, and Maryland, having no private territorial disputes, were in a more favorable postion to oppose the claims of the larger states.

During the discussion of the Articles of Confederation, Maryland was active in endeavoring to curtail the boundaries of the larger states, and to hold the lands beyond for the benefit of the Union.[1] The feeble support lent by the others revealed a lack of unanimity as to detail even among them. The position of Rhode Island was indicated in the third of the proposed amendments accompanying her ratification. She was firmly of the opinion that the vacant lands should constitute a national domain, but expressly denied any intention that jurisdiction should vest in Congress.[2] New Jersey held a similar opinion.[3] After hesitation she yielded on November 26, 1778. The object of both Rhode Island and New Jersey was to secure a revenue for the payment of the war debt. It was unequal wealth rather than unequal political power that they feared. Delaware considered the articles " in divers respects unequal and disadvantageous," but convinced that the interests of particular states should subserve the good of all, she, on February 1, 1779, instructed her delegates to sign the articles. Maryland alone had not given her consent, nor would she do so until some

---

[1] *Journals of Congress*, ii, 290.

[2] *Acts and Resolves of the General Assembly* (*MS.*), *1778*, Feb. 16, 1778.

[3] *Journals of Congress*, ii, 603.

means should be found to limit the boundaries of the larger states. Her contention was that both title and jurisdiction should vest in Congress. Strongly intrenched in this position, Maryland held out until New York, Connecticut, and Virginia had taken steps towards ceding to the national government their western lands, when, on March 1, 1781, her delegates signed the Articles of Confederation. At last the Confederation became a legal fact.

Throughout the whole constitutional movement, from the first steps toward union till the adoption of the Articles of Confederation, the colony and state of Rhode Island had pursued a consistent policy of co-operation. In the acts of her legislature, and in instructions to her delegates, she had ever been in the forefront of patriotism. In fact, from the beginning of the Stamp Act difficulties, harmony had marked all her relations with the other states. There had been a common enemy to oppose, common rights to maintain, and a common existence to perpetuate, but nowhere was there a surrender of individuality.

CHAPTER III

A PERIOD OF DISCORD

THROUGHOUT the struggle with England the thirteen commonwealths had acted harmoniously. While asserting repeatedly their complete independence of each other and of Britain, they had allowed the assumption by Congress of many attributes of sovereignty, made necessary by the exigencies of war. The inadequacy of the first formal statement of the relations between the states and the United States was perceived even before it was adopted. At the close of 1780, it seemed as if a crisis had arrived. With demands on the states for money availing little, and credit almost gone, Congress found itself helpless. The army was suffering to the point of mutiny, from the lack of pay, provisions, and clothing. Heroic measures were necessary. "If we mean to continue our struggle," said Washington, "we must do it upon an entirely new plan. Ample powers must be lodged in Congress, as the head of the Federal union, adequate to all the purposes of war."[1] Again, "There can be no radical cure till Congress is vested by the states with full and ample powers to enact laws for general purposes."[2] Only then would ruinous delays cease. As a step toward greater efficiency Congress, on the third of February, 1781, took into consideration a resolution offered by Dr. Witherspoon of New Jersey, that it was absolutely necessary that Congress have power to superintend the commercial regulations of every state, and to lay duties on all

[1] Ford, *Writings of Washington*, ix, 13.   [2] *Ibid.*, ix, 126.

imported articles, with the consent of nine states. Though
this was lost, Congress, on the same day, recommended to
the states that it was absolutely necessary that it be vested
with power to lay a duty of five per cent. ad valorem on all
goods, with certain exceptions, imported after May 1, 1781,
and to lay a similar duty on all prizes condemned in any port.
The revenue so raised was to be employed in discharging the
principal and interest of the public debt incurred on account
of the war. The duration of the grant was to be until such
debt should be paid.[1] This resolution, together with urgent
solicitations that it be adopted, was sent at once to the
states.[2] The necessity of the case was set forth so forcibly
that responses began at once to come in. Connecticut led,
on March eighth, closely seconded by New York. New
Hampshire and Pennsylvania signified their acquiescence in
April, followed by New Jersey two months later. Though
Virginia ratified in May, her grant was not to take effect until August. North Carolina and Delaware gave their consent in the autumn. South Carolina and Maryland came in
laggardly in February and April, 1782. Massachusetts did
not make the grant until 1782, and then reserved the right to
appoint the collectors. Georgia had given evidence of a
favorable disposition, but Rhode Island remained silent.

Here is the point at which Rhode Island departed from
that hearty acquiescence which she had shown in everything
tending to united action. The cause of such a departure
must involve some new element now entering for the first
time into inter-state relations. What was that new element?
Congress had had the general direction of the war, of foreign
affairs, and of the common interests of the states while struggling for liberty. None of these involved any interference

[1] *Journals of Congress*, iii, 573.

[2] *Rhode Island Archives* (*MS.*), *Letters, 1780-1*, 24 (Circular of President of
Congress to Governors).

with the machinery of local government. The taxing power, above all, had been held in the hands of the states. Now a tax was proposed to be collected in the state by an external authority. Whatever may have been the status of the states under the Continental Congress and the Articles of Confederation, according to modern theory, from the express terms of the Articles of Confederation, and from the writings of that day, it is evident that each state intended to retain its "sovereignty, freedom and independence,"[1] saving the powers delegated in the articles. Among those which they did not give up was the power of the purse. It was in the demand for that power that Rhode Island saw an encroachment on her independence, a doctrine of which was expressed in the instructions to the Congressional delegates, in May, 1776, "to secure to this colony in the strongest and most perfect manner its present established form, and all the powers of government, as far as it relates to its internal police and conduct of our own affairs civil and religious."[2]

This conception of liberty is the mainspring of Rhode Island's action in 1781, and in the years that follow down to 1790. Its full import was brought out in the discussions that followed through weary months. Though the men at home were narrow and saw the world about them only through the exaggerated perspective of provincialism, Rhode Island's representatives in the hall and in the field viewed the situation aright. From these men came the first expressions of opinion on the subject. In a letter to Governor Greene, Gen. James M. Varnum, delegate in Congress, characterized as the two great points of weakness in the government, the lack of power in Congress to draw out the resources of the country, and the jealousy existing among the members of Congress. "Prudent caution against the abuse of power is very re-

[1] *Articles of Confederation, Article I.*
[2] *Rhode Island Colonial Records*, vii, 526.

quisite for supporting the principles of republican government, but when that caution is carried too far, the event
may and probably will prove alarming."[1] He realized that
it was only a matter of time when a convention must be
called to revise the frame of government.

Not until the request of Congress had been six months
before the states, does there appear the slightest evidence of
its consideration in Rhode Island.   In August, 1781, the
delegates, Varnum and Mowry, wrote from Congress to Governor Greene: " We are at a loss to conjecture the rumors
which have induced the state of Rhode Island to delay complying with the requisition of Congress respecting the five
per cent. duty."[2]   No response was vouchsafed until October, when in a letter to Robert Morris, the Governor says of
the proposed grant: " We are unable to determine on the
utility of that measure . . . We shall wait until our sister
states have adopted the same, and whatever is for the advantage of the union, we shall cheerfully accede to."[3]   So
the matter rested until General Varnum, relieved by the
presence of his colleagues from attendance in Congress, returned home at the close of 1781, to exert his inflence for
the impost.

Productions from the pen of the opposition were not
wanting before Varnum entered the arena.   A letter which
appeared in the *Providence Gazette* of January 26, 1782,
over the signature, " Dixit Senex," is typical of the attitude
of the party.   " Congress," said this writer, " may call on us
for money, but cannot prescribe to us methods of raising it;
that is within our sovereignty, and lies wholly in the power
of our own legislature."[4]   He anticipates the introduction of

---

[1] *Rhode Island Archives (MS.), Letters, 1780–1, 47.*

[2] *Rhode Island Archives (MS.), Letters, 1781–2, 3.*

[3] *Rhode Island Colonial Records, ix, 485.*

[4] *Providence Gazette, Jan. 26, 1782.*

strange tax-gatherers and excisemen, and would debar all members of the legislature from holding any revenue office. In a series of articles over the signature of " Citizen," Varnum demonstrates the desirability of a stable revenue, which, if easily collected, would prove a great blessing, essential to the ending of the war.[1] The theory of American nationality developed by him was purely federal. He says: " Were we to contemplate the United States separately, as composing thirteen distinct sovereignties unconnected with and independent of each other, the requisition in question would appear totally absurd and ridiculous. This, however, is not the case."[2] From the union under the Continental Congress, the Declaration of Independence, and the harmonious action of the states, he drew the conclusion of the existence of a single nation, and denied the independence of the states.

Such utterances called forth a champion for the opposition, hitherto unknown to political fame, in the person of David Howell, a lawyer of Providence, and a professor in Brown University. It is in his writings that we find the most able presentation of the opposition cause.[3] The first of his letters in the *Gazette*, in reply to Varnum, compared the impost proposition to the Stamp Act. On the strict construction of the Articles of Confederation he relied for proof of the sovereignty of the states, and he utterly denied any inherent sovereignty in Congress. As a restriction on commerce, he opposed the impost. For, said he, " It is against the welfare of any commercial state to clog and

---

[1] The articles of Varnum, signed " *Citizen*," are in the *Providence Gazette* of Mar. 2, 9, 16, 23, and 30, Apr. 20, and May 18, 1782.

[2] *Providence Gazette*, March 16, 1782.

[3] Howell's articles in the *Gazette* over the signature " *A Farmer*," appeared March 23 and 30, and April 6 and 10.

embarrass trade with any restrictions or duties whatsoever."[1] If duties were necessary, Rhode Island should lay her own. On the assumption that import duties are borne by the importer, he argued that when duties were levied under the Articles of Confederation, Rhode Island paid one-fiftieth of the whole amount, but under the proposed plan, granting that she owned one twenty-fifth of the shipping of the states, she would pay one twenty-fifth of the tax. In another letter Howell gives a resumé of his objections to the impost. He acknowledges Rhode Island's duty to pay her quota, but only according to the method prescribed in the Articles of Confederation. He considered it the most precious jewel of a state's sovereignty that it could not be called on to open its purse but by the authority of its own legislature. Should customs officers be introduced from without, there would be no means of controlling them. The funds collected would be turned into the general treasury, where the taxpayers could not observe their disbursement. If there was any benefit to be derived from the power to lay duties, the state should retain it, for the inland states in their turn would not surrender their peculiar privileges. The grant was further considered too indefinite. The time was not specified and the grant was irrevocable. In short, Rhode Island admitted her duty to pay her quota of taxes, but would brook no departure from the terms of the Articles of Confederation.[2]

Here the controversy rested for a brief time. The Fabian policy of the opposition had kept the question out of the assembly for more than a year. The first result of this struggle was the retirement of Ellery, Varnum and Mowry from Congress, and the election of delegates less favorable to the impost. These were John Collins, the future paper money governor, General Ezekiel Cornell, Jonathan Arnold,

[1] *Providence Gazette*, March 30, 1782.

[2] *Ibid.*, April 13, 1782.

and, most notable of all, David Howell. The latter was instructed to proceed at once to Congress, where he soon had occasion once more to defend the position of his state, this time before a Congressional committee. At the request of a committee appointed to inquire why Georgia and Rhode Island had not granted the impost, Howell appeared to defend his state. As in his newspaper writings he had spoken to his neighbors, so now he spoke to the whole country. His objections, as expressed before the committee, were four in number:

1. The proposed system tended to raise a revenue for the use of the general government and not of the state. This would be paid by the merchants, and, should they be unable to obtain a correspondingly higher price for their goods, they would be crushed out of existence. Such a burden would rest more heavily on Rhode Island than on any other state, from the preponderance of the mercantile and manufacturing classes, and her inability to produce agricultural products sufficient for her own markets.

2. Rhode Island had suffered heavily from the ravages of war. Newport, which in 1774, sent out one hundred and fifty sail, now sent out but three. To compensate for her losses, the state should retain the power of laying duties. More especially should this be done in self defense, so long as the larger states persisted in claiming western lands.

3. It would be derogatory to the dignity of a state to permit foreign officers within her boundaries, collecting a revenue under some external authority. All revenue collected in the state should be handled by her own officers, and stand to her individual credit.

4. The terms of the grant were too indefinite. Though the intentions of the present Congress were honorable, their successors. by keeping the national debt outstanding, might perpetuate the impost. The states would be powerless to prevent it.

In closing, Howell suggested two amendments: first, that the states retain the power of appointing collectors; second, that the revenue collected in each state be credited to the account of that state. Thus the presence of officers of the central government would be avoided, and Rhode Island would be the gainer, owing to the position which she expected again to assume in the commercial world.[1]

To counteract Howell's influence at home, Robert Morris wrote an elaborate letter to Governor Greene, taking up the objections made by Howell and disposing of them one by one.[2] His arguments did not differ in substance from those employed elsewhere by the advocates of the measure, and were based on the propriety of the act and the exigencies of the time. He enlarged on the fact that, to continue and lighten the present burdens, the revenue was necessary. The refusal of Rhode Island would defeat the whole plan. The entreaties of Morris were of no avail, for the aversion to the impost was too strong to yield to persuasion.

On October 10, 1782, wearied at the procrastination of Georgia and Rhode Island, Congress passed a resolution demanding of those states a definite answer.[3] Repeated assurances of acquiescence left no doubt as to the final action of Georgia, but of Rhode Island there was no hope. With the question now fairly put before the state, Howell, in writing to his friend Theodore Foster, said: "The crisis has at length arrived. . . . I hope those who have undertaken to contend for the liberties of their country and retain the zeal of 1775 will [display] it on this occasion. . . . I doubt not my friend but you will make every honorable effort to prevent this fatal measure from being carried into effect. . . . I hope every exertion will be made on the occasion by the friends

---

[1] *Rhode Island Archives (MS.), Letters, 1781-2,* July 30, 1782.

[2] *Rhode Island Archives (MS.), Letters, 1782-3,* 1.

[3] *Journals of Congress,* iv, 86.

of liberty and free trade. . . . Should it be adopted, I shall
no longer consider myself as the representative of a sovereign and free state, but wish to be recalled. But I cannot
suspect the firmness of our assembly. I hope they will not
be *driven* into any measure. This is but an entering wedge,
others will follow, a land tax, a poll tax and an excise." [1]
To Moses Brown, Howell expressed his conviction that the
state of Rhode Island would support him in his opposition
to the impost.[2] Both Howell and Arnold endeavored to impress the assembly with the necessity of withholding the
impost while the western lands were still held by some states
to the prejudice of others.[3] In a last appeal the delegates
even questioned the right of the assembly to make such a
grant. Would it not, they argued, be an infringement on
the rights of future assemblies, to make such a perpetual
grant of money? Why should they not cling to the old
method, under which Rhode Island had ever been ready to
contribute to the extent of her ability?

While the impost was pending before the assembly, Congress called for the quotas of supplies from the states for the
ensuing year. Howell made an attempt to secure the collection of this tax separately from the state taxes, to be subject only to the order of Congress, or of the Superintendent
of Finance. But, instead of this, was adopted a plan embodying the same thought, and further, the appointment of
a receiver in each state to hold the funds. The receiver was
to have the rights possessed by the state treasurers against
delinquent collectors.[4] The making of collectors responsible
to a receiver, instead of to the treasurer, was considered by
Howell and Arnold a sufficient departure from established

[1] *Foster Correspondence* (*MS.*), i, 20.

[2] *Moses Brown Papers* (*MS.*), iv, 23.

[3] *Rhode Island Archives* (*MS.*), *Letters, 1782-3*, 23.

[4] *Journals of Congress*, iv, 91.

custom to warrant their strongest opposition. The appointment of a receiver was but one degree less obnoxious than
the appointment of customs officers by Congress. It would,
they contended, supersede in part one of the state officers,
and introduce a new functionary unknown to the constitution, and irresponsible to the people.[1]

The assembly met at East Greenwich on the last Monday
in October, and on the first day of November, with fifty-
three of the whole number sixty-eight present, voted unanimously against the impost.[2] In reporting the result to
Congress, Speaker Bradford stated three reasons for rejection :

1. The plan would be unequal in operation, bearing most
heavily on the commercial states.

2. It proposed to introduce into the state, officers unknown
and irresponsible to the state government. Hence the
measure would be unconstitutional.

3. The grant was not limited in time. Since Congress
was not accountable to the states for its expenditures, it
would be placed in an independent position, repugnant to
the liberties of the state.

The writer hastened, however, to assure Congress of the
loyalty of the state, and her willingness to bear her share of
the burdens of the nation.[3] Along with the rejection of the
impost, as if in anticipation of the tumult that act was to
excite, instructions were sent to the delegates in Congress,
" To vindicate and support with a becoming firmness on all
occasions, such of the acts of the General Assembly of this
state as respect the United States at large, and to use their

[1] *Rhode Island Archives (MS), Letters, 1782–3*, 30.

[2] *Providence Gazette*, Nov. 2, 1782. As the question did not come before the
upper house, it does not appear on the MS. records.

[3] *Journals of Congress*, iv, 116.

utmost exertions to prevent any infringement being made on the sovereignty and independence thereof." [1]

The scene now changes to the halls of Congress, where Bradford's official announcement was not read until December twelfth. The unofficial report had been but a few days in reaching the expectant ear of Congress. When, on December sixth, a resolution was passed, urging compliance with the requisition for 1783, a provision was inserted that a deputation be sent to Rhode Island to impress the necessity of the impost.[2] In spite of the protest of Howell and Arnold, such a deputation was appointed.[3] The action of Rhode Island becoming known unofficially, a committee, on December eleventh, reported a letter to be sent to the governor of that state remonstrating against such action, and demanding a special session of the assembly to reconsider the question and receive the message of the deputation.[4] On receipt of Bradford's letter, a long reply was at once drawn up to disprove the allegations contained in it.[5]

Rumors now began to come in that Maryland was meditating a revocation of her grant. Delaying their departure to learn the truth, the Rhode Island deputation did not set out until December twenty-second. Half a day's journey from Philadelphia, they were overtaken by the news that Virginia had repealed her grant. They at once returned and two days later were discharged from their mission. The response of Rhode Island was a new departure. No other state, however it hampered its grant, had refused outright. Though it had almost been assured that she would reject the impost, still the announcement that she had actually done so created a profound sensation. As the news spread through

---

[1] *Acts and Resolves of the General Assembly (MS.),* Nov. 2, 1782.

[2] *Journals of Congress,* iv, 115; Gilpin, *Madison Papers,* i, 225.

[3] *Rhode Island Archives (MS.), Letters, 1782-3,* 33.

[4] *Journals of Congress,* iv, 116.   [5] *Ibid.,* iv, 118.

the states, comment was by no means in all cases depreca-
tory. Many people were, in the words of a Pennsylvanian,
"pleased to find that the State of Rhode Island . . . . have
unanimously resolved not to invest them with the power of
levying five per cent."[1]

Through the whole struggle, David Howell had stood out
as the chief opponent. Again and again he had obstructed
the cherished plans of the government. Now he had defeated the most important of all. His own feelings at the
defeat of the impost found expression in an address to the
people of Rhode Island, wherein he declared that their opposition to British oppression would not rank the state
higher in the annals of America, than the firmness and unanimity with which they rejected the impost.[2] With Howell's
influence predominant, it was felt that hope for a change of
sentiment in Rhode Island was vain. To destroy his influence, on the same day that the deputation to Rhode Island was
appointed, a committee was chosen to inquire into the authorship of certain statements which had lately appeared in the
newspapers. Through these publications it was feared that,
"as well the national character of the United States and the
honor of Congress, as the finances of the said state, may be
injured and the public service greatly retarded."[3]

The committee reported that they had particularly noted
a letter in the *Boston Gazette* of November 10, 1782, under
the heading, *Providence*, purporting to have been written
from Philadelphia to a man in that town. The questionable
passage was in these words: "This day letters have been
read in Congress from Mr. Adams of the sixteenth of
August, and Mr. Dumas, his secretary, of the nineteenth.

[1] *Providence Gazette*, Dec. 18, 1782.

[2] *Ibid.*, April 12, 1782.

[3] Gilpin, *Madison Papers*, i, 223; *Rhode Island Archives* (*MS.*), *Letters, 1782-3,*
33, 44, where there is a certified copy of the motion.

The loan he is negotiating fills as fast as could be expected. The national importance of the United States is constantly rising in the estimation of European powers and the civilized world. Such is their credit that they have of late failed in no application for loans, and the only danger on that score is that of contracting too large a debt."[1] Investigation, said the committee, had proved the statements ill founded and untrue. From internal evidence it was suspected that the author was a member of Congress. To reach the truth in the matter, the Secretary of Foreign Affairs was directed to request from the executive of Rhode Island the discovery of the author. That such a course was unnecessary, there is good evidence, for Madison says: "The unanimous suspicions were fixed on Mr. Howell." But it was thought that a detection of the person suspected "would destroy in that state that influence which he exerted in misleading its counsels with respect to the impost."[2]

Mr. Howell having acknowledged the authorship of the writings in question, it was moved that the Secretary of Foreign Affairs be discharged from his instructions, because of " Mr. Howell, a delegate from the State of Rhode Island, having acknowledged himself the author of the extract of the letter quoted in the report of the committee."[3] Howell at once moved to postpone this motion which placed his name on the journal in such a connection, to consider a similar motion, accompanied by a formal acknowledgement of the writings with his justification. He denied the authority of Congress over his correspondence with the state executive. ·The very existence of such a committee, he declared, was

[1] For this and other extracts appearing in the newspapers, and the proceedings of Congress thereon, see certified copy of the proceedings of Congress in *Rhode Island Archives (MS.)*, *Letters, 1782-3;* also *Journals of Congress,* iv, 118. For publication see *Providence Gazette,* Nov. 2, 1782.

[2] Gilpin, *Madison Papers,* i, 223.

[3] *Journals of Congress,* iv, 120; Gilpin, *Madison Papers,* i, 223.

derogatory to the dignity of Congress, and tended to establish a precedent dangerous to the freedom of the press, the
palladium of liberty both civil and religious. He maintained
that the writings in question were substantially true, as could
be proven by documents then in the possession of Congress.
But he protested against the publication or placing on the
journal of one's utterances in a mutilated form. The original
motion prevailed, followed by another, made by Hamilton,
that "Congress having, in respect to the Articles of Confederation, admitted on their journals an entry of a motion
made by Mr. Howell, seconded by Mr. Arnold, highly derogatory to the dignity and honor of the United States in
Congress assembled: Resolved, that a committee be appointed to report such measures as it will be proper for
Congress to take thereon." [1] Accordingly the Secretary of
Foreign Affairs was directed to transmit Howell's motion,
together with a statement of the foreign loans to the executive of Rhode Island, with a view of proving the falsity of the
writings.[2] But when, two weeks later, Arnold moved to forward to his state executive certain letters substantiating
Howell's disputed statements, the motion was postponed.
That the circumstance might not be used by Howell in justification of his action, the matter was referred to a committee,
and the proceedings on the whole affair were placed on the
secret journal.[3] Such procedure was irregular and adopted
only in the last extremity, to baffle Howell in attempting to
make his position secure at home. It was even doubted by
some, whether it was within the jurisdiction of Congress to
do so.[4] Realizing that they had overshot the mark, and fear-

[1] *Journals of Congress*, iv, 122; *Rhode Island Archives (MS.), Letters, 1783-5,* 2.
[2] *Journals of Congress*, iv, 122-3.
[3] *Secret Journals of Congress*, i, 249; *Rhode Island Archives (MS.), Letters, 1782-3,* 45.
[4] Gilpin, *Madison Papers*, i, 246.

ing that greater harm than advantage would come from the affair, Congress, on January fourteenth, voted to transmit to Rhode Island Arnold's motion, with the documents therein mentioned.[1]

When the contest was virtually at an end, the whole matter was laid before the assembly. The expression of that body's approbation of the acts of the delegates was made in a series of resolutions, transmitted to Congress. These were:

(1) "That the motion containing a declaration and protest made by Mr. Howell and seconded by Mr. Arnold, as entered on the journals of Congress, of the eighteenth day of December, in the year 1782, appears to be just, true and proper, aud that this general assembly do highly approve of the conduct of the delegates in making said motion, declaration and protest."

(2) "That the extracts of letters from the secretary of foreign affairs, laid before this general assembly, do fully justify the representations made by this state to its delegates in regard to the success of the late applications of Congress for foreign loans, and in regard to our credit and reputation in Europe."

(3) That this general assembly entertain a high sense of the meritorious services rendered to the state and to the cause of freedom in general by the firm and patriotic conduct of the said delegates, particularly in their strenuous exertions to defeat the operations of measures, which the state considered dangerous to public liberty.

(4) That his excellency, the governor of this state, return an answer to the aforesaid letter of his excellency, the president of Congress, enclosing a copy of these resolutions."[2]

Rhode Island had repeatedly declared her willingness to

[1] *Journals of Congress*, iv, 142.

[2] *Acts and Resolves of the General Assembly (MS.)*, Feb. 8, 1783.

raise her quota of the national revenue, provided it could be raised by state authority. Having carried her point against the five per cent. impost, she at once laid an import duty exactly like that proposed by Congress.[1]

The contest over the import duty had proved the Rhode Island champion to be the ultra state-rights member of the Continental Congress. Holding strong opinions, and forced often to maintain them against great odds, he sometimes overstepped the bounds of parliamentary courtesy, and practiced a vigorous obstruction policy. Of his sincerity and singleness of purpose there is ample evidence, not only in his own public writings, but in his private correspondence. To Theodore Foster he wrote: "I wish my constituents to know every sentiment I have advanced and every vote I have given. If I have been wrong I may then be informed of it and put right. If I have been right I shall receive that approbation from the good and virtuous which every earnest servant of the public is entitled to. This is the reward I covet."[1]

Were further evidence required, it could be found in the letters of his colleague, Dr. Arnold. Of Howell he said: "It appears to have been his first and only wish to serve his country generally, and especially his constituents, with unshaken fidelity. . . . He clearly understood the Articles of Confederation, and distinguished between the rights relinquished and those retained. . . . He has vindicated himself with a firmness becoming a representative of a free state."[3]

In reviewing Rhode Island's action on the impost, its motives may be reduced to three:

(1) A misunderstanding of the effects of an import duty.

(2) Anxiety respecting the disposal of western lands.

[1] *Providence Gazette*, March 15, 1783.

[2] *Foster Correspondence* (*MS.*), i, 20.

[3] *Rhode Island Archives* (*MS.*), *Letters, 1782–3*, 34.

(3) A jealousy of yielding to outside authority any power over her internal affairs.

In relation to an impost, Rhode Island stood in a peculiar position. She was the only small state in which commerce and manufactures predominated. No state was so dependent on its neighbors for agricultural products. To restore the former commerce of the state was the dream of the new race of merchants. Free trade was to be the foster-mother of their enterprise, but, they agreed, should a duty be levied, it must be paid by the importer. He might or might not be able to add this to the price of his goods. In case it was added, the neighboring states would probably raise correspondingly the price of their products. The proceeds from the duty, instead of remaining in the state to balance this enhanced price, would be withdrawn for the use of the general government. Should the neighboring states be provoked to lay an embargo against her, the state would be in a sorry plight.

The attitude of the state toward the public domain was similar to that of New Jersey, in that she did not contend for national jurisdiction over the territory.[1] She simply demanded that the proceeds from the sale of such lands should accrue to the benefit of the general treasury. In accordance with their instructions from the first discussions of the subject her delegates contended earnestly " for this state's proportion of vacant or back lands."[2] Filled with this plan for the solution of the financial difficulties of the nation, Rhode Island refused to yield her peculiar advantages until she was assured of a fair share of the proceeds of this great domain.

The extreme individualism developed in the people of Rhode Island by their history and surroundings was a marked trait in their character. A century of constant

---

[1] *Journals of Congress*, ii, 605.

[2] *Acts and Resolves of the General Assembly* (*MS.*), Nov. 2, 1782.

struggle to preserve their chartered rights had created a jealousy of all outside interference in their affairs, which it required but the proposition to transfer to Congress the power
of collecting a revenue within the state to rouse.   In her refusal to grant this power to Congress, Rhode Island for the
first time opposed the united will of the states.

But as the prospect of securing the grant of the impost
faded, the necessity of a stable revenue became more and
more painfully evident.   The opening of the year 1783
found the revenue the topic for consideration before Congress.   To heighten their anxieties, a memorial was presented from the officers of the army, setting forth in the
strongest terms their desperate situation.   Dissatisfaction
was gaining ground in the ranks on account of the pay
which was in arrears.   It was fully realized that the public
debt must be paid or the interest met.   The former was out
of the question; the latter became an imperative necessity.
Under the existing powers of Congress, this interest must
be met by requisitions, or by the establishment of permanent funds in the states.   The first had proved impracticable;
the second would rouse state jealousies.   The late experiences with Rhode Island made hope in this direction
almost vain.   The only resource left was to obtain, through
additional powers conferred on Congress, a general revenue,
but under such restrictions as would make it acceptable to
the unwilling members.   The declaration by supporters of a
liberal construction of the powers of Congress that, as that
body was authorized to borrow money, it had the power to
raise money to repay it, stirred the strict construction spirit
of Rhode Island.[1]   Her delegates asserted that no power
not expressly authorized by the Articles of Confederation
could be exercised, and that any argumentative construction
was abhorrent to freedom.

[1] Gilpin, *Madison Papers*, i, 296.

The deliberations of Congress crystallized into a resolution, proposing to the states for their ratification a plan for raising a revenue, which was adopted on April eighteenth, 1783. The Rhode Island delegates, together with Hamilton, and Higginson of Massachusetts, voted in the negative.[1] As it went out to the states, the scheme included:

(1) A duty on imports.

(2) A permanent revenue, to continue twenty-five years, to be raised by the states to meet the annual quotas of fifteen million dollars.

(3) An amendment to the Articles of Confederation changing the basis of apportionment of taxes among the states from that of real estate to an apportionment according to population.

This plan, which was to take effect when agreed to by all the states, was essentially a revival of the plan of 1781, modified in some particulars. It provided for a specific duty on liquors, tea, coffee, cocoa, pepper, and sugar, and an ad valorem duty of five per cent. on all other imports. The proceeds were to be employed in paying the debt incurred by the war. In the discussion of the plan of 1781, objection had been made, particularly by Howell, that the term of the grant was too indefinite; that by neglecting to discharge the public debt the grant might be made perpetual. To obviate this objection, the act was limited, illogically perhaps, to twenty-five years. Again, it had been objected, that there would be introduced into the state officers appointed by Congress and unaccountable to the state government. But since, to have left this function to be exercised by officers both appointed by and responsible to the state would have been to continue the old system, a compromise gave the appointment of these officers to the state, but retained the control of them in Congress. Profiting by another

[1] *Journals of Congress*, iv, 190.

criticism of the former plan, the states were to receive an annual statement of the receipts under the law. To say that Rhode Island was the cause of the features peculiar to this plan, would be too sweeping an assertion. It is interesting to note, however, that every change in the part providing for an impost, excepting the introduction of a specific duty, was suggested by that state in her objections to the impost of 1781.

Along with this scheme was issued an address to the states, emphasizing the desperate circumstances of the national finances, as well as the relief to be expected from the proposed measure. The situation was brought out more clearly by accompanying documents, among which was the letter sent to Rhode Island, on December sixteenth, 1782, in answer to that state's rejection of the impost, inserted as containing a most carefully prepared reply to the objections to the plan of 1781. This is the letter which Howell said would " remain on the journal of Congress as a monument of the ingenuity and zeal of the day in which it was written.'" It was hoped that with so many concessions, the new impost might receive the support of all. But that this letter should now be reissued and brought to the notice of all the states, did not tend to incline Rhode Island toward compliance. That it was not merely the specific duty that displeased the delegates of that state, but that they were firmly set against the whole system, was soon evident. The only specific objection made by them still remaining, was that the collectors were removable by Congress. Now they took refuge behind this single point, and fought as hotly as ever. Expressing their strong disapproval of the plan, they laid it before the general assembly for their consideration. The appointment of customs officers under this system, they alleged, would be incompatible with the state constitution,

---

[1] *Rhode Island Archives* (*MS.*), *Letters, 1783-5*, 22.

which provided for annual appointments. The appointment of officers to become independent of the authority appointing them would be a constant menace to justice.[1]

The proposition so vigorously urged upon the states was first acted on by Delaware, followed in early summer by Pennsylvania. In Rhode Island, for a whole year, no official notice of the matter was taken. The only references to it are in the letters of the delegates, and in brief notes in the newspapers. It was on September eighth, 1783, in a letter reviewing the subjects then before Congress, that Howell and Ellery first commented on the measure.[2] A memorial from Massachusetts, protesting against the half pay of army officers and the prevailing high salaries, furnished the text of their discourse.[3] That state enumerated her grievances, and applied for redress, but at the same time carefully kept her grasp on the purse-strings. Herein, it was thought, lay the protection of the states. " Had the state of Massachusetts granted Congress the revenue they request, what would have remained in their hands to give weight to their remonstrances against the commutation and high salaries, or against any other grievance?"[4] In other words, the custom followed by the British House of Commons of voting annual supply bills, was the proper mode of curbing authority. " The power of the purse," said the delegates, " is the touchstone of freedom in all states. If the people command their own money they are free; but if their sovereign commands it they are slaves. All other strings in government take their tone from the mode of raising money. An alteration, therefore, in the mode of raising money, is an alteration of

[1] Staples, *Rhode Island in the Continental Congress*, 435.

[2] Letter to Gov. Greene, *Rhode Island Archives (MS.)*, *Letters, 1783–5*, 6.

[3] *Journals of Congress*, iv, 276.

[4] Letter from delegates to Gov. Greene, *Rhode Island Archives (MS.)*, *Letters, 1783–5*, 2.

the Constitution.   It is an essential and radical change. . . .
It is altering the center of gravity.   It is like transferring the
fee simple of an estate.   It is like putting your weapon of
defense into another man's hand."[1]   The doctrine of implied
powers was particularly to be reprehended.   Grant the power
of laying an impost, and admit of powers by implication, and
liberty would take its flight.   Should such pernicious doc-
trines be recognized, the future would see " Continental taxes
collected by continental officers, under the laws of Congress,
and offenders against these laws . . . liable to be carried
into any part of the United States for trial, and that before
continental judges appointed by Congress.   Such in time
might be the bitter fruit of this evil tree—a continental impost."[2]

Again, on the fifth of the following February, Howell in-
veighs against the impost.   This time it was a remonstrance
from Connecticut on the same question of half pay, which
called up the matter.   His imagination pictured the Congress
of the future, holding in one hand the purse, and in the other
a sword above the heads of the trembling and impotent
states.   For " if the states give up to Congress the power of
raising money from them, and of disposing of that money,
their particular sovereignty will, in fact, be all absorbed in
one mighty sovereignty, against the abuses of which they
will retain only the power of complaining, and receiving for
answer that they can have no remedy."[3]   The opprobrium
cast upon the state at the present time would find its ample
compensation in the approbation of the future.   Then, said
he, let the states " govern themselves—maintain their separate sovereignties—and adhere strictly to the principles of

[1] Letter from delegates to Gov. Greene, *Rhode Island Archives* (*MS.*), *Letters,
1783-5,* 2.

[2] *Ibid.*   [3] *Ibid.,* 22.

their union and alliance with each other, and in a word, do justice."[1]

To the influence of these leaders of opinion were added occasional contributions to the public press, on the question of the hour. As early as May, 1783, Madison wrote to Edmund Randolph of the impost: "In Rhode Island they are attacking it in the newspapers."[2] Yet, considering the importance of the question, and the active part taken by the Rhode Island delegates, the papers are strangely silent. Perhaps the leaders believed that their views on the whole question of a Continental impost had been sufficiently emphasized on previous occasions. The attack of which Madison wrote was made by " Dixit Senex" in the *Gazette*. He contended that not only taxation, but every power of government, should reside in the legislature. This position was characteristic of Rhode Island, for her assembly had always been and was long to continue to be the most absolute legislative body in America. Taxation, he declared to be the natural instrument of tyranny. Said he, " I never wish for the power of raising devils I have not the power of laying."[3]

" Casca," in the *Gazette* of October eleventh, admitted that the promoters of the impost were honest, but dishonesty might follow. After risking everything to establish "free republics," it seemed folly to part with everything "to establish one great sovereignty. Difficulty in obtaining money is the best assurance of its wise use."[4]

Another writer, more than a year later, congratulated the nation on the fact that there were thirteen republics instead of one. To him, the only logical outcome of the measure of

[1] Letter from delegates to Gov. Greene, *Rhode Island Archives (MS.)*, *Letters, 1783–5*, 22.

[2] Gilpin, *Madison Papers*, i, 547.

[3] *Providence Gazette*, May 10, 1783.

[4] *Providence Gazette*, Oct. 11, 1783.

February third, 1781, and April eighteenth, 1783, would be to create a mighty Continental legislature, in time to merge and swallow up the legislatures of the particular states."[1]

When, in reply to Rhode Island's inveighings against the impost, the distress of the public treasury was pleaded, the constant rejoinder was that the relief was to be found in the public lands. Among the amendments proposed by Rhode Island to the Articles of Confederation, was one providing for the cession of western lands to the general government.[1] During the year 1782, the public domain became a leading question in politics.[2] An inclination among the large states was manifested to accede to the demands of the smaller ones. Tenders of cession made by New York[3] and Virginia[4] came before Congress for debate in the spring of 1782, at the time when Howell made his first appearance in that body. Soon after the election the Rhode Island delegation was advised in regard to the vacant lands, that " this state conceives itself to be invested with a perfect and indisputable right, in common with her sister states, to the said lands."[5] In the instructions given at the time of Rhode Island's rejection of the impost, the delegates were again charged " to contend earnestly for this state's proportion of vacant or back lands."[6]

Owing to the strength of opposing factions the prospects of success were not flattering. Howell, as a member of the committee on public credit, proposed to bring up the subject of the back lands, for he thought they would undoubtedly furnish a means of restoring public credit. But, though the question was debated long and hotly, and on some occasions

---

[1] *Providence Gazette*, Apr. 9, 1785.

[2] *Rhode Island Colonial Records*, viii, 365.

[3] *Journals of Congress*, iv, 582.

[4] *Journals of Congress*, iv, 68.

[5] *Rhode Island Colonial Records*, ix, 561.

[6] *Acts and Resolves of the General Assembly (MS.)*, Nov. 2, 1782.

the claimants were outvoted, yet nothing definite was accomplished.[1]

The possibilities of revenue from the public domain were no less vivid to the Rhode Island delegates when the second impost proposition was before them than before. This was the alternative suggested on all occasions, and the end persistently sought for. So long as this resource remained a possibility, it was thought to be folly to resort to another, which was uncertain and dangerous to liberty.[1] In the plan for the government of the western lands, of the committee to prepare which Howell was a member, his idea found expression in the provision that nothing should interfere with the disposal of the soil by the United States.[2] By this means he proposed to secure a revenue which should pay the debt of the nation, and leave Rhode Island a free mart of commerce. The happy influence of the possession of a national domain upon the national spirit, inspires a peculiar interest in this earliest attitude of the states on the question. Oddly enough, the measure with which Rhode Island was closely in sympathy, was a potent factor in bringing about the very condition which she, of all the states, most feared, viz., a truly national spirit.

While ignoring the measure proposed by Congress, Rhode Island had gone on with her own methods of raising a revenue. A duty of two per cent. on the list of enumerated articles was imposed.[2] This duty was, after July first, to apply to all foreign goods which had not already paid duty in another state. The proceeds were specifically appropriated to the payment of the interest on the state debt.

The legislature did not take up the proposal of Congress until June twenty-eighth, 1784. On that day it resolved

[1] Letter from delegates to Gov. Greene, Oct. 13, 1782. *Rhode Island Archives* (*MS.*), *Letters, 1782-3*, 23.

[2] *Schedules of the General Assembly*, June Session, 1783, 26.

that the basis of taxation prescribed in the Articles of Confederation was preferable to that proposed by Congress.
They showed their adherence to the old method by ordering
a new assessment on that basis. The impost clause was debated in the lower house at the same time, and rejected by
a majority of forty. In its place, the duty of the previous
year was raised to two and one-half per cent. As in the
year before, dependence was placed on direct taxes to meet
the requisitions of the general government.[1]

By the end of 1784, there began to appear, however, a
weakening in the ranks of the opposition. In this emergency Ellery wrote to Green, "I trust that nothing but the
last necessity will embrace it in its present form, if at all. It
is probable that this state [New York] will not come into it,
and if it should not, I think we ought not to be scared into
it by the inefficacious act of Connecticut."[2] At its February
session, the assembly was induced to pass an act which was
a step toward the request of Congress. It was but a halting
attempt, but was secured by the friends of the impost as an
entering wedge. The act imposed the same specific duty, and
on the same articles, as that proposed by Congress, and likewise a five per cent. duty on all other imports. The collectors
were appointed by and amenable to the general assembly.
Of the proceeds, eight thousand dollars was appropriated
annually to pay the share of the state in the foreign debt of
the United States. The remainder was to be devoted to the
payment of the proportion of the domestic debt held in
Rhode Island. A poll tax of one Spanish milled dollar was
imposed, and a like tax on every hundred acres of land, and
on every house over two years old. This act was to take
effect when all the other states should accept the plan of
Congress, and should continue twenty-five years.

[1] *Acts and Resolves of the General Assembly* (*MS.*), *1784–5, 3.* July 2, 1784.
[2] *Rhode Island Archives* (*MS.*), *Letters, 1783–5,* 51.

It was only after a struggle that the assembly was induced to yield so much. Even that was done only under the strongest pressure. The greater share of those who had looked with horror on the proposition for a general impost now felt that the door was open to evils innumerable. But their hearts were soon made glad by the news that New York had failed to pass the impost by a vote of thirteen in the senate, and that the popular current in that state was setting against the measure.[1] This postponed indefinitely the operation of Rhode Island's late act, leaving in effect only the impost of two and a half per cent. In July, 1785, the number of articles paying the duty was greatly increased,[2] and in October of the same year the act was again amended.[3]

In the meantime, Congress was staggering on beneath its burden of debt. Since the last of October, 1781, requisitions on the states had been made to the extent of over $16,670,000. To meet these, there had been paid in by the states only $2,419,000, of which neither North Carolina nor Georgia had paid one cent. For the ensuing year, it was estimated that there would be necessary $2,508,327 to pay the public service, and the interest on the public debt. Besides, there would fall due during the year a part of the principal of two foreign loans and many domestic obligations.[4] The question of means was well nigh incapable of solution. The consummation of the impost plan appeared the only hope. An examination of the acts of the various states showed that New Hampshire, Massachusetts, Connecticut, New Jersey, Virginia, North Carolina, and South Carolina had granted the impost clause in such manner that,

[1] Howell to Gov. Greene, *Rhode Island Archives* (*MS.*), *Letters, 1783–5,* 66.
[2] *Acts and Resolves of the General Assembly* (*MS.*), *1784–5,* 109.
[3] *Schedules of the General Assembly,* Oct. Session, 1785, 42.
[4] *Journals of Congress,* iv, 614.

should the other six states do likewise, that clause might become operative at once. Delaware and Pennsylvania had granted the impost, but had attached provisos that withheld its operation until the whole system should be adopted by all the states. Neither Maryland, Georgia, nor New York had passed any act whatever in conformity with the plan. Rhode Island's act was so different from the form desired, and so insufficient, that it was not considered a compliance. In view of this state of affairs, Congress again presented the plan of April, 1783, to the states, calling on them with the earnestness of despair to adopt it.[1] This call came like the last appeal of a drowning man to the Rhode Island assembly at its February session, 1786. Summoning all their forces, the friends of the measure secured the passage of an act granting the full measure of power over imposts which was desired by Congress. The act granted " power to levy and collect within this state, for the use of the United States, for the special purpose of paying off the principal and interest of the debt contracted during the late war with Great Britain, the following duties upon goods imported into this state from any foreign port or island or plantation whatever, to be collected under such regulations as the United States in Congress assembled shall direct."[2] This power was granted under the provisions and limitations stated in the recommendation of Congress.

The impost had not absorbed the undivided attention of the American people during these stormy years. Our commercial relations with the rest of the world were in a condition to demand immediate action. It is from a study of America's commercial relations, that Rhode Island's attitude upon the questions of the day is best comprehended. Therein may be seen why a state which had been so violently

[1] *Journals of Congress,* iv, 614-5.
[2] *Acts and Resolves of the General Assembly (MS.),* Feb. Session, 1786, March 3.

L. of C.

opposed to granting to Congress power over the revenue, should have come finally to grant all that was asked.

As the negotiations for peace passed through successive stages, the commercial relations between Great Britain and America proved a bone of contention. The local policy of Pitt and Shelburne would not only have granted to Americans equal rights with other foreign nations, but would have allowed American ships and goods the right of entry into British ports on payment of the same duties that were imposed on British subjects. The opposition in Parliament declared this to be a revolution in commercial policy, and a violation of the Navigation Acts. In case of its adoption, they prophesied the absorption of the West India trade by America, to the detriment of the mother country. Against this opposition Pitt and Shelburne were not to prevail. By an order in council of July second, 1783, trade between America and the British West Indies was restricted to British ships, owned and manned by British seamen. America was thrown into consternation. Never before had the American people understood what it implied commercially to be separated from England. Before the war one-third of British tonnage was of American build. The West India trade had been in the hands of merchants in the northern colonies, and had proved most profitable. It had been the hope of the commercial interests centering in New York, Boston, Providence, and Newport, that at the close of the war this profitable occupation might be resumed. With the proceeds of this trade flowing into their coffers, and the power of levying duties carefully retained by the states, an era of prosperity was open before them. But just as the danger of a Continental impost was removed for the time being, their dreams were dispelled by the order in council.

Great quantities of English goods were flooding the country, underselling and exterminating domestic manufactures.

Specie was drained out of the country, while the American merchant who took his goods to England to sell for specie was met by a heavy tariff. On the arrival of the news that the order had been promulgated it was appreciated that action was necessary. To prevent the violation of existing treaties, and protect the country from British commercial invasion, was the duty of Congress. As early as September, 1783, Madison prophesied that Congress would recommend some defensive plan against the navigation laws of England.[1]

This took form in a request made by Congress, on April 30, 1784, for power to prohibit for fifteen years, any goods from being imported into or exported from any state in vessels owned or navigated by subjects of any foreign nation, with whom the United States had not formed treaties of commerce; and further, to empower Congress, during the same time, to prohibit the subjects of any foreign nation, unless authorized by treaty, from importing any goods not the produce of their own country.[2] All the provisions of this act had to receive the consent of nine states.

The commercial party, strong in the North, now hoped to see their interests established on a firm basis; but the country at large was not yet ready for concerted action. It was early prophesied that Rhode Island would not this time offer any serious resistance.[3] As for nine months nothing was accomplished toward alleviating the growing evil, a movement was set on foot to change some features of the recommendation, to make it more acceptable to the states. It was now proposed to vest Congress with power to regulate foreign and coast-wise trade, and to regulate the duties on foreign importations. It was provided that all ordinances on the subject should have the consent of nine states in Con-

---

[1] Gilpin, *Madison Papers*, i, 573.

[2] *Journals of Congress*, iv, 392.

[3] Gilpin, *Madison Papers*, i, 573.

gress, and of the legislatures of the same number; that the grant should be for a limited time, and that all duties should be collected under the authority and for the use of the state in which they should be paid.[1] This alternative act seemed especially calculated to conciliate Rhode Island. The assent of nine states insured deliberation. Rhode Island had, in 1781, feared that if a duty were collected in her ports, Connecticut would retaliate. Now that would be forbidden. The new plan was to give Congress the right to fix the duty, but the incongruity of a duty collected in the state by an outside authority was removed. Howell, losing no time in reporting this plan to his governor, wrote of it: "I trust in the wisdom of the public councils to devise a system of commercial regulations which will answer every reasonable object of the mercantile part of the community, without endangering the liberties of this country. But if I am called upon either to part with my freedom or foreign commerce, I shall want no time to deliberate."[2] During all this time the trade laws of Britain were bearing more and more heavily on the people of America, fostering a feeling that power must be given to Congress to enact retaliatory measures. The mercantile class in the seaboard towns, believing at first that their interest lay in retaining for the state its power to maintain free trade or to lay its own duties, were now brought by the hardships of the British trade laws to realize that their safety lay in maintaining the public credit, and presenting a united front to British aggression. Reluctantly they acknowledged that the desired end must be sought through the propositions of April 18, 1783, and April 30, 1784. Through the efforts of the commercial element, the opposition of the other classes to those measures began to weaken. The per-

---

[1] *Journals of Congress*, iv, 392.

[2] *Rhode Island Archives (MS.), Letters, 1783-5*, 53.

sistency of this opposition is revealed by the piecemeal manner in which the grants were secured.

The friends of the measures of Congress had first succeeded in securing the inefficient grant of the impost at the February session, 1785. At the same session Congress was given power to "regulate, restrain, or prohibit the importation of all foreign goods in any ships or vessels other than those owned by the citizens of the United States or any of them, and navigated by seamen, citizens of the United States."[1] This grant, which was restricted to twenty-five years, was full enough in regard to imposts, but did not touch upon exports. Though this was but a small result, other states did not even do as much as this.

The next step was taken when it was found that her grant would not become operative in the near future. Several of the commercial states had, for self-preservation, passed laws in restraint of British trade. The Rhode Island assembly, following their example, in May, 1785, imposed an additional duty of seven and a half per cent. on goods imported in British ships.[2] An act of this nature, involving no concession to Congress, met with no opposition, and passed by acclamation.

The election of members of the assembly to sit at the October session, resulted in a house of deputies of sixty-one members, of whom twenty had not sat in the last assembly. Whereas the commercial party had, at the last session, been able to grant to Congress power over imports in foreign vessels, they were now able to empower the delegates to prohibit the importation of foreign goods in vessels owned by citizens of the United States. Congress was at the same time to regulate trade between the different states.[3] Still the

[1] *Acts and Resolves of the General Assembly* (*MS.*), *1784-5*, 69.

[2] *Ibid.*, 91; *Providence Gazette*, May 2, 1785.

[3] *Acts and Resolves of the General Assembly* (*MS.*), *1784-5*, 128.

request of Congress was not fully granted. Even in this small concession may be seen a compromise. Nothing was yet said concerning exports. The fear that the neighboring states would impose restrictions on trade must be allayed. To effect this, the clause concerning inter-state trade was inserted in the grant of power over American shipping, and the whole passed together. As a measure of urgency, while the Congressional grant was inoperative, the legislature laid a prohibition on the exportation of American goods in British ships, and all entries of British ships from ports of that nation were forbidden under pain of forfeiture of ship and cargo.[1] Howell himself could now allow that power to regulate trade might be granted to Congress with safety, but he insisted that a line should be sharply drawn between this power and that of raising a revenue by means of duties. The latter must be tenaciously retained by the states.[2] Encouraged by their success in passing the impost act, and impelled by an urgent appeal from Congress, the commercial party in the assembly advanced to the final grant. The appeal from Congress was the result of an investigation of the laws passed by the states in conformity with the recommendation of April 30, 1784. The committee appointed for the purpose found that Massachusetts, New York, New Jersey, and Virginia had passed acts in conformity with the recommendation of Congress, but had made them inoperative until all the states had consented. Connecticut, Pennsylvania, and Maryland had passed laws that fixed the date of taking effect differently, while New Hampshire's grant was limited to fifteen years. Rhode Island and North Carolina had given power over imports only. Delaware, South Carolina, and Georgia had done nothing. It was voted that the recommendation

---

[1] *Acts and Resolves of the General Assembly (MS.), 1784–5,* 145; *Providence Gazette,* Nov. 12, 1785.

[2] Letter to Gov. Greene, *Rhode Island Archives (MS.); Letters, 1783–5,* 94.

be again presented to the three latter states, and that New
Hampshire, North Carolina, and Rhode Island be asked to
reconsider their acts.[1]
The scale was turned by this appeal, and the legislature,
on March thirteenth, granted to Congress full power over
imports and exports, but attached the condition that it
should not take effect until Congress was given power over
inter-state trade.[2] This act, though saddled with a condition,
was accepted by Congress as fulfilling its demands.[3]
As it was the fear of retaliation on the part of Connecticut
that had been a potent factor in the opposition to the imposts, it was a sense of close relationship with that state,
which now induced a suspension of the embargo act of October, 1785, until a similar act had been passed by Connecticut.
Thereupon the law was to become operative by proclama-
tion of the governor.[4]
The five years which had passed since the first proposal
of an additional grant of power to Congress had witnessed a
rude awakening of the people of Rhode Island. They had
found that to stand alone fighting the battles of commerce
would be quite another thing from resting beneath the
shelter of the British crown. It was a sacrifice of their ideas
of local independence and constitutional liberty, to yield those
powers which, under the influence of the commercial towns,
the state had been led to confer upon Congress. The state
of Rhode Island had yet to learn that among states, as
among men, "none of us liveth to himself." She must
yet receive her purification by fire, before entering into

---

[1] *Journals of Congress*, iv, 622.

[2] *Acts and Resolves of the General Assembly* (*MS.*), *1786-7*. 15.

[3] *Journals of Congress*, iv, 715.

[4] *Schedules of the General Assembly*, Feb. Session, 1786, 37; *Providence Gazette*,
March 11, 1786.

the blessings of the Federal Union. A popular frenzy was destined to engulf her mercantile power, which had brought her into line on the questions of impost and commercial regulations.

CHAPTER IV

THE PAPER MONEY ERA

GREAT popular upheavals in any community do not arise upon the impulse of the moment, nor are they the result of an inherent tendency to anarchy. Behind every such expression of the popular will, examination will reveal a train of events and antecedent conditions silently at work, culminating in a sudden and violent outbreak. Such was the case on the occasion of the political revolution which took place in Rhode Island in 1786. It has been seen how a steadily increasing sentiment among the mercantile interests had by successive grants, bestowed on Congress the additional powers sought by that body. This was done in opposition to a large class in the rural towns, who were to lead in the approaching convulsion. It needed only the aggravation of the economic conditions which had for a decade prevailed in America, to precipitate a crisis.

The antecedent conditions in America, so far as they concern Rhode Island, must be reviewed. The exertions of the infant nation were enormous. The country emerged from the war with industries paralyzed and a debt with which she was incompetent to grapple. Rhode Island had early felt the rigors of war, for during the first week of December, 1776, a British fleet had appeared off Newport, and proceeded to garrison the town with eight thousand troops. From these unwelcome visitors she was not free until October, 1779. The approach of the British caused a general emigration of the inhabitants, not only of Newport, but of many of the coast towns. For three years the shores of Narragansett Bay were kept in a state of defense. By the British occupation of the island, their raids on the neighboring mainland, and the maintenance of the patriot troops, the fairest portions of the state were laid waste or drained to the last degree in providing supplies. By the British occupation, the metropolis of the state, where centered wealth and commerce, was lost. The remaining commercial towns, though not actually occupied by the enemy, were blockaded. The portion of the commonwealth remaining free from British domination was the interior country towns which were wholly unable to bear the burdens of a commonwealth. But in any case the burden of expense would have been heavy.

Repeated disaster had not shaken the faith of the people in paper money. The first resort of Congress to obtain money was through an emission of paper.[1] On receipt of the news of this issue, the general assembly of Rhode Island promptly made the bills a legal tender at the rate of six shillings to the dollar.[2] The expenses of the state, for the years preceding the Revolution, had not greatly exceeded two thousand pounds per year. During the years 1775 and 1776, the expenses of war and the unwillingness of the people to submit to direct taxation led to the issue of one hundred and fifty thousand pounds in paper.[3] The issues of the states and of Congress creating an over-supply of money brought on depreciation.

A New England convention held at Providence to seek a means of sustaining prices recommended that the states cease to issue paper and resort to taxation. This was reiterated by a convention at Springfield, in July, 1777.[4] Con-

[1] *Journals of Congress*, i, 87.

[2] *Acts and Resolves of the General Assembly* (*MS.*), *1775*, Aug. 26.

[3] *Rhode Island Historical Tracts*, viii, 139.

[4] Arnold, *Hist. of Rhode Island*, ii, 404.

gress, in the call for supplies of November twenty-second, 1777, reached the same conclusion; wherefore it was recommended that the states cease to issue bills of credit; that they take up all their issues except those of fractional currency, and that in the future all money be raised by taxation.[1] Before this recommendation had been received, Rhode Island voted to cease issuing bills, borrowing on six per cent. notes to meet current expenses.[2]

Realizing the evil consequences arising from so much paper in circulation, Congress called on the states to raise as much money by taxation as they might think proper, for the use of Congress.[3] This was met in the state by a tax of sixteen thousand pounds. The natural aversion to taxation, heightened by the distressed condition of the coast towns, led Providence to secure the passage of the act, by which she assumed an increase of one hundred thousand pounds in her valuation.[4]

The inhabitants of the southern towns were constantly taking refuge from the British marauders in the more northern towns. By the loss of their lands and the sale of their effects at a sacrifice, they were thrown almost upon charity. It was estimated that there were two hundred and fifty refugees in Providence without the means of support during the winter of 1777–8. Many of the coast towns were almost deserted.[5] In September, 1777, the inhabitants of Rhode Island, Conanicut, and Block Island were exempted from taxes on all personal property except cattle.[6] The tax of sixteen thousand pounds was followed by others in

[1] *Journals of Congress*, ii, 346.

[2] *Acts and Resolves of the General Assembly (MS.), 1776, Pt. ii*, Dec. 31.

[3] *Journals of Congress*, ii, 12.

[4] *Acts and Resolves of the General Assembly (MS.), 1777, Pt. i*, Mar. 23.

[5] *Rhode Island Colonial Records*, viii, 151.

[6] *Schedules of the General Assembly*, Sept. Session, 1777, 5.

August[1] and December,[2] bringing the taxes of the year up to ninety-six thousand pounds. It must be borne in mind, however, that at this time, as in following years, taxes laid and taxes collected were very different things.

The devices of Congress for obtaining money through loan offices and lotteries having been unproductive, and the depreciation of bills of credit having become alarming, recourse was had, on November twenty-second, 1777, to requisitions on the states for specific sums.[3] The first three requisitions were made in paper and were as follows:

Date.	Paper Value.	Specie Value.
1777, Nov. 22	$100,000	$36,363.64[4]
1779, Jan. 2–5	300,000	37,688.44[5]
1779, May 21	750,000	64,878.45[6]
	$1,150,000	$138,930.53

On October ninth, 1779, Congress made a requisition for $15,000,000 per month, to be paid in paper,[7] to begin February first, 1780, and to be continued until October first of the same year. This was later extended to April first, 1781.[8] The quota of Rhode Island for each month was $200,000. A requisition for $6,000,000 per year, for eighteen years, seems never to have received attention from anyone after its passage, and is therefore excluded.[9] To meet these requisitions, the reports to Congress show that Rhode Island actually paid in paper as follows:[10]

[1] *Acts and Resolves of the General Assembly* (*MS.*), *1777, Pt. ii*, Aug. 23.

[2] *Ibid.*, Dec. 6.   [3] *Journals of Congress*, ii, 345.

[4] *Ibid.*, ii, 345.   [5] *Ibid.*, iii, 176.

[6] *Ibid.*, iii, 284.   [7] *Ibid.*, iii, 373, 376.

[8] *Ibid.*, iii, 442.   [9] *Ibid.*, iii, 174.

[10] *American State Papers, Finance*, i, 60.

Date of Warrant or Receipt.	Paper Value.	Specie Value.
1778, June 26	$50,000	$11,763.29
1779, July 23	195,018	12,599.35
" Nov. 12	300,000	12,330.45
" Dec. 14	100,000	3,658.98
1780, Jan. 1	75,000	2,407.70
" Jan. 20	175,000	5,617.97
" Feb. 28	80,000	2,000,00
" April 11	204,000	5,100.00
" April 14	100,000	2,500.00
" June 9	114,732	2,868.30
1782, Feb. 23	8,238	205.95
	$1,402,788	$61,051.99

In 1787, when the paper was practically of no value, Rhode Island turned in $2,593,353.30 on the requisition of March 18, 1780.[1] The embargo which had been laid at the suggestion of Congress on the export of all provisions from the states, was inflicting great hardship on the people of Rhode Island.[2] So heavily did the Connecticut embargo rest on the people that a request was sent to the governor of that state, asking that it be suspended in favor of Rhode Island.[3] The scarcity of provisions, he explained, was due to the expedition to Rhode Island, which had prevented the people from sowing grain, as well as to the drought of the summer and the absence of the men at harvest time. One-fourth of the land suited to agriculture was either occupied or controlled by the enemy, from whom the inhabitants were refugees without the means of livelihood. Receiving no response, the destitute situation

[1] *American State Papers, Finance*, i, 58; Specie values determined from tables of depreciation in *American State Papers, Finance*, v, 722 et seq.

[2] *Journals of Congress*, ii, 581; *Acts and Resolves of the General Assembly* (*MS.*), *1778*, June 30.

[3] *Rhode Island Colonial Records*, viii, 499.

of the state led again in January, 1779, to an appeal for aid.[1] The delegates in Congress were instructed to obtain a suspension of the embargo in New York and Connecticut, in favor of Rhode Island. Governor Greene, in his letter, said that the number of refugees was constantly increasing; that the state had never been able to produce grain sufficient for her own use, and that now the state was deprived of all imports except small amounts obtained from Massachusetts. "If some relief is not speedily granted," said he, "many of the poorer sort of inhabitants, especially those that have come off from Rhode Island, must inevitably perish of want."[2] To Governor Clinton, on the same day, he wrote: "There are several thousand of the inhabitants of Rhode Island come off, that must be supported among us. Your excellency will be able to judge, from what your own inhabitants suffer, how hard the lot of these poor people must be, when I inform you that corn nor flour cannot be purchased for money at any price whatever."[3]

To the assembly of Connecticut he writes that storms and force of military duty had ruined the crops of the last summer so that the product was even less than usual. "The most obdurate heart would relent to see old age and childhood, from comfortable circumstances, reduced to the necessity of begging for a morsel of bread."[4] A committee was appointed to wait on the Connecticut assembly to impress the necessity of the case.

Nor were these efforts unsuccessful. The assembly of Connecticut allowed seven thousand bushels of grain to be exported to Rhode Island, and in compliance with a recommendation of that body, contributions were taken up to the

---

[1] *Acts and Resolves of the General Assembly* (*MS.*), *1779,* Jan. 3; *Rhode Island Archives* (*MS.*), *Letters, 1779,* Jan. 7.

[2] Staples, *Rhode Island in the Continental Congress,* 209.

[3] *Rhode Island Colonial Records,* viii, 499.   [4] *Ibid.,* viii, 500.

amount of five hundred bushels of grain and four thousand three hundred pounds in money. Moreover Congress, on the second of March, relieved the state of fifty thousand dollars of her quota, that sum being generously assumed by South Carolina.[1] In New York the embargo was in like manner suspended.

The issue of state paper having been abandoned, and taxes not yielding the necessary funds, recourse was had to borrowing on treasury notes bearing interest. The interest on these of the face value of one hundred and sixty thousand pounds was added to the burden of the state. Every other means was taken by Congress to avoid a further emission of paper. A loan of $20,000,000 through the loan offices was authorized.[2] The loans came in so slowly that the assembly recommended that subscription lists be opened in every town.[3] As in the other colonies at the opening of hostilities, the Tories had sought refuge with the British. Their estates, which had been taken possession of by the state, were, by act of the assembly, confiscated to the public use.[4]

During the year 1780, the "Forty for One Act" practically repudiated thirty-nine fortieths of the bills of credit.[5] They were then made receivable only for a special tax laid for the purpose of calling in the notes. From that date the requisitions of Congress were made in specie. Many of the states took measures to relieve the soldiers who had received paper in payment for service, and who were placed in an especially unfortunate position by the act. In Rhode Island a tax of sixteen thousand pounds was laid, of which six thousand pounds was devoted to the payment of one-fourth

[1] *Journals of Congress*, iii, 216.   [2] *Ibid.*, iii, 306, 316.

[3] *Acts and Resolves of the General Assembly* (*MS.*), *1779*, Aug. 21.

[4] *Rhode Island Colonial Records*, viii, 609.

[5] *Journals of Congress*, iii, 442.

of the depreciation of the pay of the Rhode Island soldiers.[1] The remaining three-fourths was to be paid out of the proceeds of the confiscated estates of the loyalists.

With the appointment of Morris as Superintendent of Finance something like order was brought into the administration of the treasury. Specie requisitions were made by Congress, but the waning influence of that body is evident in the laxity of the states in complying with its demands. A treasury statement shows that of the requisitions made from October 31, 1781, to August 20, 1788, against $5,900,349.20 paid by all the states, there remained unpaid $9,463,660.70. Of these sums Rhode Island had paid $87,-950.83, against $268,088.14 yet unpaid.[2]

Upon the call of October 3, 1781,[3] for $216,684 from Rhode Island, the delegates were instructed to obtain relief for the state.[4] Accordingly, following the request of the delegates, Morris wrote that a commissioner would be appointed to direct the expenditure of Rhode Island's contribution within the state, so that so much specie might not be drawn out of her boundaries.[5] By these means the state was enabled to meet her obligations in such a way that Morris, in a letter to Edmund Randolph, in June, 1782, said that New Jersey and Rhode Island were the only states which had made payments on the requisitions due that spring.[6]

To show the relative contributions of the States from 1781 to August, 1783, in proportion to assessments, Morris transmitted to the president of Congress the following statement:[7]

---

[1] *Schedules of the General Assembly*, Nov. Session, 1780, 30.

[2] *American State Papers, Finance*, i, 56–7.

[3] *Journals of Congress*, iii, 683.

[4] *Rhode Island Colonial Records*, ix, 502.

[5] Staples, *Rhode Island in the Continental Congress*, 364.

[6] Gilpin, *Madison Papers*, i, 142.

[7] Sparks, *Diplomatic Correspondence*, xii, 395.

South Carolina...................................All.
Rhode Island....................................Nearly ¼.
Pennsylvania ....Above ⅛.
Connecticut ....⅛.
New Jersey......................................⅛.
Massachusetts...................................⅛.
Virginia ....⅛.
New York..1/20.
Maryland ....1/20.
New Hampshire...................................1/21.
North Carolina ....Nothing.
Delaware..Nothing.
Georgia ....Nothing.

The British evacuated Newport on the twenty-fifth of October, 1779, leaving the town prostrate. A report to the legislature, in June, 1782, estimated the damage done by the British at nearly twenty-five thousand pounds. The same report states that five hundred houses had been destroyed,[1] the forests which had abounded on the island cut down, and farms and fields of the state's most prosperous region laid waste. Probably no less than two thousand persons fled from their homes on the shores of Narragansett Bay.

But among the losses to the state, none could compare in after effects with the loss of Newport's Hebrew population. The enterprise which had made that town the commercial metropolis of the north was due chiefly to the Jews. Twenty square-rigged vessels, besides many smaller ones, were kept in commission by one house. Of this wealthy class few returned at the close of the war. Their name was only to be preserved by tradition and by the monuments of their benevolence in the town, from whose docks trade had forever departed.[2]

Allusion has already been made to the new race of merchants, the foundation of whose prosperity was laid during

[1] Arnold, *Hist. of Rhode Island*, ii, 447.

[2] *Providence Gazette*, Sept. 6, 1782.

the war, and who were now rising to wealth at the expense
of the producing class.   In the agricultural districts great
distress prevailed.   For several years taxes had been heavy.
Cheap foreign goods were tempting the purses of the common people.   Debts increased on all sides and lawyers
throve.   Paper money had not only depreciated in the hands
of the people, but, in October, 1781, was declared no longer
legal tender in payments of debts to the state, or of taxes.[1]
At the opening of the war the statute of limitations had been
suspended,[2] but on the return of peace, creditors began to
make new and strenuous demands.   At the May session,
1784, the statute was reenacted, bringing hardship to the
debtor class.[3]   Under the existing law, should the town treasurer fail to pay the town's quota of taxes to the state, he was
liable to imprisonment.   He must look for relief to the collector of taxes.   The imprisonment of the treasurer of South
Kingstown, and the subsequent levy by the collector on the
stock owned in the town, led to a petition from the people
declaring that "one universal scene of distress is spread
throughout the said town."[4]   From Scituate came another
petition to the same effect.   The treasurers of other towns
met with the same fate, until a general act of the assembly
gave relief for a time while renewed efforts were making.[5]

In southern Massachusetts there was formed, in the
winter of 1882–3, a combination to resist the collection of
taxes.   At Killingly, just across the Connecticut line, a
meeting was held to extend the movement to that state.
The disaffection was spreading into Rhode Island, but by the
prompt action of Deputy Governor Bowen, seconded by the

[1] *Schedules of the General Assembly*, October Session, 1781, 20.

[2] *Acts and Resolves of the General Assembly (MS.), 1774-5*, Nov. 6, 1775.

[3] *Acts and Resolves of the General Assembly (MS.), 1785*, May 2.

[4] *Rhode Island Colonial Records*, ix, 513.

[5] *Schedules of the General Assembly*, Oct. Session, 1782, 14.

assembly, the offenders were brought to justice.[1] About the same time, certain inhabitants of the border towns of Massachusetts came across into Rhode Island and rescued prisoners who were on trial for attempting to seize cattle held for taxes. The wave of open resistance was first seen in Massachusetts in 1784, when the towns of Medway and Wrentham issued a call for a convention to secure redress for the commutation of officers' half-pay, and the tariff. A convention at Hartford condemned the senate and courts, and denounced Continental taxes. In the county of Hampshire, a mob seized the court house, preventing the sitting of the courts.[2] In May, 1783, a mob prevented the sitting of the courts at Springfield. Conventions followed in quick succession. Attempts to alleviate the distress by passing tender laws, whereby debtors might pay their debts in cattle and produce, only postponed the difficulty. In this condition of growing discontent and confusion the state continued until Shay's Rebellion broke out in August, 1786. A convention which met at Leicester, composed of delegates from thirty-seven towns, formulated a statement of the causes of the present troubles, alleging them to be: the want of a circulating medium; abuse in the practice of law, and the exorbitance of legal fees; the existence of the Court of Common Pleas in its present form; the appropriation of the revenue arising from import duties to the payment of interest on the state debt; the number of high salaries paid in the state; and the payment of money to Congress while the public accounts remained unsettled. To promote these sentiments, disturbances took place in the western and southern counties of Massachusetts, culminating in the organization of Shay's force. The vigorous action of

[1] *Schedules of the General Assembly*, Feb. Session, 1783, 5.

[2] Bradford, *Hist. of Massachusetts*, ii, 211, 260.

the authorities effectually discouraged any further resort to arms.

In New Hampshire the popular malady took the form of a demand for paper money, and a petition to that effect was presented to the legislature. Measures taken by the state to relieve those who were her own creditors did not satisfy the demands. Demagogues incited the people to assert their rights. Following these demands, the legislature made a tender of real or personal property an exemption from imprisonment for debt. Following the example of Massachusetts, the legislature at last passed a tender law. A plan for an emission of paper, when submitted to the people, was rejected, and the commotion subsided after a mob had been dispersed from the neighborhood of the legislature at Exeter.

The general discontent and anarchic tendencies, so powerful in other parts of New England, were reinforced in Rhode Island by local conditions. Her state rights advocates, the country party, hampered by debts, watched with envy the rise of a prosperous commercial class, the very cause of whose prosperity seemed the cause of their own misery. They saw this power wax in strength in the assembly, granting in spite of opposition the requests of Congress. Impelled by their mistaken notions of self-interest, they at length rose against their opponents and inaugurated an era as disgraceful as it was dishonest.

Beginning in meetings in the towns and in instructions and petitions, the movement gained such power as to make it possible to seize the government by constitutional means, whereas in Massachusetts the lack of a majority on the part of the opposition drove them to arms. The colonial days had witnessed many issues of paper in Rhode Island. The excessive issues of Continental money, and the consequent depreciation, led a convention assembled at

Providence to recommend that the states issue no more
paper.[1] Accordingly the issues ceased and recourse was
had to borrowing on treasury notes. On these notes $94,-
500 was borrowed prior to 1780, when the issue of paper
was resumed. The sentiments of the better class in the
state prevented further issues until 1786. Their views were
expressed by Governor Cooke in a letter to the delegates in
Congress on June twenty-second, 1777. He confessed that
the support of the state soldiers had already so exhausted
the treasury that, unless relief was granted by Congress, the
state must again resort to paper. "You are fully sensible,"
said he, "of the almost irreparable mischiefs that have been
already occasioned by such large emissions of bills, and of
the fatal consequences that will attend further emissions."[2]

William Ellery wrote, in May, 1779, in explanation of the
large requisitions made by Congress: "The more that is
collected by taxation, the less it will be necessary to loan in
order to put a stop to further emissions, which is the wish of
all. A stoppage of the press once effected, our liberties are
effected, and an end is put to the war. Our enemy's whole
dependence now rests upon our being crushed with whole
reams of depreciated paper money.[3] To base the credit of
the government on a more substantial foundation, the delegates were instructed, in October, 1782, "to press the redemption of the outstanding Continental bills of credit."[4]

The rejection of a petition to the assembly, signed by
many citizens of the state, for an emission of paper, was the
sign for opening a campaign against the party in power.[5]
The deputies chosen to the assembly in October, 1785,

[1] *Rhode Island Colonial Records*, viii, 75-7.

[2] *Acts and Resolves of the General Assembly* (*MS.*), *1777*, *Pt. ii*, June 22.

[3] Staples, *Rhode Island in the Continental Congress*, 235.

[4] *Rhode Island Colonial Records*, ix, 612.

[5] Arnold, *Hist. of Rhode Island*, ii, 511.

though largely in sympathy with the commercial policy, numbered in their ranks several of the radical party. To the February session came several bearing instructions on the subject of the popular discontent. Foster, Gloucester, Smith-field, Coventry, Middletown, and Tiverton favored an emission of paper.[1] Gloucester suggested, as a plan for the more easy payment of debts, that there should be a light tax to pay a part of the foreign debt annually; there should be a duty laid by the states to pay interest on loans; the vacant lands should be sold to pay the national debt, reserving grants for soldiers; and an excise similar to that in force in Massachusetts should be laid.[2]

The Smithfield instructions enumerated the grievances of the people at length. They were alleged to be: that the payment of interest on loan office certificates made the rate of interest too high; the outstanding treasury notes yielded too much revenue to the holders; on account of the scarcity of money, all public securities yielded too much; the scarcity of money made it impossible to pay taxes; the impost and excise, as the easiest way of raising a tax, should be increased, and that real and personal property should be made a tender in payment of debts.[3] Richmond and Charleston voted against paper, the latter by a vote of thirty-nine to seven.[4] Cumberland complained that from the scarcity of money, many debts had been contracted, and at the same time the ability to pay had been lessened. Suits at law were increasing, debtors were thrown into prison and their goods sold. Though many objections were evident, yet the freemen considered that an issue of paper was necessary.[5]

These expressions roused the fears of the people of both

[1] *Papers relating to the Adoption of the Constitution.* 59, 47, 50, 63, 60, 58.

[2] *Ibid.,* 47.   *Ibid.,* 50.

[4] *Ibid.,* 53, 59.   *Ibid.,* 42.

Providence and Newport, to the point of remonstrance. The debt of the United States to the state, urged the Providence remonstrants, would relieve Rhode Island of all except the regular governmental expenses. These could be met by taxation. Should an emission take place, the result would be to drain away gold and silver, and divert trade to other channels.[1] In the memorial from Newport, one hundred and fifty signers declare that there is no scarcity of money. If any need to mortgage their farms, it can be done with an issue of paper. The depreciation which would surely follow an issue would destroy trade and credit.[2] The more thoughtful everywhere saw plainly the ruin that would ensue to those commercial towns whose supplies and goods for export were drawn from the neighboring states.

In the midst of these demands for paper all eyes were fixed on the assembly, as it came together at its March session. When a vote was reached on a motion to issue, it was defeated by a vote of forty-three to eighteen. It is an interesting coincidence that the number voting for paper on this occasion was the same as that of the opponents to the impost which was passed at the same session.[3]

In accordance with the suggestion of Providence, an act was passed making real, and certain articles of personal property, at an appraised value, a tender for debt on execution. This act, the preamble recites, was passed because of the scarcity of a circulating medium, and the frequency of forced sales at a serious loss. The act provides not only for a tender of property, but that, should a creditor refuse the tender, upon the payment of all interest on the judgment to date, the debt would be discharged and the judgment remain simply a debt on interest. In case a debtor possessing real

[1] *Providence Gazette*, Mar. 4, 1786.

[2] *The de Island Historical Society's MSS.*, iii, 110.

[3] *Ibid.*, iii, 110; *United States Chronicle*, Mar. 2, 9, 1786.

estate refuse, after three months, to give satisfaction, the creditor might, on application to the court, have satisfaction out of the estate.[1]

This did not produce the desired result. The clamors grew. The instructions given by Smithfield to her deputies on April nineteenth, exhibit the prejudices of the country districts against the creditor class.[2] They complain of many and unjust taxes laid, especially to pay interest on loan office certificates, which had become so depreciated that often the interest in silver was of greater value than the face of the bill. Moreover the assembly had granted the five per cent. impost. If the assembly wanted an impost they should have insisted on having it collected by state officers, and paid into the state treasury. For these reasons the town directed its deputies to strive: (1.) To stop the payment of interest or principal of the loan office certificates until their just value should be determined; (2.) To secure a repeal of the grant to Congress of power to lay an import duty, and to give the assembly control over revenue officers; (3.) To see that the accounts of the state with the United States be ascertained, and that in the meantime no money be paid to Congress; (4.) To move for a more equitable representation in the assembly.

The first charge originated from the most apparent of the evils arising out of the financial system of the war. The third, likewise, had its origin in the financial chaos of the Revolution, coupled with the feeling that Rhode Island was a creditor state. The second point in the instructions was the final protest of the minority who had so long prevented the granting of the impost. The apportionment of members of the assembly as provided in the charter had never been changed. Newport had six, Providence, Portsmouth, and Warwick four

[1] *Acts and Resolves of the General Assembly (MS.), 1786–7,* Mar. 16, 1786.
[2] *Papers relating to the Adoption of the Constitution,* 54.

each, and all other towns two each. It had long been felt
that this was unjust, and movements had been set on foot for
a reform, but to no purpose. The feeling still existed as an
undercurrent helping to swell the tide of discontent.[1]

The third Wednesday in April saw the opposition in full
force at the polls. The result was a complete overthrow of
the party in power. The new assembly which came together
at the general election in May contained seventy members,
of whose names forty-five do not appear on the roll of the
March session. Of the assistants, five of the ten were new.
Neither the governor nor the deputy governor were re-elected.
The towns which returned substantially the same deputies as
to the previous assembly were Newport, Providence, Bristol,
Westerly, Warren, Hopkinton, North Providence, Cumberland, Richmond, Foster, Gloucester, and New Shoreham.
These towns, it is probable, were of two classes, those which
retained their old deputies of the commercial party, and
those other towns which had at the former election chosen
representatives of the opposition. The remaining towns may
fairly be taken to represent the extent of the change in opinion during the winter of 1786.

The assembly at once entered on the work for which it had
been chosen. On Friday, the fifth of May, a deputy from
Warwick moved that an issue of paper be authorized, basing
his motion on the facts, that there was little money in the
country; that the lands and stock of the farmers was being
seized and sold at forced sale at a great loss; that silver
could not be hired on the best security, and that distress was
everywhere.[2] The result of the motion was an act for emitting one hundred thousand pounds in paper. The act relates that, "Whereas, From a variety of causes, political and
mercantile, the currency of this state, now in circulation has

[1] *Foster Papers* (*MS.*), ii, 11.
[2] *United States Chronicle*, May 11, 1786.

become altogether insufficient in point of quantity, for the purposes of trade and commerce, and for paying the just debts of the inhabitants thereof, to establish a circulating medium, upon the firmest and most equitable principles that may be, and for facilitating that change of property so essential to a commercial state, and a people circumstanced as are the inhabitants of this state, Be it enacted," etc.   Then follows the act emitting the paper, based on the security of clear landed property of twice the value of the emission.   Each freeholder was to receive an equal share of the paper, which was to be repaid into the treasury in seven equal annual payments, the first to be made at the end of seven years.   During the first seven years the holder was to pay interest at the rate of four per cent.[1]   This act created, in short, a loan of one hundred thousand pounds to the people, in paper at four per cent. for which the state took as security mortgages on lands.   The fearful consequences which might follow the passage of such an act, which in the confident language of its authors, would " have the greatest tendency of anything within the wisdom of this legislature to quiet the minds and alleviate the distressed situation and circumstances of the good people of this state,"[2] were set forth in a protest against it from the deputies of Providence.[3]   In view of the proposed issue of one hundred and sixty thousand pounds, they objected to the excessive amount, declaring that to make it a legal tender in satisfaction of past contracts would be an injustice, and a violation of the rights of mankind, and that it would not only not be received by the United States in payment of taxes, but work to defraud creditors outside the state, where the paper would be worthless.   Industry, commerce, and public credit would be destroyed, and the state would be unable to pay for those necessaries of life

[1] *Acts and Resolves of the General Assembly* (*MS.*), *1786-7*, May 3, 1786.
[2] *Ibid.*, May 3, 1786.   [3] *Ibid.*, June 26, 1786.

which she must purchase outside her boundaries. Instead of being intended to relieve distress, they boldly declared it to be "calculated only to accommodate certain persons who, being deeply in debt for real estates and other property purchased under contracts to be paid for in solid coin, and who now have promoted this measure to serve their own private purpose, and although we are willing to unite in every reasonable act to relieve the distress, yet we are fully convinced that passing this bill is a measure that will not have that tendency." The propriety of these apprehensions was proven by the fearful experience of the following months. That the measure was supported by a large mass of the freemen who sincerely believed that in paper was a relief from the intolerable burdens of poverty and taxation, is as certain as the fact that among its supporters were many who supported it as a means of extricating themselves from debt.

The clause in the act which struck dismay to the hearts of creditors was that providing that, should any creditor refuse to receive the paper, the debtor might discharge the debt by depositing the same with one of the judges of the court in the county. That official was then to give public notice through the newspapers and by a personal notice to the creditor to appear and receive the paper. Should the creditor fail to appear, the debt was declared cancelled.

Those who prophesied depreciation had not long to wait to see their prophecy fulfilled. Within two months after issue the bills had so depreciated that a forcing act was deemed necessary by its supporters. Under a pretense of great respect for law, was perpetrated one of the greatest acts of injustice in the history of paper money. It was insisted that the laws must be kept in high esteem and veneration, and the paper as good as gold. Again a deputy from Warwick, on the plea that "various attempts have been made by a certain class of men, who for mistaken principles, suppose the said currency to be injurious to their interests, and from an inclination to render invalid such laws and regulations of this assembly as may not quadrate with their interest, judgment and opinion of things,"[1] introduced a bill providing that any person who should thereafter refuse to take the paper in exchange for any article for sale at face value, or should make any difference between paper and coin, or tend to depreciate or discourage the paper money, should be fined one hundred pounds for the first offense, and for the second be fined the same amount and be rendered incapable of voting or holding office in the state.

The minority, led by Providence, Newport, and Bristol, sought to avert serious consequences by a compromise. They asked to that end, that a conference be arranged to discuss the embodiment in the act of a provision that, forty thousand pounds having been issued, the emission should cease; that the clause making paper a tender in payment of past contracts be omitted; that the necessaries of life be permitted to be bought for silver and gold, and that the citizens of other states be relieved from the penalties imposed by the act. But the attempt was in vain, and the bill passed by a majority of six.[2]

John Brown, a prominent citizen of Providence, and a member of the assembly, characterizing this as a country measure, says; " I have ever wished to reconcile the landed and mercantile interests throughout the state from the beginning, and having real estate in twelve different towns, was in hopes of bringing about some conciliatory measure."[3] But conciliatory proposals were lost on a majority deter-

---

[1] *Acts and Resolves of the General Assembly* (*MS.*), *1786-7*, 32, June 30; *United States Chronicle,* July 6, 1786.

[2] *United States Chronicle,* July 6, 13, 1786.

[3] *Providence Gazette,* July 8, 1786.

mined to carry its point at any cost. A period of absolute stagnation in business began. Rather than sell their goods and receive in return paper bills, merchants closed their stores. It was only with the greatest difficulty that provisions could be obtained. Many people removed to the neighboring states. The farmers who had mortgaged their farms to secure paper, being unable to purchase goods without it, sought to compel the townspeople to accept it by withholding produce from the market. Few farmers from the neighboring states could be induced to bring their produce into Rhode Island, where they might be obliged to accept worthless paper for it. It was said that a boy bringing in a load of potatoes, was compelled to sell his load against his will and accept paper in payment.[1] To devise some means of providing the people with the necessaries of life, a town meeting was held in Providence on the twenty-fourth of July. The penal law was denounced. Producers were besought to bring corn and meat to market, and should any one be fined for refusing to receive paper, the town would pay the fine. A subscription was opened to raise five hundred dollars with which to purchase corn for those in immediate want. Resolutions were also adopted recommending that no one be molested for bringing goods to market, nor for selling them for any price, or in any manner.[2]

These measures of the townspeople roused the wrath of the country party. South Kingstown, in town meeting, recommended that as some of the merchants had refused to sell goods for paper, every one ought to refuse to sell them cheese, flaxseed, barley, oats, horses, or lumber.[3] The farmers of Providence county, in convention at Scituate, on the tenth of August, sought to concert measures for promoting

[1] *Providence Gazette*, July 8, 22, 1786.
[2] *Providence Town Meeting Records (MS.)* vii, 69.
[3] *Providence Gazette*, Aug. 5, 1786.

the paper circulation.[1] Providence sent a committee to
make overtures to this body for restoring confidence and
harmony between city and country. The convention adjourned without taking action, to meet with a state convention to be held on the twenty-fourth of August at East
Greenwich, " to consider the propriety of making some
alteration in the principles of, and laws relating to, the late
bank of paper money."[2] The action of this convention
shows that the changes contemplated were not of the nature
of relaxations in severity. The delegates from sixteen
towns who gathered there recommended to the deputies in
the assembly that they use their utmost endeavors to support the acts of the assembly on paper money; to take into
consideration the public securities, and liquidate them at a
stipulated value, and to withhold the staple farm products
from those who violated the paper money acts.[3] The assurance that in case the penal laws were repealed, and the use
of paper restricted to the satisfaction of judgments, the principal merchants would aid in giving circulation to the paper,
had no effect to alter their recommendation.[4]

The assembly was convened in special session to devise
further means of enforcing the circulation of paper. The
amendment now made to the law recited that, whereas " the
usual and stated methods and times of holding courts within
this state is impracticable, inexpedient and inapplicable to
the true intent and meaning of the said act, and altogether
insufficient to carry into effect the good purposes of this legislature touching the same," it was enacted that any com-
plainant might lodge his complaint with a judge of any court
in any county. It should be the duty of this judge to sum-
mon the offender to appear within three days for trial, with-

---

[1] *Providence Town Meeting Records* (*MS.*), vii, 71-2.

[2] *Providence Gazette*, Aug. 19, 1786.   [3] *Ibid.*, Aug. 26, 1786.

[4] *United States Chronicle*, Aug. 26, 1786.

out jury, before a court of three judges. The decision of a majority of the court should prevail. This judgment was to be final and without appeal. No delay, protection, privilege or injunction should be asked or granted. The penalty for the first offense was fixed at not less than six nor more than thirty pounds, and for the second offense not less than ten nor more than fifty pounds.[1] At the same time the paper was made a tender in payment of continental taxes.[2]

It seems as if the advocates of paper had reached the end of their course. They had made the paper money law retroactive by making it a tender in contracts made before May, 1786; they had deprived the citizens not only of trade, but of the necessities of life; they now violated the very principles of Magna Carta by suppressing trial by jury. Their relations with the Confederation, they now disgraced by proposing to pay their quota of taxes in depreciated paper. Thirteen members of the assembly, representing the towns of Providence, Newport, Bristol, Warren, and New Shoreham, entered a protest against this latest legislation. In their opinion, this was a violation of the natural and constitutional rights of the people, a violation of the Articles of Confederation, and an evasion of the obligation toward the national government. It was a violation of existing treaties with foreign states, was destructive of trade credit, and was a denial of the right of trial by jury.[3]

To restore credit and harmony, they proposed that both the tender and penal clauses be repealed; that when tender of paper was made and refused, it should be sufficient warrant for returning a writ as unsatisfied, and that those who had mortgaged their lands to receive paper might take up the mortgages at once upon paying back the paper. An increase in taxes was at the same time suggested.[4] The

---

[1] *Acts and Resolves of the General Assembly (MS.), 1786-7, 59, Aug. 25, 1786.*
[2] *Ibid.,* 55, Aug. 25, 1786.   [3] *Providence Gazette,* Sept. 2, 1786.   [4] *Ibid.*

propositions of the protestants were of course indignantly rejected. On the other hand, the assembly lent a more willing ear to addresses comporting with their own desires. The addresses of Governor Collins to the legislature, assigning as the cause of the special session of the assembly, the demands of many citizens on account of the unsettled state of the currency arising from a combination of influential men against the laws of the state, is a fair example of the arguments which sustained and incited the majority. Said he, " if there is no check to the present combination against the laws, your lives are unsafe, and your liberties are at a fatal, a final and a melancholy end."[1]

To complete the work of this extraordinary session, a select committee reported a bill to repeal the statute of limitations then in force, as inconsistent with the laws of the state, inexpedient and altogether impracticable. Promissory notes were henceforth not to be negotiable, and the time for bringing action upon them was limited to six months.

There were enacted in almost every town in the state, after these laws were passed, scenes which, had not their consequences been so serious, would have been most amusing. Debtors were everywhere eager to pay their debts. Creditors scarce dared show themselves on the street for fear of meeting a debtor with the paper money in his hand, but the care of the legislator had left no mode of escape for the creditor. Early in the summer debtors began to deposit paper with the courts. Notices began to appear in the newspapers summoning creditors to appear and receive the same. These notices, with their bold headline " Know Ye," of which no less than twenty-six appeared in one issue of the *Gazette*, became notorious throughout the state. " Know

---

[1] *United States Chronicle*, Sept. 7, 1786.

Ye Men" and " Know Ye Measures," were synonymous with rascality and dishonesty.[1]

A convention, held at Smithfield on the thirteenth of September, devised a scheme by which it was hoped to extricate the state from its present predicament. This was to be accomplished by the establishment of a " State Trade," a sort of socialistic scheme, to be conducted by a committee of the assembly, by which produce and lumber received in payment of taxes was to be exported. The specie so gained was to be devoted to paying the foreign debt. To consider this plan a special session of the assembly was asked for, but no response was made to the suggestion and the matter was dropped.

The paper money power had now reached its height. The exertions of its advocates had forced upon the state a policy repeatedly proven to be disastrous. It was left to the judicial power to inflict upon the system the blow which should break the hold of paper. This was brought about through the case of *Trevett vs. Weeden*, brought by John Trevett against John Weeden, of Newport, butcher, for refusing to receive paper money at par with specie. The excitement created in the state by this case was only equalled by the importance of the principles involved. Its importance arises from its connection with both the paper money legislation and the question of the independence of the judiciary. Each faction in the state felt that on the result of this trial depended the fate of its cause.

The information was exhibited before Paul Mumford, chief justice, but as the superior court was then sitting, the case was heard before the full bench, on the twenty-fifth of September.[2]

[1] *Providence Gazette*, Aug. 12, et seq.

[2] The details of this case are taken from a pamphlet report by Gen. J. M. Varnum, printed soon after in the *Providence Gazette* of Sept. 30 and Oct. 7, and the *American Museum*, v, 36.

Despite the fact that Weeden was in the deepest poverty, the best legal talent in the state was at his service. His counsel were Gen. James M. Varnum, of East Greenwich, and Henry Marchant, of Newport. The plaintiff's case rested on proof of the violation of the statute. The defendant's plea covered three points, in these words: " It appears by the act of the general assembly whereon said information is founded, that the said act hath expired, and hath no force; also, for that by the said act the matters of complaint are made triable before special courts, incontrolable by the supreme judiciary court of the state; and also for that the court is not, by said act, authorized and empowered to empannel a jury to try the facts tried in the information; and so the same is unconstitutional and void: all which the said Weeden is ready to verify. Where he prays judgment of the court here, that they will not take further cognizance of the said information." [1]

When General Varnum arose to defend his client, it was not so much, as he said, " in the line of my profession, as in the character of the citizen deeply interested in the constitutional laws of a free, independent and sovereign state." [2] The parties to this action, said he, " are of no further consequence than as the one represents the almost forlorn hope of a disappointed circle; the other as a victim, the first destined to the fury of their intemperate zeal and political phrenzy." [3]

The obscure phraseology of the act, which left it open to the construction that the penalties and forms prescribed were to be valid for only ten days, was the first point of attack. It was argued that the case at bar, being outside the limit set in the act, would not be cognizable under it.

Upon the plea that the trial was to be before a special court, without appeal, it was argued that the constitution

---

[1] Varnum, *Trevett vs. Weeden*, 2.

[2] *Ibid.*, 3.   [3] *Ibid.*, 7.

was subverted. The efficacy of the judiciary, as Varnum pointed out, depends on uniformity of decision, which can exist only in the presence of a single supreme court of appeals. This would be impossible in the presence of the court provided for in the act. The act of 1729 had established one " Supreme Court of Judicature, Court of Assize and General Gaol Delivery, over the whole colony, for the regular hearing and trying of all pleas, real, personal and mixed, and all pleas of the crown."[1] This court must be supreme, and any special court over which this court had no jurisdiction must be unconstitutional.

The last plea involving the right of trial by jury, was defended in a speech, the like of which had not been heard before at the Rhode Island bar. The development of the right, its assertion in Magna Carta, its reiterations down to the granting of the charter of 1663, and even to the present, were arrayed as proof of its existence as a right of the people. This right could be alienated only by a change in the constitution. The legislature possessed no such power except by the express consent of the people. This they had never given.

The advocate then entered on a fervid plea for the independence of the judiciary. He said : " The legislative have the uncontrollable power of making laws not repugnant to the constitution. The judiciary have the sole power of judging those laws, and are bound to execute them, but cannot admit any act of the legislature as law which is against the constitution."[2] A double tie binds the legislature to observe the constitution, " but if the general assembly attempt to make laws contrary hereunto, the court cannot receive them."[3] In developing this idea, Varnum applies the quotation from Bacon's Abridgment, that " if a stat-

---

[1] *Laws of Rhode Island*, 1730.

[2] Varnum, *Trevett vs. Weeden*, 27.　　　[3] *Ibid.*, 28.

ute . . . be repugnant, or impossible to be performed, the common law shall control it and judge it to be void." [1] "This act is repugnant when it authorizes the judges to proceed without a jury, according to the law of the land." The jury being the judges as to fact, and the court as to law, it would be impossible for judges to try a man without a jury and yet according to the law of the land. "This act therefore is impossible to be executed." [2] By this argument this case is directly linked with the "Case of the Convent Seals, and the Statute of Carlisle," the first case in which a common law court said that an unrepealed statute was void for cause judicially ascertained. [3] The whole argument closed with an appeal once more for an independent judiciary, for dependence of that department is the high road to tyranny. The decision of the court was "that the information was not cognizable before them." [4]

The decision was hailed with joy in Providence and Newport. Business at once awoke, and for a short time paper circulated freely, since it was known that it could be accepted or refused at will. From the point of view of the hard money people, the chief trouble was past. The paper could no longer be forced on an unwilling people. But on the part of the defeated party, momentary dismay was turned to wrath against the superior court. The assembly, the willing instrument of the paper money policy, was now called into service. The assembly, at its October session, peremptorily called the judges of the superior court before them in the following words: "Whereas it appears that the honorable, the justices of the Superior Court of Judicature,

[1] Bacon's *Abridgment*, iv, 635; Varnum, *Trevett vs. Weeden*, 30.

[2] Varnum, *Trevett vs. Weeden*, 30. See discussion in Brinton Coxe's *Judicial Power and Unconstitutional Legislation*, 234-48.

[3] *Statutes of the Realm*, i, 150.

[4] Varnum, *Trevett vs. Weeden*, 1.

Court of Assize, etc., at the last September term of the said court declared and adjudged an act of the supreme legislature of this state to be unconstitutional, and so absolutely void; and whereas it is suggested that the aforesaid judgment is unprecedented in this state and may tend directly to abolish the legislative authority thereof; it is therefore voted and resolved that all the justices of the said court be forthwith cited by the sheriffs of the respective counties in which they live or may be found to give their immediate attendance on the assembly to assign the reasons and grounds of the aforesaid judgment; and that the clerk of the said court be directed to attend this assembly at the same time, with the records of the said court which relate to the said judgment."[1]

The original summons, as it passed the lower house, contained also these words, which were stricken out by senate amendment: "In order that this assembly on proper information may adopt such measures as may establish the supremacy of the legislative authority."[2]

Two judges being detained at home by illness, the hearing was adjourned until the last Monday in the month, when all the judges appeared before the assembly.

This summons was but the logical result of the position always assumed by the legislature of the colony. It had always maintained that it was the source of all power as the representative of the popular will. It has already been noticed how, under the provision of the charter of 1663, empowering the general assembly "to appoint, order and direct, erect and settle, such places and courts of jurisdiction for the hearing and determining of all actions, cases, matters and things, happening within the said colony and plantation," a "General Court of Trials" had been created, composed of

[1] *Acts and Resolves of the General Assembly* (*MS.*), *1786-7*, 61.

[2] *Ibid.*, 61.

the governor or deputy governor and at least six assistants.[1] In 1678, the general assembly refused in terms "to judge or reverse any sentence or judgement passed by the general court of trials, according to law, except capital or criminal cases, or mulcts or fines."[2] In May, 1781, it was voted that, "if either plaintiff or defendant be aggrieved, after judgment entered in court, they may have liberty to make their appeal to the next general assembly for relief."[3]

In a letter to the Lords of Trade and Plantations, from the Earl of Bellomont, under date of November twenty-seventh, 1699, that official reports that the assembly of Rhode Island has judicial power of hearing and determining causes, of taking them out of the courts of law, and reversing judgments without regard for the rules of the common law.[4]

In consequence of a decision of the Privy Council, on an appeal from a judgment of the assembly, the latter body repealed the act, assuming for itself chancery powers, and provided that a court of chancery should be established.[5] At the same time, petition was to lie to the assembly and the petitioner was to have relief "in any matter or thing that may be cognizable before them, or that may at any time hereafter, when a proper court of chancery be stated, have their appeals continued for relief, if they shall think fit to prosecute the same."[6] Appeals thus continued to come before the assembly, and no court of equity was established until 1741.[7] Then it was done because attention to such cases impeded the public business. The court of equity was soon abolished and a writ of review substituted, whereby in certain cases a new trial might be secured.[8] It is certain

[1] *Rhode Island Colonial Records*, ii, 26.   [2] *Ibid.*, iii, 19.
[3] *Acts and Laws, 1745, 19.*
[4] *Rhode Island Colonial Records*, iii, 386.
[5] *Ibid.*, iii, 550.   [6] *Ibid.*, iv, 136.
[7] *Acts and Laws, 1745,* 239.   [8] *Ibid.*, 282.

from the records that from this time onward, as long as the
state continued under the charter, judicial power was exercised by the general assembly. It was not until the year
1856, that this power was finally taken from it.[1]

When on the thirtieth of October, 1786, the judges appeared before the legislature, each party was nerved for a
bitter fight. David Howell, the youngest judge on the bench,
whose reputation as a legislator had been won in Congress,
first addressed the assembly.[2] The order on which the judges
were then before the assembly, said he, might be considered
either as calling on them to assist in legislation, or to give
the reasons for their decision, as if accountable for it to the
legislature. Upon the first supposition, the court was ever
ready to give its counsel to the assembly on points of law;
but for decisions rendered in cases heard before them, they
were accountable only to God and their own consciences.

After a résumé of the arguments which proved that the act
"was unconstitutional, had not the force of law, and could
not be executed,"[3] he observed that in the summons they
had been alleged to declare the act unconstitutional and so
void, whereas this was simply found in the plea, while the
judgment was "that the information is not cognizable before
them." Whatever the private opinion of the judges might
be, they could be held only by their record. This, however,
he denied the right of the legislature to question.

Judge Tillinghast expressed his feeling of independence in
his sphere of duty, for, said he, " melancholy indeed would
be the condition of the citizens, if the supreme judiciary of
the state was liable to reprehension, whenever the caprice or

---

[1] *Rhode Island Reports*, iv, 324.

[2] The sources of information on the trial of the judges are: *Acts and Resolves
of the General Assembly* (*MS.*), 1786–7 ; *Providence Gazette*, Nov. 11, 1786, and
Varnum, *Trevett vs. Weeden.*

[3] Varnum, *Trevett vs. Weeden*, 38.

resentment of a few leading men should direct a public inquiry."[1]

The words of Judge Hazard are of peculiar interest as coming from a friend of paper money. "It is well known," said he, "that my sentiments have fully accorded with the general system of the legislature in emitting the paper currency; but I never did, I never will, depart from the character of an honest man, to support any measures, however agreeable in themselves. . . . The opinion I gave upon the trial was dictated by the energy of truth; I thought it right—I still think so."[2]

After long discussion the question was put "whether the assembly was satisfied with the reasons given by the judges in support of their judgment?" It was decided in the negative. A motion to dismiss the judges from office evoked a protest, signed by Judges Hazard, Tillinghast, and Howell, wherein they insisted on their full power in construing the laws of the state as a court of last resort. As no charge had been brought against them in their true judicial capacity, if such was to be brought they demanded trial before some legal tribunal. Without such trial and conviction, they denied the right of the legislature to convict them.[3] Upon the request of the assembly for counsel from the three lawyers sitting in that body, it was given as their opinion that without impeachment or other regular process of law, the judges could not be removed from office. Thereupon it was voted by a large majority, "that as the judges are not charged with any criminality in rendering the judgment upon the information *Trevett vs. Weeden*, they are therefore discharged from any further attendance upon this assembly, on that account."[4]

[1] Varnum, *Trevett vs. Weeden*, 43.   [2] *Ibid.*   [3] *Ibid.*, 45.
[4] *Acts and Resolves of the General Assembly (MS.), 1786–7*, Nov. 3, 1786; *Providence Gazette*, Nov. 11, 1786; *United States Chronicle*, Nov. 9, 1786.

Though baffled in this direction, the legislature had remaining a weapon to be wielded by their constituencies in
the form of the ballot at the annual election. But though
the assembly, for three score and ten years, continued to review the work of the courts, yet never again did they presume to hold a court answerable for its decisions.

The dominant party, chagrined at the failure of its endeavors to coerce the courts, as well as at the demonstrations
following the decision in *Trevett vs. Weeden*, now chose another line of aggression. The assembly that issued the summons to the judges, resolved that the text of an act entitled
" An act to stimulate and give efficacy to the paper bills
emitted by this state in May last," be forwarded to the several towns to be submitted to the freemen in town meeting,
and an opinion returned to the assembly at its next session
in the form of instructions to the deputies.[1] The proposed
act declared in its preamble, that whereas certain persons
had accumulated great wealth by depreciating securities and
buying them at a reduced price, and were now attempting to
depreciate the paper, therefore it was proposed to require
every citizen to take a test oath to make every endeavor that
paper money should have an equal value with specie, and to
sell or expose for sale no article for which he would not take
in payment either paper or gold at the same rate. Every
person taking the oath was to be enrolled at the town clerk's
office, and to receive a certificate of having complied with
the law. All incumbents in office as well as all newly elected
officers, together with practicing lawyers and all persons entering or clearing vessels at any port were to be obliged to
subscribe. No person was to be eligible to office until the
oath had been taken. Violations of the law were to be ac-
tionable as perjury.[2]

[1] *United States Chronicle*, Oct. 12, 1786; *Providence Gazette*, Oct. 14, 1786.
[2] *Ibid.*

Alarmed at the prospect, the leaders of the opposition, together with the more moderate of the party in the ascendancy, again attempted to effect a compromise whereby the penal laws might be repealed. Further, they proposed that a tender of paper be not made to work a discharge of the debt, but simply to stop the accumulation of interest; that the excise be revived and made payable in paper; that the state tax be made higher and paid more punctually, and that the principal and interest of the state debt be paid in paper.[1] By making paper acceptable in payment of certain taxes, and leaving it at the option of creditors to accept or reject this medium, it was hoped that a certain currency might be given it. But with the trial of the judges still pending, and the test act before the people, and a chance of its ratification, the country party were encouraged flatly to refuse a conference.

Though its devotees in the assembly were still confident, public opinion on the forcing acts was undergoing a change. The distresses of the past summer, the decision in *Trevett vs. Weeden*, and, above all, that inherent sense of justice which, though dulled for a time, is sure at length to assert itself in the public mind, had prepared the people to receive with detestation the proposition to carry forward the system. Replies in the form of instructions began to appear at an early date. Providence, at a town meeting on October seventeenth, judging the act to be "unconstitutional, unjust, impolitic, tending to drive people into parties violently opposed to each other,"[2] and declaring that when a man loses the right to buy and to sell, he becomes a slave, directed its deputies to oppose this almost proscriptive act. In the sister capital, it was thought that this test might lead to others,

---

[1] *United States Chronicle*, Oct. 12, 1786; *Providence Gazette*, Oct. 14, 1786.

[2] *Providence Town Meeting Records*, vii, 73–4.

religious or political, or would at least tend to subvert the liberties of the people and lead to an aristocracy.[1] East Greenwich, adopting a similar course, directed her deputies to work for a settlement of the difficulties concerning the paper money, a renewal of the excise and high taxes, and the preservation of the right of trial by jury.[2] Cumberland, which eight months before had been vociferous for paper money, decided that the passage of a test act would appreciate the paper in the hands of the present holders, multiply oaths, make the people familiar with excessive punishments, embarrass commerce by excluding imports, and raise the price of necessities.[3] Even Gloucester, the stronghold of the country party, realizing that commerce had been destroyed, voted that they wished the bill " to be forever rejected." [4]

Only three towns in the state placed themselves on record as favoring the act. These were Scituate, Foster and North Kingstown. The act so universally censured was quickly disposed of by the assembly at its meeting on November second.[5]

The acquittal of the judges, supported by the sentiment displayed on the proposed test act, made the whole series of force acts practically inoperative. Though still upon the statute books, friend and foe alike knew that they would never again become operative. In the December session the assembly attempted to deal with the changed condition of affairs. The force act of June, which made it a crime to refuse paper on a par with specie, together with all subsequent addi-

---

[1] *Papers Relating to the Adoption of the Constitution* (*MS.*), 40.

[2] *Ibid.*, 44.   [3] *Ibid.*, 43.

[4] Warwick, Bristol, North Providence, Tiverton, Cranston, Exeter, Hopkinton, and Portsmouth. *Ibid.*, 41.

[5] *Acts and Resolves of the General Assembly* (*MS.*), 1786–7, 70; *United States Chronicle*, Nov. 2, 1786.

tions and amendments, was repealed.[1]   Paper was still, by the act of May, a legal tender, and deposits with the courts still operated to discharge the debt.   As some of the judges now began to receive such deposits, and to give notice of their intention to do so, it was enacted that a debtor might make his deposit with any judge.[2]   In their attempts to relieve the condition of debtors, two suggestions of the Smithfield convention of September thirteenth were acted upon by the assembly. The English statute limiting the time of bringing personal actions, which had been repealed during the war, but reenacted in 1785, was now amended so that all actions on promissory notes and book accounts must be brought within two years.[3]   The negotiability of promissory notes was destroyed by making it necessary that action upon them be brought in the name of the original promisee.[4]

The friends of sound money began to look forward to the April election as the next occasion on which an attack could be made upon the party in power.   In the meantime, paper was to reign in the session of the assembly which met on March twelfth, and to reflect both the narrowness and the meanness of the cause which it upheld.   Several acts, among which were the removal of the postmaster at Newport for an alleged insult to the governor in detaining letters addressed to him until postage was paid, and the withdrawing of the charter of the city of Newport on a petition representing one-seventeenth of the taxable property, stand as evidences of their capacity in other directions.[5]   That its members were in sympathy with the riotous conduct of the masses in the neighboring states was made evident by their refusing to deliver up to the Massachusetts authorities some of the offenders in Shays' rebellion.

[1] *Acts and Resolves of the General Assembly* (*MS.*), *1786–7*, 92, Jan. 6, 1787.

[2] *Ibid.*, 80, Dec. 29–30, 1786.   [3] *Ibid.*, 82, Jan. 6, 1787.   [4] *Ibid.*, 82.

[5] *Rhode Island Colonial Records*, x, 233.

In pursuance of a line of policy adopted in October of the previous year, and followed out in the late session, the object of which was to ascertain the public debt with a view to extinguishing it, the assembly had at the last session made provision for paying one-fourth part of such debt in the money received as state taxes, that is, in paper.[1] Now the act was extended to cover all forms of securities held against the state. Creditors were notified to present their securities and to receive one-fourth payment on them or to forfeit all claim to such part thereafter. Here was a simple proposition whereby one-fourth of the state debt was to be repudiated; for to make payments in the paper was repudiation and nothing less.

Thus closed the last session of the year 1786-7. No more disastrous year is recorded in the annals of Rhode Island. Her reputation in the community of states was gone. To a nation prejudiced by the state's opposition to the salutary measures of Congress, her name became a synonym of all that was disreputable and dishonest. Allusions of this nature are to be found in almost every publication of the day. The *Connecticut Magazine* added to these a poetical effusion :

> " Hail, realm of rogues, renowned for fraud and guile,
> All hail, ye knaveries of yon little isle.
> *   *   *   *   *   *
> Look through the state, the unhallowed ground appears
> A nest of dragons and a cave for bears;
> A nest of vipers mixed with adders foul.
> *   *   *   *   *   *
> The wiser race, the snares of law to shun,
> Like Lot from Sodom, from Rhode Island run."[2]

The existence of the tender law made the administration

---

[1] *Schedules of the General Assembly*, October (2d) Session, 1786, 86; *Ibid.*, December Session, 1786, 21.

[2] *Providence Gazette*, Apr. 14, 1787.

of justice almost farcial. The superior court which, since its encounter with the assembly, had not sat with a full bench, was adjourned at its March term for three weeks because the depreciation of paper made the administration of justice impossible. At this adjourned session all cases involving large amounts were put over until a future term, probably in the hope that a change in affairs might be brought about in the meantime. At the April term in Washington county more than twenty bills in equity were heard for the redemption of mortgaged estates. The paper for redeeming these estates was brought into court by the sackfull. Determined not to make a farce of justice, the judges refused to record these tenders, and put over all such cases until the next term. They hoped that at the coming election an assembly would be elected which would sweep away the paper money laws. If this was not accomplished the court knew very well that their removal would be sure, and the responsibility of the whole matter would be cast on other shoulders.

The general election had for some weeks been the center of expectant interest. Two tickets or "Proxes" were in the field. That of the party in power bore the legend "Liberty and Property secured by Perseverance." The name of John Collins headed the ticket, supported by that of Daniel Owen, for deputy governor.[1] The opposition ticket bore the names of William Bradford and John Malbone.[2] Collins and Owen had proved to be a strong combination in the year that was closing. The former, a man of moderate views, was calculated to hold the wavering spirits; the latter was the acknowledged leader of the paper money party in its stronghold, Gloucester. In William Bradford the sound money party put forward a man who had been identified with every step in the Revolution. He was a member of the committee

---

[1] *Rhode Island Historical Society's Collections* (*MS.*), vii, 31.

[2] *Ibid.*, 32.

of correspondence appointed in 1773, of the committee of safety in 1775, and of the Hartford Convention of 1780, of which latter body he was president. He was chosen a member of the Continental Congress as the successor of Stephen Hopkins, and served as deputy governor from 1775 to 1778. John Malbone, a representative of one of Newport's oldest mercantile houses, stood for the commercial interests of the colony.[1]

The opposition sought to rally supporters to their standard through the press. An address issued to the free electors averred that the character of the state was already so debased that to be an inhabitant of Rhode Island was synonymous with being a villain. The continuation of the tender laws in the face of depreciation was cited as proof of the dishonest motives of the party in power. It was charged that a law to prevent bribery and corruption passed by the last assembly had been put forward with the hope of preventing the Quakers from voting.[2] " A Farmer " confessed that in 1786 he had voted for paper, partly because he considered the old administration opposed to the interests of the people at large. The people had wanted a legal tender paper founded on landed security and redeemable, but the emission had been too large. The penal acts, the test oath bill, the act annulling the indorsement of notes, and the change in the statute of limitations, had overdone the matter. They had all been fabricated with the sole purpose of making a tender

[1] The remainder of the paper money ticket was: For Assistants, Joseph Staunton, John Williams, Sylvester Sayles, James Arnold, Caleb Gardner, John Cook, William Congdon, Joseph Tweedy, Thomas Coggeshall and Thomas Hazard; for Secretary, Henry Ward; for Attorney-General, Henry Goodwin; for Treasurer, Joseph Clarke. Opposed to them were, for Assistants, John Jenks, Simeon Perry, John Smith, Richard Searle, Thomas Rice, William Hammond, Gideon Clarke, Henry Bliss, Joseph Baker, and Peleg Arnold; for Attorney-General, William Channing. Henry Ward and Joseph Clarke had no opposition.

[2] *Providence Gazette*, Apr. 7, 1787.

and refusal an extinguishment of a debt. He suggested
that the compromise proposed in the previous June might
still solve the difficulty.[1]

The April election came and went, and left the paper
money party still in power. Of the eighty assistants and
deputies who assembled at the May session of the legislature, only twenty-four were new comers. From Jamestown, Cumberland, Cranston, Barrington, and Warren new
delegations appeared. How much of this change was due
to a change in public sentiment on paper money is unknown.
The strength of the majority in the north, west, and south remained unbroken. The judges of the superior court were
made to pay the penalty of their insubordination. Chief
Justice Mumford alone was re-elected.

Encouraged by this victory, the party in power felt prepared to hold out not only against their own fellow-citizens,
but against public sentiment in the other states. But though
possessing a majority in the assembly, they attempted no
new measures for promoting the paper money, but confined
themselves to carrying out the work of repudiation already
begun. The paper money movement from this time is the
record of a gradual recession from a policy which was soon
to be gradually abandoned.

The payment of the state debt in paper, which had been
begun in March, was continued at the June session, 1787,
when a second quarter of all securities held against the state,
excepting certain four per cent. notes, to be ordered paid.[2]
In November of the same year, a third quarter was discharged,[3] and on May tenth, 1788, the last quarter was ordered to be paid.[4] To complete the work of repudiation, in

[1] *Providence Gazette.* Apr. 14, 1787.

[2] *Acts and Resolves of the General Assembly (MS.), 1786–7,* June 16, 1787.

[3] *Ibid.,* Nov. 3, 1787.   [4] *Ibid.,* 1788–90; May 10, 1788.

March of the following year, those notes which had been heretofore excepted were called in.[1]

On the approach of the April election, the position of the towns was in several cases set forth in instructions to their deputies. Providence declared that the tender laws, and the present statute of limitations, ought to be repealed.[2] On the very same day, South Kingstown instructed her delegates to oppose the repeal of any of the acts of issue.[3] Midway between these stood Westerly, when she demanded a continuance of the tender laws but a repeal of the statute of limitations.[4] A call for the repeal of one or both of these laws was re-echoed from Jamestown, Middletown, Bristol, Little Compton, and Hopkinton.[5] South Kingstown found as a supporter of her position West Greenwich.[6] The larger share of the country towns seem to have trusted to the well known sentiments of their deputies. At the session which preceded the election, the opposition only succeeded in securing the extension of the time for bringing personal actions from two years to four.[7] A motion to repeal the tender law was defeated by a large majority.[8]

As the third year of the sway of paper money drew to its close the dominant party weakened perceptibly. In March, 1789, a motion to repeal the tender law was lost by a vote of nineteen to thirty-seven.[9] In June of the same year the vote on a similar motion stood twenty to thirty.[10] The assembly in September, confessing that as the bills of credit had depreciated, great injustice would result unless some-

[1] *Acts and Resolves of the General Assembly* (*MS.*), *1786–7*, Mar. 14, 1789.

[2] *Providence Town Meeting Records*, vii, 118.

[3] *Papers Relating to the Adoption of the Constitution* (*MS.*), 63.

[4] *Ibid.*, 60.   [5] *Ibid.*, 49, 62–4.   [6] *Ibid.*, 65.

[7] *Schedules of the General Assembly*, March Session, 1788, 11.

[8] *United States Chronicle*, Apr. 10, 1788.

[9] *Ibid.*, May 19, 1789.   [10] *Ibid.*, June 18, 1789.

thing was done, suspended the act making a tender and lodgement of the paper a discharge of the debt, until the rising of the next session.[1] At the next session, as was anticipated, the assembly proceeded to do that long deferred act of justice, and repealed the act of May, 1786, which made paper a legal tender at par with coin.[2] The scarcity of specie and the accumulation of debts having made it impossible for debtors to meet their obligations in hard money, it was enacted that real estate and certain articles of personal property might be tendered in payment of debts. The rate of acceptance of paper was fixed at fifteen of paper for one of silver. But for all contracts made since November, 1786, unless specified to be in gold or silver, paper was to be taken at par.[3]

So closed the drama of paper money in Rhode Island. Conceived in ignorance, and supported by folly and dishonesty, it had brought discord, repudiation and misery. It disappeared, leaving a disorganized finance and a majority in power inflamed by passion, whose persistence in opposition to salutary national measures was bringing Rhode Island to the verge of war with her sister states. However just her motives, however steadfast her hold on principle, still the work of the year 1786 so lowered her in the eyes of her neighbors that only bad and perverse motive could be seen in her acts respecting the federal constitution. It is owing to prejudice and distrust it aroused against the state and to its influence in preparing the way for strife over the constitution, that this episode has its vital connection with the relations of Rhode Island to the union.

[1] *Acts and Resolves of the General Assembly* (*MS.*), *1788-90*, 117.
[2] *Ibid.*, 128.   [3] *Ibid.*, 128.

CHAPTER V

RHODE ISLAND AND THE CONSTITUTION

THE Confederation had, in the first five years of its existence, proved its inadequacy. Even before it went into effect, the far-reaching political sense of Hamilton saw its weakness, and suggested a remedy.[1] Half a decade and a succession of fortuitous events were necessary to bring public opinion to the point of action. The remoter cause of the convention of 1787 was the fact and growing conviction of the inefficiency of the Articles of Confederation. The immediate antecedents were the Alexandria and Annapolis conventions. The development of the remoter cause was, in each state, the resultant of the forces of local politics working therein.

In Rhode Island those forces received their impetus far back before the Revolution, when the rivalry of Providence and Newport had created two parties. Newport, the historic, commercial, and social metropolis of the colony, watched the rise of Providence with a jealous eye. The natural consequence of growth was a demand on the part of Providence, for recognition in politics. Consideration she won for herself when, in 1755, Stephen Hopkins was elected governor over a candidate put forward by Newport. This was the signal for the opening of hostilities between the two towns under the leadership of Stephen Hopkins and Samuel Ward. These northern and southern parties, the one dominant in Providence county and the adjoining towns in Kent and Bristol, the other strong in Newport and Kings counties,

[1] Letter to Duane, Sept. 30, 1780. Lodge, *Works of Hamilton*, i, 203.

struggled with varying success until 1768, when impelled by a common sentiment against ministerial oppression, a compromise was effected. The progress and outcome of this struggle has been traced in an earlier chapter. At the close of the war, old party divisions reappeared, but dividing lines were drawn differently from those of former days. Newport had lost her prestige. Her commerce was ruined and her most influential citizens gone. Providence, which had grown in importance, became the center of the descendants of the old Ward party. The old Hopkins party, deprived of the support of its chief town, welcomed to its fold Kings, now Washington county, from which the Ward influence had departed. The seaport or town party soon saw that their commercial prosperity depended on the stability and credit which could only be gained through a strong central government. The quiet advances of this really numerical minority are marked by grants to Congress bit by bit of the powers desired by that body.

The economic and industrial conditions which resulted in social convulsions in all the northern states in 1786–7, manifested themselves in Rhode Island in the overthrow of the town party and the accession of the country party to power, with its accompaniment of paper money, repudiation and distress. As no unjust and unnatural system is destined to long life, the fall of paper money was swift and complete. But the party which instituted the policy, plunged into deeper misery by its course, met all measures tending toward a stronger government with bitter hostility. The remnant of the paper money party formed a nucleus about which all opponents of a closer union grouped themselves.

It was the Annapolis convention that directly led to the Federal convention. As a prelude to this, there was held at Mount Vernon, in March, 1785, a meeting of commissioners from the states of Maryland and Virginia, which drew up an agreement concerning the navigation of the Potomac and the opening of a road to the Ohio. Further than this, they recommended that the states arrange similar duties, a uniform system of dockage, a uniform currency and an annual meeting of commissioners to discuss the commercial policy of the two states.[1] Both states having ratified the work of the commissioners, Virginia, on January twenty-sixth, 1786, elected eight delegates to meet the delegates of the other states " to take into consideration the trade of the United States; to examine the relative situation and trade of the said states; to consider how far a uniform system in their commercial regulations may be necessary to their common interest and their permanent harmony, and to report to the several states such an act relative to this great object as, when unanimously ratified by them, will enable the United States in Congress assembled effectually to provide for the same." [2]

A circular letter was sent by the commissioners to the other states, asking that delegates be appointed, naming the first Monday in September, 1786, as the day, and Annapolis as the place of meeting. On the eleventh of September, delegates from five states met for organization. New York, New Jersey, Pennsylvania, Delaware and Virginia were represented; Connecticut, Maryland, South Carolina and Georgia appointed no delegates; Massachusetts elected delegates, but at so late a day that they did not arrive until the convention had adjourned.[3] In Rhode Island no movement was made to elect delegates until June, when Jabez Bowen and Samuel Ward were appointed to attend, with instructions similar to those given to the Virginia delegates.[4] But, like

[1] *Virginia State Papers*, iv, 80; *Pennsylvania Archives*, x, 511; Henning, *Statutes at Large*, xii, 50.

[2] Elliot's *Debates*, i, 112–116.   [3] *Ibid.*, 115.

[4] *Schedules of the General Assembly*, June Session, 1786, 5.

Massachusetts, they were met on the way by the news that the convention had adjourned. The avowed objects of this convention contained nothing which could rouse the opposition even of Rhode Island. Moreover, whatever might be suggested would have effect only after ratification by all the states. The tardiness of both Massachusetts and Rhode Island can probably be explained by the dilatory manner in which representative bodies of that day usually met. They thought that the convention would likewise be late in organizing.[1] The work of this body, so important as a step toward the convention to follow, was embodied in a report addressed to the states represented. This report, reviewing the defects of the confederation, recommended that all the states choose delegates to a convention to meet at Philadelphia on the second Monday in May, 1787, " to take into consideration the situation of the United States, to devise such further provisions as shall appear to them necessary to render the constitution of the federal government adequate to the exigencies of the Union." [2] The results of this meeting were to be reported to Congress, and after its ratification by that body and by the states, was to become effective.[3] On February twenty-first, Congress resolved that a convention of delegates should be held on the second Monday in May at Philadelphia, " for the sole and express purpose of reviewing the Articles of Confederation, and reporting to Congress and the several legislatures such alterations and provisions therein as shall, when agreed to in Congress, and confirmed by the states, render the federal Constitution adequate to the exigencies of government and the preservation of the Union." [4]

The states led by New Jersey, on November twenty-third,

---

[1] Gilpin, *Madison Papers.* ii, 700; *Providence Gazette*, July 8, 1786.

[2] Original copy sent to Rhode Island is in *Rhode Island Archives, Letters, 1785–8*, 56.

[3] Elliot's *Debates*, i, 116.   [4] *Ibid.*, i, 119.

had begun to appoint delegates even before the passage of
the resolution by Congress. By the day set for the convention, nine states had chosen representatives. Connecticut,
Maryland, and New Hampshire made their appointments before the end of June. Rhode Island alone was unrepresented.
Emphasizing the necessity of a convention, her delegates
wrote of the government: "We think it our duty to inform
the state that it is totally inefficient for the purposes of the
union, and that Congress without being invested with extensive powers must prove totally nugatory."[1] They declared
their willingness to retire to private life if only they could
"see such a degree of energy infused into the Federal government as may render it adequate to the great ends of its
original institution."[2] These were the sentiments of a man
of culture, uttered by James Manning, president of Brown
University, who looked with disfavor upon the popular
movement in Rhode Island.

The question of appointing delegates to the Philadelphia
convention first came before the general assembly at that
March session of 1787 which was infamous for repudiation,
and was rejected by a majority of twenty-three.[3] This action,
though not unanticipated, caused Rhode Island to become
a pariah among the states. Madison said: "Rhode Island
alone refuses her concurrence. A majority of more than
twenty in the legislature of that state has refused to follow
the general example. Being conscious of the wickedness of
the measures they are pursuing, they are afraid of everything
that may become a control on them."[4] Again he wrote:
"Nothing can exceed the wickedness and folly which continue to reign there. All sense of character, as well as of

[1] Staples, *Rhode Island in the Continental Congress*, 566.

[2] *Ibid.*   [3] *Ibid.*, 572.

[4] Letter to Col. J. Madison, Apr. 1, 1787. Gilpin, *Writings of Madison*, i, 286.

right, is obliterated. Paper money is still their idol, though it is debased to eight for one."[1]

To her immediate neighbors, Rhode Island appeared responsible for the evils of the present and of the past. A writer from Salem, Massachusetts, realizing that perhaps the political existence of the union depended on the results of the convention, said: " Rhode Island has refused to coöperate in this business. From her anti-federal disposition nothing better could have been expected. To that state it is owing that the Continental impost has not taken place. To her may be charged the poverty of the soldiers of the late army, the heavy taxes of our citizens and the embarrassed state of the public finances. It is however hoped and wished that her dissent will never more be permitted to defeat any federal measure. Rather let her be dropped out of the Union, or appropriated to the different states that surround her."[2]

The feelings of the minority, who in shame and impotent wrath saw the finger of scorn pointing from all sides, can hardly be described. "A Freeman," reviewing the relation of the state to the union, and giving voice to the sentiments of his party, cited the act to pay the state's quota of federal interest in paper, and the refusal to join in the Federal Convention, as presenting " a prospect too serious not to excite our attention."[3] "Can any palliation or excuse," said he, " be offered by a line of policy so inconsistent with our true interest, and that respect we owe to Congress and our sister states? . . . Does it not argue great obstinacy as well as ignorance of the true interest of the state to refuse to join in a convention recommended by Congress and approved by all the other states? It must be confessed that these meas-

---

[1] Letter to Edmund Randolph, Apr. 2, 1787. Gilpin, *Madison Papers*, ii, 629.

[2] *American Museum*, i, 290.

[3] *Providence Gazette*, Apr. 14, 1787.

ures have a direct tendency to dissolve that bond of union
by which we confederated with our sister states, and to induce them to consider us as having derelicted the confederacy, and not entitled to its assistance or protection; or
rather, will they not divide our territory and subject it to the
jurisdiction of the neighboring states?"[1]

The letters of the delegates in Congress breathed a pure
spirit of Federalism from the first. To Governor Collins
they did not hesitate to say: "This period forms a most serious crisis in our political existence. The avowed objects of
this new assembly, sanctioned by general opinion and pointing to the great interests of the whole Union, are too momen-
tous not to claim the attention of the state of Rhode Island."[2]

The Anti-Federalists were loud in their protestations of
adherence to the Articles of Confederation, from whose weakness they saw power accrue to the separate states. The
reply of the Federalists was: "How far an entire adherence
to the Articles of Confederation may justify the policy of any
one or two states in remaining indifferent spectators, to the
probable events of these arrangements, we shall not presume
to decide; but common safety, and the relation the part
bears to the whole, should have their due influence upon
this occasion."[3] Imbued with these sentiments, members of
Congress from Rhode Island most seriously recommended
the appointment of delegates to the convention.

The Federalists, both within and without the state, were
agreed that morally at least, Rhode Island was bound to join
in any measure for establishing the union more firmly. The
Anti-Federalists, wasting few words, relied on their professed
consideration for the Articles of Confederation, to conceal
any unworthy motives and justify their course. Oblivious
of criticism and supported by the popular vote, the assembly

---

[1] *Providence Gazette*, Apr. 14, 1787.

[2] *Rhode Island Archives (MS.), Letters, 1785-8*, 68.   [3] *Ibid.*

continued to "trample most sacred obligations, and defy the United States to arms."[1]

The proposition made at the May session to appoint delegates, was lost in the upper house by a majority of two, after it had passed the lower house by the same majority.[2]   The question, revived again in the upper house at the June session, passed by a majority of five, but because of factional struggles was defeated in the lower by a majority of seven.[3]

The natural effect of such continued obstinacy was to raise a wave of hostile comment.   Washington observed with pain that the state persisted in that "impolitic, unjust, and one might add without much impropriety, scandalous conduct which seems to have marked all her public councils of late."[4] The *Newport Herald*, a journal recently established in support of Federal principles, declared the object of this administration to be the freeing the people from debt.   Though an object commendable in itself, the continuance of the tender laws showed that they would not scruple as to the means employed.   There were, it was asserted, Tories still in the state who were only too glad to aid the Anti-Federal movement to serve their own ends.[5]   At a celebration of Independence day in a certain New Jersey town twelve guns had been fired and twelve toasts drunk, totally ignoring the existence of the despised state of Rhode Island.[6]   Indeed, public opinion ran so high that Lord Temple was led to write to Lord Cærnarvon : " It is already seriously talked of, the annihilation of Rhode Island as a state, and to divide that territory (I mean the government of it) between Massachusetts and Connecticut."[7]

[1] "A Friend to this State," in *American Museum*, iv, 320.

[2] *United States Chronicle*, Aug. 2, 1787.   [3] *Ibid.*

[4] Letter to David Stuart, July 1, 1787.   Ford, *Writings of Washington*, xi, 159.

[5] *Providence Gazette*, June 30, 1787.   [6] *Ibid.*, Aug. 4, 1787.

[7] Bancroft, *Hist. of the Constitution*, ii, 425.

Madison, who was watching the progress of events, afterwards wrote: " Rhode Island was the only exception to a
compliance with the recommendation from Annapolis, well
known to have been swayed by an obdurate adherence to an
advantage which her position gave her, of taxing her neighbors through their consumption of imported supplies, an
advantage it was foreseen would be taken from her by a revision of the Articles of Confederation."[1] By this statement
the writer reveals his lack of information on the subject in
question. From the acknowledged fact that in 1781 and
1783 the merchants of Rhode Island had hoped by retaining the power of laying duties, to reap a benefit as the port
of entry for the surrounding states, he concludes that now
the opposition is from the same quarter. It is evident that
he is not aware that the commercial leaders who were most
powerful in the opposition to the impost were now the
strongest advocates of union. He overlooked the fact that a
letter from Providence had been read in the convention, on
May twenty-eighth, from "the merchants, tradesmen, and
others of this place deeply affected with the evils of the present unhappy times,"[2] giving it as the general opinion in Providence, and of the well informed throughout the state, that
the full power over commerce, domestic and foreign, should
be given to the general government, and that the powers of
Congress in the matter of requisitions should be made effectual. The purpose of the communication was to prevent any
unfavorable opinion in the other states which might be prejudicial to the commercial interests of Providence. The influence and exertions of the memorialists were pledged to
work for the adoption of the results of the convention, which
should tend to strengthen the union, promote the commerce,

[1] Gilpin, *Madison Papers*, ii, 709.

[2] Elliot's *Debates*, v, 578; Gilpin, *Madison Papers*, iii, Ap. 1.

increase the power and establish the credit of the United States." [1]

Accompanying that from Providence was a letter from General Varnum, who had just returned from Congress. He had found that the measures of the legislature did not represent the real character of the state. "They are equally reprobated and abhorred," said he, "by gentlemen of the learned professions, by the whole mercantile body, and by most of the respectable farmers and mechanics. The majority of the administration is composed of a licentious number of men, destitute of education, and many of them void of principle. From anarchy and confusion they derive their temporary consequence; and this they endeavor to prolong by debauching the minds of the common people, whose attention is wholly directed to the abolition of debts, public and private. With these are associated the disaffected of every description, particularly those who were unfriendly during the war. Their paper money system, founded in oppression and fraud, they are determined to support at every hazard; and rather than relinquish their favorite pursuit, they trample on the most sacred obligations. . . . It is fortunate, however, that the wealth and resources of this state are chiefly in the possession of the well-affected, and they are entirely devoted to the public good." [2]

During all this storm of hostile criticism no official defence or explanation was offered until at last, in September, a letter was dispatched to the president of Congress in explanation of the position of the assembly. Therein it was asserted that they have been actuated by "that great prin-

[1] *Ibid.* The signers of this letter were John Brown, Joseph Nightingale, Levi Hall, Philip Allen, Paul Allen, Jabez Bowen, Nicholas Brown, John Jencks, Welcome Arnold, William Russell, Jeremiah Olney, William Barton, and Thomas L. Halsey.

[2] Gilpin, *Madison Papers*, iii, Ap. 1; Updike, *Rhode Island Bar*, 300.

ciple which hath ever been the characteristic of this state, the love of true constitutional liberty, and the fear we have of making innovations on the rights and liberties of the citizens at large."[1]   While Rhode Island granted the power over import duties and the regulation of trade, the recommendation to appoint delegates to the convention had not been complied with because the legislature did not conceive it in their power to do so.   By law, the delegates in Congress were chosen by the freemen, and for the assembly to appoint delegates to the convention when they could not appoint delegates in Congress was held to be inconsistent. It would, moreover, be improper to appoint delegates to a convention that might result in the dissolution of Congress, and the existence of a confederation without that body. "You will impute it, sir," the letter concludes, "to our being diffident of power, and an apprehension of dissolving a compact which was framed by the wisdom of men who gloried in being instrumental in preserving the religious and civil rights of a multitude of people, and an almost unbounded territory, that said requisition hath not been complied with; and fearing that when the compact should once be broken, we must all be lost in a common ruin.   We shall ever esteem it a pleasure to join with our sister states in being instrumental in whatever may be advantageous to the Union, and add strength and permanence thereto, upon constitution-principles."[2]

    This letter, in so far as it spoke of fear of invading liberty or abridging the civil or religious rights of individuals, strikes an old key-note.   The rights, civil and religious, for which the fathers had struggled, and of the existence of which they were justly proud, seemed amply secured in the Articles of Confederation.   The deliberate discarding of such

[1] *Acts and Resolves of the General Assembly* (*MS.*), *1786–7*, July 15, 1787.
[2] *Rhode Island Colonial Records*, x, 258.

a constitution to make way for another whose terms were as yet unstated, appeared most dangerous to a large class. These individuals hesitated to resign rights which, if once released, the state's tiny influence might not again succeed in regaining. It would have strengthened the position of the assembly had the remainder of its argument been based on equally valid grounds. The inconsistencies of this line of reasoning were brought out in a protest entered by the deputies from Providence and Newport against this letter.[1] The appointment of delegates to attend conventions of the states had never before been held an assumption of power, even when they were given authority to declare independence, or form Articles of Confederation. The acts granting control of imports and of commerce proved the power of the assembly to amend the constitution without resort to popular vote. The Articles of Confederation themselves provided for amendment by the legislature. But in any case it appeared to the protestants that it would do much more honor to the state to join heartily with the other states in promoting this reform. In fact it was apparent to the minority that this argument was put forward to take the place of a better one, which they had not.

The Federal Convention finished its task on the seventeenth of September, 1787, and transmitted the results of its deliberations to Congress, recommending that it should afterward be submitted to a convention of delegates in each state, chosen by the people thereof, under recommendation of the legislature. Each state, having ratified, was to inform Congress that that body might take steps for putting the same in operation.[2] The constitution, with the accompanying letter, was received in Congress on September twenty-eighth. Thereupon it was at once resolved to transmit all

[1] *Rhode Island Colonial Records*, x, 259.

[2] Elliot's *Debates*, i, 317.

the papers thereon to the state legislatures, which were in
turn to submit them to conventions in each state.

The time of action on the constitution was influenced by
several causes: the date when the state received the official
notice; the time when the legislature would be again in session; the date set for the convention; and the time consumed
in the convention.   All these opportunities for delay did in
fact have much influence on the time of adoption.   Delaware and Pennsylvania led the way early in December, followed by the unanimous vote of New Jersey soon after.
Georgia did likewise on the second day of the new year.
Connecticut, the fifth state, ratified by a vote of one hundred
and twenty-eight to forty.   In none of these states, except
Pennsylvania, had the opposition been formidable.   There,
by the force of leaders like Wilson and McKean, the opposition was overcome.   The next state to consider the question was Massachusetts, whose convention met on January
ninth, 1788, and continued in session until it ratified the
constitution, on February sixth, by a vote of one hundred
and eighty-seven to one hundred and sixty-eight.   But with
her ratification Massachusetts brought forward certain amendments which were recommended to Congress for adoption.
Maryland, on April twenty-sixth, ratified without proposing
amendments, by sixty-three to eleven.   Three steps in the
process of ratification by a state may be distinguished:
first, action in the legislature on the question of calling a
convention; second, in the choice of members to attend the
convention; and third, in the convention on the question of
ratification.   In South Carolina an attack was made at each
stage.   Again the value of competent leaders was shown,
and under the guidance of the Pinckneys and Rutledges
ratification was secured by a vote of one hundred and forty-
nine to seventy-three, on May twenty-third.   New Hampshire, as the ninth state, ratified on the twenty-first of June.

Four states yet remained to be heard from. Virginia and New York were already considering the great measure in convention when that of New Hampshire closed its labors. In Virginia were enacted the most dramatic scenes of the whole series of conventions. On each side were men famous in the nation's history. After a session of twenty-three days a majority of ten was given for ratification. The last state to ratify before the inauguration of the new government was New York. Her convention assembled on June seventeenth and saw both Virginia and New Hampshire ratify before her. After a protracted struggle that state ratified on July twenty-sixth. North Carolina came into the union on November twenty-first, leaving Rhode Island alone outside the fold.

The new constitution, which was sent out on September twenty-eighth, was not long waiting attention from Rhode Island. No sooner had the assembly at its October session taken the matter into consideration than all parties knew that a long battle was begun. Even before the assembly met, Madison, reviewing the probable attitude of the states, said, "Rhode Island is divided; the majority being violently against it. The temper of this state cannot yet be fully discerned. A strong party is in favor of it. But they will probably be outnumbered, if those whose numbers are not yet known should take the opposite side."[1] The first action of the majority revealed two facts: that, though in a majority, they did not feel strong enough summarily to reject the constitution; and that they proposed to enter upon a long course of filibustering. Instead of an act calling a convention, it was voted that about a thousand copies of the new constitution should be struck off and distributed, "that the freemen may have an opportunity of forming their sentiments of the pro-

[1] Letter to Edmund Randolph, Oct. 21, 1787, Gilpin, *Madison Papers*, ii, 649.

posed constitution."[1]   The "sentiments" so formed were to be communicated in instructions to their deputies before the February session.

The friends of the constitution, chafing at the delay, found vent for their feelings in numerous appeals to the people through the columns of the newspapers. The letters of "Cincinnatus," then appearing in the New York *Journal*, furnished them with texts and an abundance of quotations. The majority, neither at this time nor at any other period during the struggle, seemed inclined to carry on a journalistic war.

Instead of following any line suggested by the few instructions given to the deputies, the assembly resolved that, as they could not make an innovation on the constitution without the consent of the freemen, the proposed constitution must be submitted to them directly in town meetings. This resolution passed by a vote of forty three to fifteen. An amendment making the vote upon the question of calling a convention was lost by a majority almost as great.[2]   In these debates Bradford of Bristol, Marchant and Champlin of Newport, and Arnold and Bowen of Providence, were the champions of the constitution. The opposition was led by Hazard of Charlestown, Joslin of West Greenwich, and Comstock of East Greenwich.

The conscience of the assembly had grown tender since the occasions only a year before, when they had felt no hesitation in depriving the citizen of some of his most valuable rights. In view of these events, their present consideration for personal rights is almost ludicrous. With a governor at heart favorable to the constitution, and an upper house divided, there was a much greater chance of the con-

---

[1] *Acts and Resolves of the General Assembly (MS.), 1786-7,* 150.

[2] *United States Chronicle,* Mar. 6, 1788.

stitution being rejected by a popular vote than by the assembly. Of this fact the opposition were well aware.

During the month that intervened before the town meetings, it was decided by the minority to show their disapproval of this unusual proceeding by staying away from the polls. On March twenty-fourth, the day appointed for the town meetings, in Bristol, Little Compton, Tiverton, and Hopkinton alone was there any contest. In the two former towns the federal party were in a slight majority. Providence held closely to the agreement. Not a single vote was cast in its favor, and there was but one against it. Newport cast but one vote for the constitution. The total vote was two hundred and thirty-seven for, and two thousand seven hundred and eight against.[1] This result among a population of over six thousand freemen could scarcely be taken as displaying the true sentiment of the community.

Instead of votes, the towns of Providence and Newport gave instructions in favor of calling a convention.[2] Fifty of the freemen of Bristol petitioned the assembly for the same end.[3] At an adjourned meeting on March twenty-sixth, the town of Providence adopted a petition to the assembly, in which five of her most prominent citizens presented the arguments in favor of a convention.[4] In view of the fact that an assembly of the whole people was impracticable, they deemed that the representative principle was sufficiently well established to warrant its use at this time. For many reasons the means taken by the assembly for taking the sense of the people was inadequate. The commercial and country towns

[1] *Papers Relating to the Adoption of the Constitution* (*MS.*), 16–37.

[2] *Providence Town Meeting Records* (*MS.*), vii, 118.

[3] *Papers Relating to the Adoption of the Constitution* (*MS.*), 109.

[4] *Providence Town Meeting Records* (*MS.*), vii, 120. This committee was composed of David Howell, John I. Clark, Thomas Arnold, Theodore Foster, and Benjamin Bourne.

had had no opportunity to discuss the question together, and become informed of the needs of the various sections of the state, as they might in a convention. Likewise conditions in the other states must be taken into account to determine how far it was advisable to sacrifice state interest to the common welfare. Though state rights must be preserved, other factors must be taken into consideration. There were, moreover, many documents which would throw light on the situation which, though impossible to present to the freemen, would influence the action of a convention. The very fact that Congress had recommended and the other states had taken affirmative action made it the more fitting that Rhode Island should acquiesce. The possibility of following the example of Massachusetts and Virginia in proposing amendments was suggested for her. Now that the state had had voice in framing the constitution, it seemed a double hardship for the freemen to deny them the privilege of proposing amendments to the constitution to which she must finally accede. Said the petitioners, "Have not the freemen of our sister states a right to claim this service at our hands, and have not the freemen of this state a right to demand it? This state, however sovereign and independent, cannot exist without a connection with her sister states."[1]

A memorandum containing eleven amendments which was brought to light after the town meeting in Providence, probably expressed the ideas of those who spoke of the desirability of amendments. These propositions in connection with subsequent events are of interest. They were, that liberty of the press and of conscience should be secured; that no standing army should be kept in time of peace; that the militia should not be called to serve outside the state except in an emergency; that appropriations should be for one year

[1] *Providence Town Meeting Records (MS.)*, vii, 120; *United States Chronicle*, Apr. 10, 1788; *Providence Gazette*, Apr. 12, 1788.

only; that the terms of senators should not be more than two years, and no direct tax should be levied except after a requisition had been made on the states. The federal judiciary should have no jurisdiction in minor cases between citizens of different states, nor should any one be tried for an infamous crime except on a presentment of a grand jury, and all questions of fact should be decided by a jury. Finally, all powers not expressly delegated should be withheld from the general government.[1]

The position of the Federal party may, from their instructions and public writings, be comprehended with tolerable accuracy. The opposition was kept busy in counteracting the moral force exerted by the ratifications of the other states. Every argument was employed in their cause. One of the few put in print appeared in the *Gazette* of March fifteenth, characterizing the new constitution as a scheme to lord it over the common people. A convention should be avoided, because artful men, lawyers and ministers, might win over the most steadfast opponents.[2] The motion was again renewed for a convention, on the last day of March, but was defeated by a majority of twenty-seven.[3] The result of the popular vote having proved as anticipated, it was reported to Congress under date of April fifth.[4] The fact that the manner of consideration had been peculiar, it was hoped would not give offense, for it was based on the truly democratic principle that all government emanates from the will of the whole people. Granting the present form of government to be inadequate, they declared the state willing to acquiesce in any amendments "which would tend to regulate commerce, and impose duties and excise, whereby congress might establish funds for discharging the public debt."[5] So

[1] *Providence Gazette*, Mar. 29, 1788.   [2] *Ibid.*, Mar. 15, 1788.
[3] *United States Chronicle*, Apr. 10, 1788.
[4] *Ibid.*   [5] *Ibid.*

much, which had long since been pronounced insufficient, Rhode Island would grant, but nothing more.   To all intents and purposes this was a flat refusal.

The approach of the annual election saw a hot canvass of the state by both sides.   A division on local issues in the Federal party gave the election, by a large majority, to the Anti Federalists.

Early in the summer came the news that New Hampshire had ratified the constitution.   The Federalists were both delighted and encouraged.   Bells rang, cannon were fired, the schools were given a holiday, and the students of Brown University marched in procession about the college.   The town of Providence showed itself truly Federal.   Nowhere in the whole country was more enthusiasm displayed than in that community in preparing to celebrate the event.   It was decided to hold the celebration in connection with that of Independence Day.[1]   The interest in this event arises no more from its expression of federal sentiments, than from being the only occasion of the resort to armed violence by the opponents of the constitution in Rhode Island.

Extensive preparations were made for orations, a parade, and an ox-roast, to which the state officers and the people generally were invited.   On the festal morning, whose passing hours were marked by discharges of artillery, an oration was delivered by the Rev. Dr. Hitchcock in the First Baptist church.   A procession then marched to Federal Hill, where an ox had been roasted whole, and a table spread a thousand feet in length.   The festivities were, however, destined to receive a check from an unexpected quarter.   Toward the evening of the previous day an assemblage of men from the country towns, particularly of Providence county, had gathered on the outskirts of the town with the avowed purpose of preventing the celebration, which they insisted was an in-

---

[1] *United States Chronicle*, June 20, 1788.

sult to the majority of the people and to the legislature. Two companies were called out to protect the place. At the request of a committee of the town, a conference was held on the morning of the fourth, at which the townsmen, after a vigorous protest, agreed that the festivities should not be held in honor of the ratification of the constitution, but in commemoration of Independence Day. Thirteen cannon were to be fired and thirteen toasts drunk. A toast to " Nine States," was changed to " The Day." With these changes the invaders allowed the celebration to proceed.[1]

The original purpose of the mob appears to have been to seize the feast, as the countrymen were advised not to bring rations with them. Some expected that the governor or deputy governor would take command on their arrival. Many of those who, stirred by the representations of demagogues, were induced to join a movement led by judges and legislators, returned in disgust to their homes, while others made the best of the situation and joined in the festivities. The actual resort to violence was thus averted by compromise, never again to be threatened by the Anti-Federalists during the struggle.

Rejoicings were not confined to the chief towns, but celebrations, including orations and feasting, were held elsewhere, notably in East Greenwich and Wickford. At the former place, among the sentiments toasted at the banquet were " Independence," " Federalism," " The Federal Pillars," " The Supreme Judiciary," and " The Newport *Herald.*" At Wick-

---

[1] *Providence Gazette*, July 5 and 12, 1788; *United States Chronicle*, July 3 and 10, 1788.

The town's committee was composed of Jabez Bowen, John I. Clark, Welcome Arnold, David Howell, Benjamin Bourne, Zephaniah Andrews, and John Mason. That representing the country consisted of William West, a Judge of the Superior Court, Capt. Andrew Waterman and John Sayles, Assemblymen from Smithfield, Abraham Matthewson, a Judge of the Court of Common Pleas, John Westcott, deputy from Foster, and Peleg Fiske and James Aldrich, deputies from Scituate.

ford tributes were paid to "The Ten States," "The Three We Hope Will Join," "All Promoters of Union," and "Harmony between City and Country." Within the month, the news that New York had ratified set the bells ringing again. The fondness for symbolic representation found expression in Providence in the display of eleven flags flying from Weybosset bridge, representing the states which had ratified. A flag upon a staff inclined thirty degrees, with the accompanying motto, "It will rise," represented North Carolina, while a bare pole inclined forty-five degrees bore the legend, "Rhode Island in Hopes."[1]

The new constitution was now assured of a trial, but Rhode Island promised to be absent from that trial. To a large number the gravity of the situation was apparent. The day when Rhode Island had been invited to join in revising the constitution was past, and she was left to take it as she found it, or not at all. But should she not accept the constitution at all, her position without the prospect of a foreign alliance, in her disorganized financial condition, was one to inspire alarm in the minds of thinking men.[2] It was plainly pointed out that the aid from England, on which some relied, would only be lent with a view to the destruction of the state and the ruin of the American commonwealths.[3]

The October session of the legislature witnessed a third fruitless effort to call a convention.[4] The ratification of New York had only been secured by a compromise which provided that a circular letter be sent to the states calling for a convention to consider the amendments offered by the states. Such a proposal might be expected to receive the hearty support of Anti-Federalists everywhere. In submitting the

[1] *Providence Gazette*, Aug. 2, 1788; *United States Chronicle*, July 31, 1788.
[2] *Providence Gazette*, Aug. 2, 1788.
[3] *Ibid.*, Oct. 18, 1788.
[4] Staples, *Rhode Island in the Continental Congress*, 618.

New York letter to the towns for consideration, the same assembly that had refused to call a convention admitted that "the citizens of Rhode Island conceive it to be absolutely necessary to be connected with the other states, if it can be done on the principles of good government."[1]

At their meeting in December the assembly found that but eight towns favored the New York proposition for a convention, and others declined to do aught but adhere strictly to the Articles of Confederation.[2] Providence remained firm in her demand for a convention,[3] but was doomed to see the measure defeated for a fourth time.[4] The fifth defeat was in March, on the eve of the inauguration of the new federal government, by a vote of thirty-seven to nineteen.[5]

A new phase of the Rhode Island question now appeared. That state, in spite of all unpleasant relations, had hitherto been united to the other states by the bonds of the Confederation, a phantom to which Rhode Island clung even until the election of delegates to Congress after the new government had been inaugurated. Now the federal government was in operation, and Rhode Island stood "perfectly alone, unconnected with any state or sovereignty on earth."[6] The mercantile and other classes whose mode of life brought them in contact with people of other states, were not slow to realize the importance of the change. They saw their commerce deprived of the protection of the United States, and shorn of the benefits of her commercial treaties, languishing under the heavy duties laid on it alike by the United States and Europe. The busy ports which had lately been crowded

---

[1] *Acts and Resolves of the General Assembly* (*MS.*), *1788-9*, 57.

[2] *United States Chronicle*, Dec. 8, 1788.

[3] *Providence Town Meeting Records*, vii,139.

[4] Staples, *Rhode Island in the Continental Congress*, 618.

[5] *United States Chronicle*, Mar. 19, 1789.

[6] *Providence Town Meeting Records* (*MS.*), vii, 141.

with shipping, would henceforth give shelter to only a few fishermen. Should the legislature persist in its course, the freemen declared themselves fully persuaded that some of their number would apply to Congress that its protection be extended to their trade and navigation under such discriminations as it might impose.[1] With credit between man and man destroyed, and the most solemn obligations openly violated, nothing was to be anticipated but retaliatory legislation, which would cut off Rhode Island's commerce by land and sea.[2]

The masses of the people, particularly in the agricultural communities, were naturally slow in grasping the full significance of the events taking place at the seat of the federal government. The result of the annual election gave little indication of a change of views. No sooner had the national House of Representatives organized than the apprehensions of Rhode Island were realized by the introduction of a motion leading to the formulation of a revenue system.[3] The debate was long, as the importance of the subject demanded. In view of this measure Providence, besides instructing her own deputies, presented to the legislature a petition signed by fully five hundred citizens, portraying the evils from which they were suffering, and those which were anticipated.[4] The only response was a sixth defeat of the proposition for a convention, but by a somewhat smaller majority.[5]

The fears of the assembly were, however, sufficiently aroused to lead them to cast an anchor to windward in the form of an embargo upon the exportation of grain, flour and

[1] *Providence Town Meeting Records* (*MS.*), vii, 140 1.

[2] *Ibid.*, vii, 146.

[3] *Annals of Congress*, i, 106.

[4] *United States Chronicle*, June 25, 1789.

[5] *Ibid.*, June 18, 1789.

meal for a limited time, until the result of the deliberations of Congress should become known.[1] Such fears were not assuaged by the pens of those who, like a correspondent of the *Providence Gazette*, declared that Rhode Island would "remain to the other states and to the world at large, a spectacle of reproach and derision."[2] Said that writer: "In the ports of the Union we shall be considered as foreigners, and our commerce subjected to like duties with them."[3]

The passage of an impost law and the perfection of a system of revenue collection brought with it a visible weakening of the majority in Rhode Island. Hoping to avert discriminating legislation, the assembly had, at its May session, passed an impost law imposing on goods imported into the state the same duties that Congress might thereafter lay upon imports into the Union. The act was to take effect at the same time as that passed by Congress, and was in general to be the exact counterpart of that act.[4] This was followed in September by a re-enactment of the revenue law lately passed by Congress.[5]

The debate in Congress which resulted in the revenue act of July fourth, and the act for the collection of the same of July thirty-first, continued, from the eighth of April, seven weeks. The position of North Carolina and Rhode Island in relation to a duty on foreign importations was a disputed question. To obviate further difficulties, Benson of New York, on June fifth, presented a resolution that Congress "declare it to be their most earnest desire" that Rhode Island call a convention.[6] On the advisability of this step

[1] *Acts and Resolves of the General Assembly (MS.), 1788-9*, 98.

[2] *Providence Gazette*, Aug. 1, 1789.   [3] *Ibid.*

[4] *Rhode Island Colonial Records*, x, 331.

[5] *Annals of Congress*, ii, 2183; *Rhode Island Colonial Records*, x, 340; *United States Chronicle*, Sept. 24, 1789.

[6] *Annals of Congress*, i, 437.

opinion differed. All were agreed that Rhode Island ought
to call a convention, but the propriety of the request was
questioned. The debate was earnest on both sides. It was
argued that from Rhode Island's absence from the federal
convention, she stood in a different position from North
Carolina. The revenue act as passed by Congress revealed
a confidence that both states would soon be within the
Union, and placed both alike in a sort of intermediate position. As Congress had no authority to lay duties at the
ports of those states, it was enacted that all goods imported
thence, not the product thereof, should be subjected to the
same conditions as if imported from other foreign ports.
But by the silence of the act in respect to domestic products, they were admitted free.[1]

Sensible of the fearful disadvantage at which they were
placed, and perceiving in the result of the election of deputies to the October session of the assembly signs of a coming
change, the town of Providence memorialized Congress on
their condition. Their perception of the necessity of union
with the other states led them to ask that they and the other
seaport towns might not be made to suffer for conduct for
which they were not responsible.[2]

The assembly, too, reading the signs of the times, sent its
first flag of truce as a step toward a commercial union. The
hope was expressed that, though Rhode Island had not seen
her way clear consistently with her principles to unite with
the other states, their common sufferings in the past would
always form a bond of union between them and the other
states. Though the new government might avoid present
difficulties, it might lead to future mischiefs. The people of
Rhode Island were attached to democratic government, but
in this new constitution there was perceived an approach

[1] *Annals of Congress*, ii, 2213.
[2] *Providence Town Meeting Records (MS.)*, vii, 156.

toward the evils from which they had lately been freed. Further, they said, "We are sensible of the extremes to which democratical government is sometimes liable, something of which we have lately experienced, but we esteem them temporary and partial evils, compared with the loss of liberty and the rights of a free people."[1]

The assembly asserted that they were awaiting the day when they might again be united with the other states under a constitution which might not be liable to alteration by nine of the thirteen states. It was hoped that in the meantime they would not be treated as foreigners, but that trade might be kept free and open between them.[2]

This letter betrays a change of attitude tending towards conciliation. No longer is a continued separation spoken of as desirable. Their argument is now based on the one strong ground of fear of the subversion of the liberties of so small a state. Congress, only too glad to observe signs of a change which might extricate them from an awkward position, viewed the communication with favor. Before the letter from the assembly reached New York an act was passed suspending the impost law in favor of Rhode Island. By this law all privileges and advantages enjoyed by ships of the United States were extended to those of Rhode Island and North Carolina, until the fifteenth of January, 1790. Exception was made in the case of rum, loaf sugar, and chocolate made in those states.[3] At the same time the assembly continued to assert that it was vested by the freemen with power simply to administer the existing constitution, while the power to change the frame of government rested in the freemen alone. Owing to "grievous complaints" that the constitution had not been adopted, the freemen were called upon to instruct their deputies, who

[1] *United States Chronicle*, Oct. 1, 1789; *Rhode Island Colonial Records*, x, 356.
[2] *Ibid.*   [3] *Annals of Congress*, ii, 2235.

were to meet at the session on the last Monday in October.[1]
According to the call, town meetings were held on the nineteenth of that month. The town of Providence, disgusted at
the farcial proceedings of the assembly, left its delegates free
to act as they saw fit.[2] Whatever instructions were given by
the other towns were of no effect, and a seventh attempt to
call a convention failed like its predecessors.[3]

Just here, as at so many points in the struggle, it was the
lack of competent leaders among the Federalists which left
Rhode Island outside the pale within which the efforts of
most skillful leaders had barely succeeded in bringing some
of the other states. Several worthy and prominent men
among the Federalists were powers in their own towns, but
not one of them was able to extend his influence further.
General Varnum, the one man in whom were contained the
elements of a leader, had been called to hold a post under
the Union in the Northwest Territory, and was no longer
available.

Before the eleventh of January, to which the assembly
stood adjourned, the situation had materially changed.
North Carolina ratified the constitution on the twenty-first
of November, leaving Rhode Island alone outside the Union.[4]
Congress had been busy preparing the amendments to the
constitution, so generally demanded by the states. The results of their deliberations, and the resolutions of Congress
thereon, were transmitted, on October second, to the governors of the various states for ratification.[5] Copies of these
amendments were submitted to the freemen in town meet-

---

[1] *Acts and Resolves of the General Assembly* (*MS.*), 1788-9, 108.

[2] *Providence Town Meeting Records* (*MS.*), vii, 160.

[3] *Providence Gazette*, Oct. 31, 1789; *United States Chronicle*, Nov. 5, 1789.

[4] *Laws of North Carolina*, i, 605.

[5] *Rhode Island Archives* (*MS.*), *Letters* 1788-1800, 1½.

ings, on the third Monday in October.[1] The necessary time had now elapsed for them to become thoroughly understood. Of the amendments proposed, that securing freedom from an established church, and freedom of worship, as well as of speech and of the press, especially commended itself to the people of Rhode Island. Though not often finding expression during this period, there was a fear that through southern influence Episcopacy might be forced upon the Union. The confirmation of the right of a judicial trial in the state, by a jury of the vicinage, likewise removed a fancied danger. The provision for the reservation to the states and to the people of all powers not expressly delegated to the United States could not but gratify the advocates of state rights.

A knowledge that the suspension of the revenue laws of the United States in favor of Rhode Island was about to expire, leaving her on the footing of a foreign state, tended to stimulate the understanding of the people. Should the assembly still refuse a convention, small favor could be expected from Congress.

The assembly convened as appointed, and after four days spent in transacting routine business, the house took up a motion made by Benjamin Bourne of Providence, for calling a convention. This was debated until late in the day, when it was carried by a vote of thirty-four to twenty-nine.[2] On the transmission of the bill to the senate, it was laid on the table until the next (Saturday) morning. In the meantime the senate had passed a bill placing the question of calling a convention before the freemen.[3] This was defeated by a majority of fourteen in the house. The senate, after considering all day the house bill, reached a vote of non-

[1] *Acts and Resolves of the General Assembly (MS.), 1788–90,* 121.

[2] *United States Chronicle,* Jan. 21, 1790.

[3] *Acts and Resolves of the General Assembly (MS.), 1788–90,* 150; *United States Chronicle,* Jan. 21, 1790.

concurrence late on Saturday evening. Four senators
voted to concur, while the same number with the deputy-
governor were in opposition. The excitement was intense.
Unwilling to wait until Monday, the assembly adjourned to
meet on Sunday morning. Early in the day Marchant, of
Newport, introduced in the house a bill similar to that introduced in the house by Bourne, and secured for his measure
a majority of twenty-one. The morning's deliberations in
the senate had been upon a bill introduced by Deputy-
Governor Owen, in substance like the one already passed by
that body, with the addition of a preamble. No better expression is to be found of the arguments of those zealous
opponents of the constitution who were now forced to a
convention, provided it be demanded by the freemen. They
acknowledged that, as the constitution was already in operation in twelve states, the citizens of Rhode Island, being
treated as foreigners, would "suffer great and manifold in-
conveniences and discouragement in their trade and commerce, and otherwise."[1]   Hence it became the interest and
duty of that state "to take the most prudent measures for
acceding to the union of the said twelve states."[2]   Feeling
that to their constituencies some explanation of their change
of attitude was necessary, the preamble concludes: "This
general assembly are sensible that the accession of the state
of North Carolina to the said union, and the grievous operation of the federal government on the interest of many citizens of this state since the last measure taken by this
general assembly on the subject, have presented the same
to our view and consideration in a very different attitude
from that in which it then appeared."[3]   Thus did they attempt to harmonize theory with present conditions. The

[1] *Acts and Resolves of the General Assembly* (*MS.*), *1788–90*, 151.

[2] *Ibid.*   [3] *Ibid.*

measure was doomed to a fate in the house similar to that of its predecessor.

The Marchant bill, coming to the senate, found the personnel of that body somewhat changed. One of the senators who had voted in the negative on the Bourne bill, so runs the story, was a preacher and, objecting to the Sunday session, withdrew to minister to his congregation. When it came to a vote, four senators voted in the affirmative, while three senators and the deputy-governor voted against it. It now devolved upon the governor to give the casting vote. Though elected and re-elected by the anti-federal party, Governor Coll'ns had been a conservative in the party, and had more than once betrayed federalistic sympathies. Now, realizing the gravity of the situation, he cast his vote in the affirmative, and the first campaign was won. The freemen were summoned to meet in their town meetings on the ninth of February to elect delegates to a state convention to be held on the first day of March, at South Kingstown.[1] During the debate on Sunday the churches had been almost deserted by the people, who hovered about the state house. When the vote was announced a shout of joy arose, and that Sunday became one of general rejoicing. The people felt that the dawn of happier times was at hand.[2]

No time was lost by the assembly in announcing their action to the president, with a request for a further suspension of the revenue laws, as there was reason to hope that the constitution would soon be ratified.[3] By act of February

---

[1] *Acts and Resolves of the General Assembly (MS.), 1788–90*, 157; *Providence Gazette*, Jan. 23, 1790.

[2] *Providence Gazette*, Jan. 23, 1790.

[3] *Acts and Resolves of the General Assembly (MS.), 1788–90*, 159; *United States Chronicle*, Jan. 21, 1790.

eighth, the act suspending the revenue law was revived, to remain in force until the first of the following April.[1]

In the process of adopting the constitution by the different states, three stages have been noted. In no other state had the struggle assumed alarming proportions in the first stage. Even in Virginia, South Carolina, Pennsylvania and New York, where some opposition was encountered at this stage, the struggle was soon past. The smallest of the thirteen had, however, for more than two years refused to call a convention.

No sooner was the call issued than the combatants prepared for the second contest. This was limited by the action of the assembly to twenty-two days. The Federalists again made use of their favorite means of creating a sentiment in their favor. In the public press they portrayed the effects of a rejection of the constitution. As a result of the total estrangement of the state from the Union, which must follow rejection, the *Gazette* pictured Narragansett Bay forsaken by traders, the wharves and warehouses silent and deserted, and the people suffering for the lack of those necessities which could only be obtained through free trade with the United States. The possibility of coercion even was hinted at.[2]

In the first stage of the struggle the opposition had relied but little upon the press, trusting rather to personal work or to conventions. Accordingly a spirited agitation in the barrooms of country taverns was supplemented by a convention of freemen of Providence, Kent, and Washington counties, held at East Greenwich, on February second. The discussion of plans for concerted action resulted in an address to the freemen of the state. They were recommended to choose such delegates to the convention "as from a known and tried firmness, and integrity and attachment to the liberty and

[1] *Annals of Congress*, ii, 2259.
[2] *Providence Gazette*, Feb. 27, 1790.

indefeasible rights of this people . . . will be cautious and careful of bartering them to the politics of any people or nation on earth." [1]

The language of this address has been taken as corroborating the charge that the vote of the assembly was secured by corruption. It has been believed, though there seems to be no evidence to prove the charge, that the Federalists, becoming alarmed at the prospect before them, saw a profitable investment in the purchase of votes for a convention. An explanation equally probable, and one more creditable to the parties involved, is furnished by one of those whose opinions had undergone a change. Though the causes that had heretofore warranted rejection were still powerful, yet that the state should exist alone was impossible. In this dilemma the citizens were admonished to choose delegates to the convention who would propose amendments to the constitution. [2]

Without the state no strong assurance was felt that Rhode Island would ratify at once, though friends of the Union were rejoiced that one step had been taken. [3] The result of the election of delegates was a strong majority against ratification.   Richmond and Portsmouth alone deemed it necessary to instruct their delegates. The former, an inland town, little affected by commercial depression, directed that the constitution be not adopted, but that it be considered, amendments proposed, and an adjournment taken until a future day, that there might be time to observe the workings of the new government. [4] Portsmouth, more susceptible to commercial disorders, whose symptoms were a languishing trade and

[1] *Papers Relating to the Adoption of the Constitution* (*MS.*), 97.

[2] *United Sta'es Chronicle*, Feb. 4, 1790.

[3] Letter, Caleb Strong to Theodore Foster, Feb. 28, 1790. *Foster Correspondence* (*MS.*).

[4] *Papers Relating to the Adoption of the Constitution*, 99.

laid-up vessels, demanded adoption at the earliest possible moment. Should adjournment be proposed, no date later than April first should be considered.'

The convention met on the first day of March, 1790, in the old state house in South Kingstown. Of the seventy delegates there assembled, forty-two were members of the assembly; four had held the office of deptuy-governor, and five had been elected to the Continental Congress. Jabez Bowen of Providence, and Henry Marchant of Newport, led the Federalists. As leader of the opposing party, His Honor, the deputy-governor, was ably assisted by Jonathan J. Hazard, of South Kingstown, whose change of attitude on the final vote was to sound his political knell. There were also present William Bradford of Bristol, speaker of the House of Deputies, and a member of the Hartford Convention of 1780; Col. William Barton, the captor of General Prescott; Joseph Staunton, one of Rhode Island's first senators in Congress, and Benjamin Bourne, the state's first representative in Congress. As chairman, the convention chose Deputy-Governor Owen. Daniel Updike was made secretary.²

After two days occupied with preliminaries and general discussions, the opposition entered on a policy of procrastination. Col. Sayles, of Smithfield, moved that a committee be appointed to draft a bill of rights and amendments, and that the convention adjourn to a future day.³ This motion was tabled, and a general discussion of the constitution, section by section, followed. The manner of raising direct

---

¹ *Papers Relating to the Adoption of the Constitution*, 95.

² *Minutes of the Convention*. The minutes of the Convention were for many years lost, but were found among the effects of Daniel Updike and deposited in the state archives. The minute book is in a volume lettered "*Papers Relating to the Adoption of the Constitution of the United States.*" The book is unpaged.

³ *Minutes of the Convention; Providence Gazette*, Mar. 6, 1790.

taxes first met with objection as bearing unequally on the towns. The Anti-Federalists, when they demurred at the part taken by the executive in legislation, were shown the precedent afforded by Massachusetts. This was effective, and no further question was raised until the ninth section of the first article was reached. Here the clause relating to the importation of slaves stirred the anti-slavery sentiment of a party led by Bradford of Bristol, and Comstock of East Greenwich. In favor of the section as it stood were Bourne, Hazard, and Champlin, who supported it as the best compromise to be obtained. Hazard disliked to antagonize the southern states, for said he: " We shall have need of assistance, to have our amendments acceded to."[1] Prolonged discussion led to the reference of the question to a committee.

No serious objection was again encountered until the fifth article was reached. The assurance herein contained of the continuance of equal representation in the senate was hailed with joy. Whatever else she had been, Rhode Island had been a steadfast advocate of state rights. Those holding the balance of power had consented to a convention only at the prospect of proposing amendments. But, by the provisions of the constitution, three-fourths of the states might impose upon the remainder any amendment they wished. The only reply of the Federalists was that in amendment Rhode Island would have an equal voice with the other states. The views of the convention having been brought out by general discussion, a committee of two from each county was appointed to draft amendments.[2]

On Friday, March fifth, the committee reported a bill of rights containing eighteen sections, and with it an equal number of amendments. After debate, two of the latter

[1] *Minutes of the Convention.*

[2] *Ibid.; Providence Gazette,* Mar. 6, 1790.

were rejected.[1]   The first provided that Congress should not have power to appoint such officers as had been heretofore appointed by the state.   The second, a proposition to apportion direct taxes according to valuation, was declared as unsatisfactory as the existing arrangement.   The debate continued until the afternoon of the next day, when Marchant moved that the constitution be adopted, and that the bill of rights and amendments be transmitted to Congress with the recommendation that they be adopted.   The Anti-Federalists foresaw that, should this be carried, their amendments would be tabled indefinitely.   To defeat the motion it was moved to adjourn, and carried by a majority of thirteen.   The Federalists made an effort to limit the time of adjournment to the last Monday in March, but were overruled by a majority who selected May twenty-fourth as the day and Newport as the place of meeting.[2]   Before adjournment it was voted to submit the bill of rights and the amendments to the freemen at the election on April twenty-first.

The adjournment was the work of the Anti Federal party. Though possessing a majority against adoption without amendments, they dared not risk a trial of strength when some might rely on future amendments.   The date fixed upon for the adjourned session not only put off the evil day of ratification, but made possible a surer victory for the enemies of the constitution, after the victory which they hoped to gain at the annual election.

No sooner had the delegates returned to their homes than the excitement of an election waxed strong.   At a meeting of the Federalists at Providence, a committee was appointed to unite with friends in Newport to secure a coalition in each

---

[1] *Providence Gazette*, Mar. 13, 1790.

[2] *Minutes of the Convention; Providence Gazette*, Mar. 13, 1790.

---

town.[1] A letter was sent to Arthur Fenner, a leader of the opposite party, but who was thought to be less influenced by partisan prejudice than many of his party, asking him to accept the nomination for governor on a coalition ticket.[2] The Federalists proposed to nominate the deputy-governor from their own party, while the assistants were to be divided between the two parties.[3] Fenner in reply hesitated to commit himself, and questioned the propriety of consulting him in the matter before the freemen of the state had signified a desire in the matter.[4]

The conventions of both parties met on the same day, the sixth of April. The majority or Anti-Federal convention, dominated by deputy-governor Owen, which met at South Kingstown, nominated a "straight" ticket. Arthur Fenner was the candidate for governor, Samuel J. Potter for deputy-governor, and six of the present assistants were candidates for re-election.[5] Daniel Owen was the first choice as candidate for governor, and it was only after his refusal of the nomination that Fenner was selected. The Federalists, in their convention at East Greenwich, to which all friends of coalition were invited, called down on their heads the invectives of their opponents by nominating a "mixed" ticket, under the caption, "Coalition or Federal Prox." At the head of the ticket appeared the names of Fenner and Potter. Four of the candidates of the Anti-Federalists found a place on this ticket. The promoters of this coalition, like every body of citizens who attempt to break down party lines in

[1] *Providence Gazette*, Apr. 3, 1790; *United States Chronicle*, Apr. 1, 1790.

[2] *Providence Gazette*, Mar. 27, 1790. The committee consisted of Geo. Champlin, Henry Marchant, Geo. Gibbs, James Robinson, Isaac Senter, John Brown, Welcome Arnold, David Howell, Zephaniah Andrews, and Jabez Bowen.

[3] *Ibid.*   [4] *Ibid.*

[5] *Providence Gazette*, Apr. 10, 1790; *United States Chronicle*, Apr. 8, 1790.

[6] *Providence Gazette*, Apr. 10, 1790.

the interests of good government, were doomed to call forth
anathemas from those bound by the shackles of party.   The
leaders were accused of attempting by a trick to gain control
of the state in the interests of the mercantile party.[1] The
Federalists maintained that though the country was in the
majority, yet the welfare of that portion of the community
was so dependent on the prosperity of the towns that their
true interests could not be antagonistic.[2] Party lines were
sharply drawn, and rumors of corruption on either side were
afloat.

With the twenty-first of April came the election and a
complete victory for the Anti-Federalists.   Jubilation lighted
the country, but the towns were dark in mourning. Though
this election did not alter the composition of the convention,
it showed all too plainly the temper of the masses.

Though separated from her sisters, Rhode Island could
not be totally oblivious of what was passing within the
Union.   However right the majority in that state might have
been in their position, it was more than could be expected
of human nature that the Union should not enter a vigorous
protest against separation.   The faint mutterings of the approaching storm had long been audible to the attentive ear.
Owing to her attitude toward the imposts of 1781 and 1783, as
well as by her paper money policy, the other states were disin-
clined to await with patience Rhode Island's accession to the
Union.   Coercion was early hinted at from various quarters.
Against the paper money legislation Connecticut had retali-
ated by excluding citizens of Rhode Island from her courts.[3]
In the midst of the paper money disorders, coercion and
political annihilation were suggested.   "A Landholder," in
the *Chronicle,* said : "The singular system of policy adopted

[1] *United States Chronicle,* Apr. 15, 1790.

[2] *Providence Gazette,* Apr. 17, 1790.

[3] *Ibid.,* Feb. 28, 1789.

by your state no longer excites either the surprise or indig-
nation of mankind. There are certain extremes of iniquity
which are beheld with patience from a fixed conviction that
the transgressor is inveterate. . . . If you will not hear your
own groans, nor feel the pangs of your own torture, it must
continue until removed by a political annihilation."[1]

When, in the debate on the bill for the collection of the
revenue, Benson of New York moved to go into the committee of the whole to consider a resolution declaring the
wish of Congress that Rhode Island ratify the constitution,
the whole question of the relation of that state to the Union
was opened.[2] The opposition to the resolution was led by
Page of Virginia, who took the ground that in no way could
the worth of the constitution be shown more effectively than by
leaving Rhode Island to act freely. Were he a Rhode Island
man, he would watch with a jealous eye the action of Congress, and apprehend undue influence, were the weight of
that body thrown in the scale. "Are gentlemen afraid," said
he, "to leave them to their own unbiased judgment? For
my part, I am not."[3] Madison, realizing the delicacy of the
situation, said, "It would be improper in this body to expose themselves to have such a proposition rejected by the
legislature of the state of Rhode Island. It would likewise
be improper to express a desire on an occasion where a free
agency ought to be employed, which would carry with it the
force of a command."[4]

The nearer neighbors of Rhode Island were not disposed
to such delicacy of treatment. Sherman of Connecticut
saw no impropriety in asking for ratification. To the objection that such a request might bear the semblance of a
command, he replied, "If a wish of Congress can bring

---

[1] *United States Chronicle*, Mar. 27, 1788.

[2] *Annals of Congress*, i, 437.

[3] *Ibid.*, 438.   [4] *Ibid.*, i, 439.

them into the Union, why should we decline to express such a wish?"[1]

The idea of coercion had at this time gained little headway in Congress. When Page asked, "Suppose they decline doing what you require, what is next to be done?"[2] the strongest response was from Fisher Ames, when he said, "I should be glad to know if any gentleman contemplates the state of Rhode Island dissevered from the Union, a maritime state, situated in the most convenient manner for smuggling and defrauding our revenue. Surely a moment's reflection will induce the house to take measures to secure this object."[3] Even this language contemplated nothing more than a request which might operate as a demand. But it revealed the fact that a large party at the north, which was prepared to demand ratification, needed but a grain of self-interest involved to lead them to coercive measures. Benson's resolution failed of passage, and the matter was dropped.

The whole Union watched anxiously the course of Rhode Island as she again and again refused to call a convention. As the weeks slipped by, a feeling that coercion might yet be the only alternative, was growing. A member of Congress, writing to a citizen of Rhode Island on the fifteenth of September, expressed the hope of soon welcoming in Congress a delegation from that state. Should they not appear, extreme measures must follow. "Enemies they must be, or fellow-citizens, and that in a very short time."[4] Caleb Strong remarked to Theodore Foster, after the call for the convention had issued, that though there was but small hope of ratification, yet it was a relief that the convention was called. His conviction was that should ratification fail, Congress would be justified in proceeding to extreme

[1] *Annals of Congress*, i, 440.   [2] *Ibid.*, i, 438,   [3] *Ibid.*, i, 440.
[4] *United States Chronicle*, Oct. 1, 1789.

measures.[1] In affirming the right of Congress to call on
Rhode Island for her share of the revolutionary debt, the
Gazette asks, "Will Congress suffer a single refractory
state to embarrass its great necessary national measures?"[2]

During the last weeks of the first session of the first Congress and the early part of the second session, a new impulse
was given to the Rhode Island question in that body by the
introduction of two measures on which the country was
sharply divided. These were the question as to the permanent residence of Congress, and that portion of Hamilton's
proposed funding system which provided for the assumption
of state debts by the general government.

It is scarcely possible to conceive the importance ascribed
at that time to the location of the national capital. The
middle states were each straining every nerve to secure that
location within their own boundaries. From New Jersey,[3] Virginia,[4] Maryland,[5] Pennsylvania,[6] and Delaware[7] came overtures to Congress looking to the location of the national
legislature within their limits. Pennsylvania opened the
subject by moving that the seat of government be fixed at
some convenient place, as near the center of wealth, population, and territory as was consistent with access by water from
the ocean and easy communication with the western territory.[8] The northern states promptly followed with a resolution to place the national capital on the east bank of the
Susquehanna, in Pennsylvania, and until such place should
be in readiness Congress should remain in New York. This
was a part of the agreement under which Pennsylvania had
joined the north in laying protective duties. She was to
have the support of that section for her attempt to secure

---

[1] *Foster Correspondence*, i, 23.

[2] *Providence Gazette*, Feb. 27, 1790.

[3] *Annals of Congress*, i, 67.   [4] *Ibid.*, i, 358.   [5] *Ibid.*, i, 371.

[6] *Ibid.*, i, 802.   [7] *Ibid.*, i, 915.   [8] *Ibid.*, i, 816.

the capital. Repeated attempts by the south, in the House, failed to shake the combination of Pennsylvania and the north.[1] The motion, fixing upon the Susquehanna and New York as the permanent and temporary seats, having prevailed, a bill was introduced to that end,[2] and passed, after a vigorous debate, by a vote of thirty-one to seventeen.[3]

The Senate at once took up the bill, and, after a vain attempt to substitute the Potomac for the Susquehanna, passed the measure with an amendment setting aside a district ten miles square, on the Delaware.[4] By an amendment in the House the bill was postponed until the next session.[5]

During the following months the location of the seat of government was a living issue, though it was not a subject of debate for some time. Pennsylvania was the keystone coveted for completing two political arches. On her both parties staked their hopes. Though that state had secured such a favorable arrangement with the north, Madison, believing that the north was scheming to retain the seat of government in that section, wrote, on November twentieth, that Morris was inclined to keep alive the possibility of an arrangement with the south.[6] By this arrangement, the permanent residence would be fixed on the Potomac, and the temporary seat at Philadelphia. Should the north insist on further delay, Morris stood ready to cancel his agreement with that party.

At the re-assembling of Congress, in January, 1790, the states north of Pennsylvania had, in the House, twenty six votes, while those to the southward would have, on the arrival of the North Carolina delegation, thirty. Should

---

[1] *Annals of Congress*, i, 915–17; Gilpin, *Writings of Madison*, i, 492; *Writings of Fisher Ames*, i, 69.

[2] *Annals of Congress*, i, 927.

[3] *Ibid.*, i, 946.   [4] *Ibid.*, i, 88–91.   [5] *Ibid.*, i, 961.

[6] Gilpin, *Writings of Madison*, i, 494.

Pennsylvania remain with the north, that party would control thirty-three votes. In the Senate, with North Carolina present, and aided by Maclay, who was uncompromisingly allied with the south, thirteen votes could be brought to oppose eleven from the north. Could this state of affairs be preserved, and the question postponed until Rhode Island should come upon the scene, the vote would be tied in the Senate, and the vice-president would cast his vote in favor of the north. All seemed to depend on the speedy ratification of Rhode Island.

In the meantime the presentation of Hamilton's scheme for the organization of the finances added an element of complication. It was proposed that the United States should assume, and during the year 1791 provide for all such state debts or parts thereof, as should be subscribed to a loan to the United States. The interest was to be assumed by the United States on January first, 1792, and the amount assumed was to be charged to each state.[1] The war debts of the states were very unequal. Massachusetts, Connecticut and South Carolina were the most deeply involved, while New Jersey and New York were burdened to a much less degree. New Hampshire and Georgia were particularly free from debt. Virginia had had a large debt, but had funded securities at a low rate and relieved herself by the sale of western land. Division on lines of self interest at once became marked.

The plan of the administration found its chief supporters in Lawrence, Smith of South Carolina, Fitzsimmons, Sherman, Ames, Gerry, Goodhue and Sedgwick. Their argument was that these debts had been incurred in the common cause, and were the debt of the whole people. Before the failure of the continental currency this view had been gen-

[1] *Annals of Congress,* i, 1092; ii, 2041-74; *Writings of Hamilton,* ii, 107

erally accepted.¹ Of the opposition the leaders were Livermore, Stone, Page, White and Jackson. Madison would have preferred making provision for a final settlement and payment of balances between the states.² The chief objections expressed were, that no state had demanded assumption, and that separate undertakings had been engaged in by the states without common consent.³ That this plan would tend to bind the states more closely together, was charged as a fault on one side, and commended as a virtue on the other. The question came to a vote in committee of the whole on March ninth, when it passed by a majority of five.⁴ Though great haste was made to complete the work before North Carolina appeared, a vote for recommitment was carried by the early arrival of the delegation from that state.⁵

While the measure was still in committee, a plan was set on foot among the Pennsylvania men for bartering that state's vote for assumption and for receiving in return support for Philadelphia as the permanent capital.⁶ When the committee again reached a vote, on April twelfth, the assumption clause was lost by a majority of two.⁷ The consternation into which the assumptionists were thrown, showed the intensity of their feeling on the subject. Gerry declared that the Massachusetts delegation would do nothing until instructions were received from home.⁸ It was their avowed inten-

¹ *Annals of Congress*, ii, 1418.
² Gilpin, *Writings of Madison*, i, 508, 511.
³ *Annals of Congress*, ii, 1355, 1428.
⁴ Maclay's *Journal*, 209; Gilpin, *Writings of Madison*, i, 512.
⁵ *Annals of Congress*, ii, 1528–31; Gilpin, *Writings of Madison*, i, 514; Maclay's *Journal*, 226.
⁶ Maclay's *Journal*, 230.
⁷ *Annals of Congress*, ii, 1577.
⁸ Maclay's *Journal*, 237.

tion to oppose the whole financial plan unless assumption formed a part of it.   Rumors of disunion were whispered about.[1]

The question of residence was not forgotten.   The subject was sedulously avoided by the north, hoping that good news might come from Rhode Island.   Pennsylvania, becoming impatient at the apparent inertia of the north, was on the point of declaring her alliance with that party broken.[2]   The south, suspecting Pennsylvania's sincerity, did not take advantage of that state's indecision.

While politics at the national capital were in this attitude of suspense, Rhode Island not only adjourned her convention, but at the state election gave a substantial majority to the Anti-Federal party.   Greater zeal was infused into the assumptionists by their defeat.   But now they were obliged to proceed by a more circuitous route.   With Pennsylvania coquetting with the south, the north turned its attention to Rhode Island.   After their former experiences with that state, and when their most dearly cherished schemes were in the balance, little delicacy of treatment could be expected by the subject of their displeasure.   In the senate, on April twenty-eighth, a committee was appointed " to consider what provisions will be proper for Congress in the present session respecting the state of Rhode Island."[3]   The recommendation of this committee led to the introduction of a resolution, on May eleventh, "that all commercial intercourse between the United States and the state of Rhode Island, from and after the first day of July next, be prohibited under suitable penalties; and that the president of the United States be authorized to demand of the state of Rhode Island . . . dollars, to be paid into the treasury of the

---

[1] Gilpin, *Writings of Madison*, i, 517.

[2] Maclay's *Journal*, 192.

[3] *Annals of Congress*, i, 1003; Maclay's *Journal*, 250.

United States by the . . . day of . . . next; which shall
be credited to the said state in account with the United
States; and that a bill or bills be brought in for those purposes."[1]   By such a measure, all commercial relations between Rhode Island and her neighbors would be cut off at a
blow.   Left thus alone, a substantial payment on the Revolutionary debt was demanded.   It needed but a demand for
the whole, and the necessary failure of the state to pay it, to
offer a sufficient pretext for a resort to arms.

In accordance with the resolution a bill was reported and
read on May twelfth, carried to a second reading on the following day, and on the third recommitted.[2]   The committee
having in charge the matter were Carroll of Maryland, Ellsworth of Connecticut, Morris of Pennsylvania, and Izard and
Butler of South Carolina.   From its earliest inception, the
measure was ardently supported by Ellsworth and King,
much to the disgust of the southern members, Maclay
and Col. Gunn.[3]   While the matter was still in the hands of
the committee, Maclay vehemently opposed any action so
long as the constitution was under consideration in Rhode
Island.   It seemed improper at such a time to pass an act
bearing on its face a punishment for rejection, and all this
for fear of a decrease in the revenues.   Guilt should be
established before extreme measures were adopted.   The
whole affair seemed to him premature, and the demand for
Rhode Island's share of the public debt bore too evidently
the stamp of an attack.[4]   On the second reading of the bill
its advocates did not hesitate to admit the independence of
Rhode Island, or that she had a right either to adopt or
to reject the constitution.   Neither did they deny that these
measures were taken to force ratification.   Their arguments
were founded on the strength of the Union and the weakness

[1] *Annals of Congress*, i, 1009.   [2] *Ibid.*, i, 1011–12.

[3] *Maclay's Journal*, 251.   [4] *Ibid.*, 259.

of one state.   Morris was with the north, while Maclay continued to oppose the bill.   The latter declared that it could
not be justified "on the principles of freedom, law, the constitution, or any mode whatever."[1]   He openly declared
that the object of the "Yorkers" was to get two senators to
vote with them on the question of the location of the capital.
Izard, who was active in the matter, admitted the severity of
the measure when he said, "If gentlemen will show us how
we can accomplish our end by any means less arbitrary and
tyrannical, I will agree with them."[2]   Even Morris was con-
strained to admit that the proposition to demand twenty-
seven thousand dollars was a most arbitrary proceeding.

On the third reading of the bill, on the eighteenth of the
month, King, Ellsworth, Strong and Izard urged its passage
on the grounds of self-defense, self preservation and self-
interest.   Maclay, in opposition, reminded Congress that the
Rhode Island convention was about to re-assemble.   The
bill was evidently prepared in anticipation of that event, to
inspire the people of that state with terror.   "It was meant,"
said he, "to be used in the same way that a robber does a
dagger, or a highwayman a pistol."[3]   The bill was passed,
however, and sent to the House.

There, in committee of the whole, Page, of Virginia, moving to discharge the committee, spoke long and earnestly
against the measure.   He argued that, as the Rhode Island
convention was soon to meet, there should be nothing before
Congress to influence their choice.   Pressure would display
a wrong spirit.   In such a case, said he, "she will come with
so bad a grace into the Union that she must be ashamed
when she enters it, and the independent states must blush
when they receive her.   It becomes this House to pity the
frailty of the weak and ignorant, who know not the blessings
of our new government, to forgive the perverse and wicked

---

[1] Maclay's *Journal*, 263.   [2] *Ibid.*, 264.   [3] *Ibid.*, 266.

who oppose it from base principles, and to show generous indulgence to that jealous, cautious, republican spirit, which indeed we should cherish and revere."[1] With such a spirit manifested in Congress, it seemed to him that Rhode Island would see her interest in joining the Union, but if it should appear that Congress was more anxious to complete the Union than to preserve the rights of freemen, and the principles of the revolution, what should Rhode Island expect? In such a case would not their resistance be applauded by republicans throughout the world? Love of freedom, patriotism and humanity was invoked in an address concluding with this fervid appeal, " Let us not treat a sister state in the very manner we disdained to be treated by Great Britain."[2] The influence combined with policy prevailed, and the bill was made the order of a future day.

Rhode Island had not been permitted to remain in ignorance of the share of the time occupied in the discussion of . her affairs. Nearly every issue of the newspapers contained hints of coercion. A representative in Congress from Massachusetts wrote, on April twenty-sixth, " I have the utmost confidence in her good sense, and that she will voluntarily relieve us from all those disagreeable consequences which might result from her longer continuance in her elopement."[3] Another Congressman remarked that "the safety of this government and the collection of its revenues may require that measures disagreeable to your citizens should be adopted."[4] News of the introduction of the resolution against Rhode Island, which was first received in that state by the publication of a letter in the *Gazette*, was at first

[1] *Annals of Congress*, ii, 1672.   [2] *Ibid.*, ii, 1674.

[3] *United States Chronicle*, May 27, 1790.

[4] *Providence Gazette*, May 22, 29, 1790; *United States Chronicle*, May 20, 1790.

deemed preposterous, but subsequent advices confirmed its truth.[1]

Again, it was declared that, should Rhode Island reject the constitution, or adjourn without reaching a vote, "The government here will be justified even to the discerning people in Rhode Island, in proposing measures which under other circumstances might be thought severe."[2] By another Congressman it was announced that hope of Rhode Island was no longer entertained, and that the course to be taken to cut off commercial relations with her was already planned. Intimating that should coercion be attempted it would be carried through, he said, " I should suppose that your opposers would readily see the prudence of preventing coercion . . . What is now before the senate, and which is supported by a majority perfectly disposed to bring your state into the union, ought to be made known in your state. The people in the back parts ought no longer to be deceived with the idea, that the condition of single independence is an eligible one."[3]

It was in the sight of this threatening array that the Rhode Island convention assembled on the twenty-fourth of May. To oppose the influence thus exerted, the Anti-Federalists relied on the oft expressed sentiments of the majority, and on the prestige of the late sweeping victory in the state. A quorum was not secured until the twenty-sixth.[4] As the delegates came slowly into Newport, many of them brought instructions in respect both to the amendments and to the bill of rights, as well as to adoption. North Kingstown instructed her delegates not to vote for ratification until their proceedings should have been again laid be-

[1] *United States Chronicle*, May 20, 1790; *Providence Gazette*, May 15, 27, 1790.

[2] *United States Chronicle*, May 20, 1790.

[3] *Ibid.*, May 20, 1790.   [4] *Ibid.*, June 3, 1790.

fore the town, and the Rhode Island amendments adopted
by Congress.[1]   Middletown, Portsmouth and Providence
were, on the other hand, firm for ratification.[2]   In case of
rejection or adjournment before ratification, the latter town
instructed her delegates to enter a spirited protest.   So intense was the sentiment there against rejection, that the instructions continue, " It is our opinion that, on the rejection
of the said constitution or further delay of a decision thereon,
the respective towns of the state have a right to make application to the Congress of the United States, for the same
privileges and protection which are afforded to the towns
under their jurisdiction, and, in such case, the delegates
from this town be, and they are hereby, fully authorized and
empowered to meet with the delegates from the town of
Newport, and the delegates from such other towns as may
think proper to join them, for the purpose of consulting and
devising such mode of application as they in their wisdom
may think proper, and to carry the result of their deliberations into immediate effect, and that they make report of
their doings to the next town meeting." [3]

This was a unique proceeding.   Separation from England
had followed a difference of opinion.   Separation from the
other states was now maintained by Rhode Island on account
of a difference of opinion.   But to carry the process of dis-
integration to its logical extent, involving the secession of
towns from the state, was heretofore unheard of.   The sensation caused by such action demanded some explanation
from the towns in question.   A justification was attempted
in a set of ingenious, though inconsistent resolutions, wherein
it was assumed that at the declaration of independence the

---

[1] *Papers Relating to the Adoption of the Constitution*, 96.

[2] *Ibid.*, 96–8.

[3] *Ibid.*, 93; *Providence Town Meeting Records*, vii, 169.

people reverted to a state of natural liberty. But the people of Rhode Island had never expressly or impliedly consented to assume any authority or sovereignty separate from the other states, and owed no allegiance to their present government so long as it is disconnected with the other states. On the refusal of the convention to be reunited with the other states, which a rejection of the constitution would virtually be, the people, or any group of them, would be justified in exercising their natural rights for the security of life, liberty, and property.[1] But this was the natural result of the prevailing political tendencies and theories. If the state was the result of a social compact, the right by which the colonies broke the compact with England must remain to the people of Providence to break their compact with the other towns. Whether the announcement of this policy was intended as anything more than a club with which to drive the convention, the action of that body in ratifying the constitution has left in doubt.

The amendments and bill of rights, imposing as they were in length, were deemed insufficient by many towns. Five towns, clinging to the idea that senators were delegates from the state governments, demanded that each state have power to recall its own, and that their remuneration be a charge to the state.[2] Charlestown desired that the executive and judicial functions of the senate be abridged, and that judicial powers in general be more clearly defined and separated from those of the states.[3] Richmond asked that power be given Congress to take immediate action against slavery. Providence entered a protest against any attempt to strike out the amendment on that subject already proposed.[4] From the opening of the convention the policy of the Federalists

[1] *United States Chronicle*, May 27, 1790.
[2] *Papers Relating to the Adoption of the Constitution*, 96, 98, 99.   [3] *Ibid.*, 98.
[4] *Ibid.*, 99; *Providence Town Meeting Records*, vii, 168.

was to press for a vote on the constitution. The Anti-
Federalists, continuing their original plan of inaction, were
working for adjournment, but were defeated on the first vote
by a majority of nine.[1] The committee on amendments,
having taken into consideration the instructions given by the
towns, brought in on the second day an amendment vesting
in the state legislatures the power of paying and recalling
senators.[2] A committee appointed to draw up further amendments presented three. The first of these gave Congress
power to enact laws for the settlement of paupers; the second prohibited Congress from conferring any exclusive
privileges of commerce, and the third provided that the yeas
and nays on any question should be entered on the journal
of either house of Congress at the request of two members.
The committee further recommended that the amendment
already proposed providing for the ratification of the amendments offered by Congress, be stricken out, and that instead
a recommendation be made to the legislature in favor of all
of them except the second.[3]

The debate continued until the afternoon of the twenty-
eighth, when, at the request of a member from Portsmouth,
the convention adjourned until the next afternoon, that he
might get further instructions from his constituency.[4] The
instructions which he received simply reiterated those given
in February and April, and further declared that their town
would hold itself blameless for any evil consequences which
might follow rejection.[5] The Middletown delegation had
taken advantage of the adjournment to secure for themselves
further instructions for ratification.[6]

[1] *United States Chronicle*, June 3, 1790.
[2] *Minutes of the Convention.*   [3] *Ibid.*
[4] *United States Chronicle*, June 3, 1790.
[5] *Papers Relating to the Adoption of the Constitution*, 94, 97; *Minutes of the Convention.*
[6] *Minutes of the Convention.*

The question of ratification was reached about five o'clock on Saturday, May twenty-ninth, and was carried by a vote of thirty-four to thirty two.[1]   The formal act ratifying the constitution, and embodying the Bill of Rights and amendments proposed, was soon passed, and after recommending the amendments proposed by Congress, except the second, the convention adjourned *sine die*.

The news of the ratification of the constitution was received with the greatest demonstrations of joy in many parts of the state, for even those who had been in opposition had begun to weary of the suspense.   The governor lost no time in communicating the news of ratification to the President, and a special session of the legislature was at once called. That body proceeded to the election of senators, and the people at their town meetings in August chose their first representative in Congress.   Rhode Island was once more one of the United States of America.

[1] *Minutes of the Convention.*

CHAPTER VI

CONCLUSION

So did Rhode Island at last ratify the constitution and once more place herself in that harmony with her neighbors which had been broken since her refusal to grant the impost of 1781. But attached to and forming a part of Rhode Island's act of ratification was a Bill of Rights of eighteen articles. It was "Under these impressions and declaring that the rights aforesaid cannot be abridged or violated, and that the explanations aforesaid are consistent with the said constitution, and in confidence that the amendments hereinafter mentioned will receive an early and mature consideration, and, conformably to the fifth article of said constitution, speedily become a part thereof," that the act of ratification was passed. Accompanying the act were also twenty-one amendments for the incorporation of which in the constitution the representatives of the state in Congress were instructed to labor.[1]

In publishing a bill of rights, Rhode Island was following the example of New York, Virginia and North Carolina.[2] In their declarations the states had once more reiterated the fundamentals of English liberty. Many of their statements appear in the early state constitutions, and many are contained in that bill of rights which we know as the first ten amendments to the constitution of the United States. The declarations of the four states are remarkably similar. Not

[1] *Appendix A.*
[2] Elliot's *Debates* (*Ed. 1836*), i, 361; iii, 592; iv, 250.

one of those offered by Rhode Island is peculiarly its own. Each provision had been adopted or proposed by at least one of the states which had preceded her.

In proposing amendments Rhode Island had been preceded by Massachusetts, South Carolina, New Hampshire, Virginia, New York and North Carolina. In each of these states there was a party actively opposed to the constitution, a party so strong that it was only by a compromise in the form of proposed amendments that ratification could be secured. It is in the amendments offered by the states that an attempt was made to give expression to the most serious objections of the opposing party.

A comparative study of the amendments offered should then reveal not only the cause of their hesitancy, but whether there were advanced in Rhode Island objections peculiar to that state. Examination shows that the twenty-one articles offered by Rhode Island were also proposed by certain of the other states offering amendments as follows:

By Rhode Island and 6 others 2, viz., 2, 8.
"   "   "   5   "   2, "   1, 20.
"   "   "   4   "   1, "   12.
"   "   "   3   "   2, "   10, 15.
"   "   "   2   "   2, "   5, 11.
"   "   "   1   "   7, "   3, 7, 13, 14, 16, 18, 21.
"   " alone   5, "   4, 6, 9, 17, 19.

Whenever one state only is found advancing an amendment with Rhode Island, that state is in all but one instance New York.[1]

The instances in which the action of a considerable number of states was similar to that of Rhode Island can scarcely be said to contain anything distinctively characteristic of that state. In the case of amendments proposed by two

[1] Elliot's *Debates* (*Ed. 1836*), i, 363.

other states (in each case Virginia and North Carolina),[1] viz.: the 5th and 11th, a closer study may be of interest. The fifth, which seeks to cut off the retroactive power of the United States courts, "except in disputes between states about their territory, disputes between persons claiming lands under grants of different states, and debts due to the United States,"[2] should be read in connection with the third, which was also proposed by North Carolina.

The eleventh may be considered in connection with the tenth, also proposed by North Carolina and Virginia.[3] The one provided for the publication of the receipts and expenditures of the government annually, while the second called for the publication of the journal of each house at similar intervals. These arose out of a dislike of secrecy in governmental affairs. The custom of the utmost publicity of both the accounts and the journals has shown amendment in this direction to be unnecessary.

Seven of Rhode Island's amendments were proposed by one other state only.[4] In each case except that of the third the other state was New York. When that state took up the consideration of the constitution it was believed, even by the friends of the measure, that more than one-half of the state was opposed. In this condition of affairs, it was only by the superb leadership of Hamilton, supported by Jay and Robert R. Livingston, that this majority was overcome.

Of these amendments the seventh, prohibiting the laying of a capitation or poll tax, time has proven to have been unnecessary. This should be read in connection with the eighth and ninth, the former of which appeared in substance in the amendments of all six of the states, and prohibited the laying of direct taxes except after the failure of requisi-

---

[1] Elliot's *Debates* (*Ed. 1836*), iii, 594; iv, 250.   [3] *App. A.*

[2] Elliot's *Debates* (*Ed. 1836*), iii, 594; iv, 250.   [4] *App. A.*

tions upon the states. Though at that time this was so generally deemed necessary, experience has shown that our
government seldom resorts to this form of taxation. To
these safeguards Rhode Island alone would have added her
ninth amendment forbidding the laying of direct taxes except with the consent of two-thirds of the states. All three
of these amendments indicate an unwillingness to place
in untried hands so important a function as taxation. It
was the same spirit that had defeated the proposed impost
of 1781. In the matter of borrowing money as well as in
taxation distrust was shown when Rhode Island and New
York sought to limit the power of Congress by requiring a
two-thirds vote on any proposition to borrow money. On
the question of declaring war the same two states would
have required a similar two-thirds vote. Again the same
policy impelled both states to place a powerful weapon in
the hands of obstructionists, in the form of an amendment
which provided for entering the yeas and nays on the journal
at the wish of any two members.

In the history of this period, again and again there is evidence of a misunderstanding of the true theory of representation. The congresses and assemblies of the Revolution
had been composed of instructed delegates. The articles
of confederation, creating simply a delegated government,
furnished a present exemplification of the principle. The
now generally accepted theory of representation found no
place in their political science. The proposition to make
representatives independent of the state was a marked innovation, but to extend this immunity from instruction to
senators who were supposed to represent the state as a unit
was not to be thought of. The right to give instruction
must be retained as a safeguard, but how could this be made
effective without the accompanying power of recall?

To preserve judicial independence, New York and Rhode

Island did not deem it sufficient that the judges should be removable only by impeachment, but would have provided further that no judge of the Supreme Court should hold any other office under the United States or a state. To preserve the distinction between state and federal officers, and to prevent federal influence from intruding itself, Rhode Island insisted on a provision that no officer appointed by the President or Congress should hold office under a state.

The state's third amendment, which was also proposed by North Carolina, after declaring that in suits to which a state might be a party, the jurisdiction of the United States courts should not extend "to criminal prosecutions, or to authorize any suit by any person against a state," proceeds to secure the state against the interference of Congress or of the judiciary "with any one of the states, in the redemption of paper money already emitted, and now in circulation, or in liquidating or discharging the public securities of any one state; that each and every state shall have the exclusive right of making such laws and regulations for the before-mentioned purposes as they shall think proper." In the case of each state this latter part is traceable to the paper money influence which had shown itself powerful in North Carolina only less than in Rhode Island. Rhode Island was still in the hands of that paper money party which, after passing a series of abominable laws and robbing the state of her fair name, had suffered defeat at the hands of the state judiciary. For more than two years this party had struggled successfully against a constitution which created an independent judiciary capable of checking their legislative vagaries. Now, when they were forced to yield, this amendment appears as a last attempt to protect themselves. There is also in this an expression of fear that the federal judiciary would encroach too far on the sphere of state action.

The question of the suability of a state had awakened an

animated discussion in some quarters previous to 1789. In the Virginia convention Madison and Marshall,[1] and Hamilton in the Federalist,[2] had denied this interpretation of the power of the Supreme Court. When this question was raised in a concrete form by a decision of the court,[3] similar fears were aroused in Georgia, Maryland, New York and Massachusetts.

It now remains to look at the five amendments which Rhode Island alone proposed. Here if anywhere may we hope to find formulated to some extent the objections of the opponents of the measure. The ninth has already been considered in connection with the eighth, and found to be but an additional attempt to limit the taxing power of Congress. Rhode Island alone of the states sought to protect her rights by making the constitution more difficult of amendment. Owing to the difficulty of securing amendments as now provided, the tendency has been to seek for an easier method of procedure; but Rhode Island, realizing that her puny size would count but little among the larger states, sought in her fourth amendment to require after 1793 the assent of eleven of the states to any amendment which might be offered. In the Federal Convention, Roger Sherman had objected to the three-fourths provision for ratification, and was so strongly supported that a compromise was inserted in the form of a provision that no state should without its consent be deprived of its equal representation in the senate.[4]

The sixth amendment provided that no one should be compelled to do military duty but by voluntary enlistment except in time of invasion. This might be construed with the twelfth, which forbade the maintenance of a standing

---

[1] Elliot's *Debates*, iii, 533, 555.   [2] *Federalist*, no. 81.

[3] Chisholm vs. Georgia, 2 *Dallas*, 419.   [4] Elliot's *Debates*, v, 551.

army, as an expression of a vague dread of militarism and arbitrary power.

The seventeenth amendment, a movement for the immediate prohibition of the slave trade, was the product of a long and heated discussion in the state convention. There was manifested a strong hostility to slavery on moral grounds. The opponents of the measure argued that this was a question for each state to settle. Rhode Island could settle it for herself, and the southern states could do the same. It was pointed out that to arrive at any agreement all sections must yield something, and as a concession to the south this should not be pressed. As a compromise it was decided to adopt the vague wording of the amendment.

Her nineteenth amendment was perhaps unique, since it embodied an attempt to secure a national law of settlement. Why this was proposed was not evident, but it would seem that some action on the part of other states was anticipated whereby Rhode Island would be forced to bear more than her share of taxation for this purpose.

Having reviewed those amendments which in any measure bear the stamp of Rhode Island origin, what peculiarities appear? The amendments bear the impress of the genius of the state where they were proposed. Offered by the states most deeply imbued with the ideas of state rights, their purpose in each case was to preserve the individuality of the state and to exclude federal power. Rhode Island adds, if anything, a nervous dread of the overweening power of her larger neighbors, either singly or combined, in Congress.

A point has now been reached from which it may be possible to form a proper estimate of Rhode Island's relations to the Union during the Revolutionary period. In the beginning Rhode Island was the product of persecution, civil and religious. The colony was founded by men of advanced and peculiar views. They were specimens of the Puritanical aftermath of the Reformation, in whom the doctrine of individual judgment was carried to its logical results. Without a presentiment that they were founding a commonwealth for posterity, they established themselves in settlements apart and disconnected, which united their political fortunes only for self-preservation. Each step in departure from that simplest form of democracy which found favor in the infant communities was taken only after mature deliberation and with the utmost caution. Everywhere the rights of individuals and of the various communities were most carefully guarded. The popular assembly, the popular initiative and referendum, frequent election of officials, as well as the preponderating influence of the legislature, all bear witness of their solicitude.

The pressure of hostile neighbors neutralized to an extent the centrifugal tendencies of the founders. Resistance, long and stubborn, to the hostility of Massachusetts and Connecticut as evinced by their repeated attempts to gain jurisdiction over the territory of Rhode Island, laid the foundations of a deep sense of individuality as a Commonwealth.

Liberty was the presiding genius of the spiritual life of the colony. Freedom of conscience, proclaimed by the founders, formed the corner-stone of both the spiritual and the political structure. Never in the course of her history did the colony lose sight of this principle. But at the same time this liberty of conscience, giving as it did full play to personal opinion, could not but heighten that other characteristic of the colony, individualism. Individualism, democracy, and liberty of conscience, these were the guiding principles of the colony's growth. Under them developed a community whose material interests were centered in agriculture and commerce. While the conditions of colonial life necessitated that the tilling of the soil should be the most

widespread occupation, yet the excellent maritime position
of the colony early led men to seek in commerce the compe-
tence which a stubborn soil refused. In this respect she was
no mean rival of the greater colonies of Massachusetts and
New York. In the excitement attendant upon the paper
money craze of the first half of the eighteenth century, and
the Ward-Hopkins controversy of a few years later, a political sense had been developed along the line of partisan politics.

Under these conditions Rhode Island entered the Revolution. During the period of intellectual resistance to the
British ministry, during the subsequent resort to physical
force, in the breaking of the political ties which bound the
colonies to Great Britain, and in all attempts to form a con-
federate government, Rhode Island had not simply acqui-
esced in the action of her neighbors, but had been found in
the lead in proposing new measures. It was in the attempt
to give to the confederation the semblance at least of life,
that the peculiar traits of the colony asserted themselves.
Whatever was the intention of the other states, whatever
may be the conclusions of modern political science, it is certain that the people of Rhode Island considered that neither
the Continental Congress nor the Congress of the Confederation had sovereignty over them, but that sovereignty passed
from Great Britain directly to the several states, where it still
remained. The proposition to grant Congress power to raise
a revenue by an impost and to regulate commerce, roused all
the latent jealousy of outside authority, as well as that state
rights sentiment which so largely tempered the earlier efforts
toward nationalism. This display of an independent spirit
was heightened by the conviction that in the western lands
was a source of revenue not fraught with danger to the individual states. The particular form of impost was obnoxious
because of the misapprehension of underlying economic

principles. It was the moment at which the two industrial classes fancied that their interests diverged. It was the country party, conservative and particularistic, which was opposed to the project. Though baffled for a long time, the commercial interests finally won their point, but all too late to be of service to the dying confederation.

But though commerce won in this instance, it was at a fearful cost. It proved to be the spark that lighted fires prepared in the years following the Revolution. The distressing economic conditions of the decade following the declaration of independence, leading to outbursts of disorder in many states, resulted in Rhode Island in a desire for paper money. The party of unrest, seeking in a blind way for relief from their pitiable financial condition, was made up of the same class who had opposed the granting of greater powers to Congress, the country party. Gathering to themselves all the dissatisfied and turbulent spirits, they smote the commercial power and for years held it beneath their feet. The extremities to which they carried their measures of repudiation reveal the intensity of their feelings. All the examples of colonial and Revolutionary days were surpassed. The advocates of honest money and honest dealing were forced to see their state burdened with a reputation for commercial dishonor as abhorrent to them as it was fatal to their trade.

In the midst of this dark period the Federal convention was called. The avowed object of the convention met with small favor from the dominant party in Rhode Island. Much less did the results of their labors, when they assumed constituent powers and produced a new frame of government. Every interest of the dominant power was opposed to the new proposition. The prospect of a strong national government, which would exercise an unknown degree of power over the localities, had no attractions for a party conscious of the unrighteousness of its cause. Fearing a check upon its mad career, the paper money party set itself to oppose the new project at every step. Standing beside them, and in most cases identical with them, were those who were anti-federalist from principle; men who were conservative and wished to continue in the old way, though before their eyes that old way was leading to anarchy. The spirit of individualism and democracy pure and simple impelled others to look for a change. Such men could only see the dangers of the plan, the creation of a power above that of the state, which should collect taxes in the state and which might in some way swallow up the identity of a commonwealth so small as Rhode Island. By such an arrangement it was apprehended that her neighbors, from whom the state had been taught by experience to expect no favors, might be given opportunity to encroach upon her. By yielding her independence it was feared too that her liberties, civil and religious, so amply secured in her charter, might be wrested from her under the new form of government.

It was a combination of such motives, dishonorable though they may have been on the part of a few, yet in the case of a majority honest but mistaken, that kept Rhode Island out of the Federal convention. The party of paper money and anti-federalism, seeing its financial structure crumble like the sands on which it was built, wreaked their otherwise impotent wrath on the new constitution. All the suspicion toward the other classes of society, all the jealousy of external domination, all the tendency to particularism existent in the community, showed itself in opposition to the measure. Like an army without a leader, the friends of the constitution sought repeatedly, but in vain, to rally their forces. It is well known that in several states, notably Massachusetts, New York, Virginia and North Carolina, this opposition was at first in the majority. There too the struggle was fierce and long. It was only by the efforts of able leaders that this majority was overcome. It was through the lack of such leaders that Rhode Island was placed at a great disadvantage. There no Hamilton or Jay, no Madison or Randolph, arose to lead the federalist minority to victory.

Intrenched behind ignorance, suspicion and prejudice, their opponents stood firm. In April, 1789, when the federal union had become a fact, the people of Rhode Island began to realize what it meant to be outside that union. The ranks of opposition wavered but held on grimly. Congress, at first disposed to grant Rhode Island time for consideration, when it became involved in partisan strife, yielded to party interest and and resolved to end the suspense. A well-framed resolution and the unofficial statements of the probable consequences of persistence were sufficient to convince the opposition that the present dangers of refusal were greater than the possible future dangers of ratification, and the struggle was brought to a close.

In passing judgment on this episode in history, the worst that can be said is that it was the result of mistaken judgments by men of narrow horizon. This result was nothing abnormal, neither was it the product of any inherent tendency to anarchy or perversity in the people of the state. It was the natural outcome of the conditions of the times, reacted upon by the Rhode Island character which had been forming since 1636. It was the outcropping of the undying love of the people of the state for democracy and liberty, and their jealousy of all authority outside their own boundaries.

APPENDIX A

1. THE United States shall guarantee to each state its sovereignty, freedom and independence, and every power, jurisdiction and right which is not by this Constitution expressly delegated to the United States.

2. That Congress shall not alter, modify or interfere in the times, places or manner of holding elections for senators and representatives, or either of them, except when the legislature of any state shall neglect, refuse, or be disabled by invasion or rebellion, to prescribe the same, or in case when the provision made by the state is so imperfect as that no consequent election is had, and then only until the legislature of said state shall make provision in the premises.

3. It is declared by the convention, that the judicial power of the United States, in cases in which a state may be a party, does not extend to criminal prosecutions, or to authorize any suit by any person against a state; but to remove all doubts or controversies respecting the same, that it be especially expressed as a part of the Constitution of the United States, that Congress shall not, directly or indirectly, either by themselves or through the judiciary, interfere with any one of the states, in the redemption of paper money already emitted, and now in circulation, or in liquidating or discharging the public securities of any one state; that each and every state shall have the exclusive right of making such laws and regulations for the before mentioned purpose as they shall think proper.

4. That no amendments to the Constitution of the United States, hereafter to be made, pursuant to the fifth article, shall take effect, or become a part of the Constitution of the United States, after the year one thousand seven hundred and ninety-three, without the consent of eleven of the states heretofore united under the confederation.

5. That the judicial power of the United States shall extend to no possible case where the cause of action shall have originated before the ratification of this Constitution, except in disputes between the states about their territory, disputes between persons claiming lands under grants from different states, and debts due to the United States.

6. That no person shall be compelled to do military duty other than by voluntary enlistment, except in cases of general invasion, anything in the second paragraph of the sixth article of the Constitution, or any law made under the Constitution to the contrary, notwithstanding.

7. That no capitation or poll tax shall ever be laid by Congress.

8. In cases of direct taxes, Congress shall first make requisitions on the several states to assess, levy and pay their respective proportions of such requisitions, in such way and manner as the legislatures of the several states shall judge best, and in case any state shall neglect or refuse to pay its proportion pursuant to such requisition, then Congress may assess and levy such state's proportion, together with interest, at the rate of six per cent. per annum, from the time prescribed in such requisition.

9. That Congress shall lay no direct taxes without the consent of the legislatures of three-fourths of the states in the union.

10. That the journals of the proceedings of the Senate and House of Representatives shall be published as soon as conveniently may be, at least once in every year, except such

parts thereof relating to treaties, alliances, or military, as in their judgment require secrecy.

11. That regular statements of the receipts and expenditures of all public money shall be published at least once a year.

12. As standing armies in time of peace are dangerous to liberty, and ought not to be kept up, except in cases of necessity, and as at all times the military should be under strict subordination to the civil power, that therefore no standing army or regular troops shall be raised or kept up in time of peace.

13. That no moneys be borrowed on the credit of the United States, without the assent of two-thirds of the senators and representatives present in each house.

14. That Congress shall not declare war without the concurrence of two-thirds of the senators and representatives present in each house.

15. That the words " without the consent of Congress," in the seventh clause of the ninth section of the first article of the Constitution, be expunged.

16. That no judge of the Supreme Court of the United States shall hold any other office under the United States, or any of them ; nor shall any officer appointed by Congress or by the President and Senate of the United States, be permitted to hold any office under the appointment of any of the states.

17. As a traffic tending to establish or continue the slavery of any part of the human species is disgraceful to the cause of liberty and humanity ; that Congress shall, as soon as may be promote and establish such laws and regulations as may effectually prevent the importation of slaves of every description, into the United States.

18. That the state legislatures have power to recall, when they think it expedient, their federal senators and to send others in their stead.

19. That Congress have power to establish a uniform rule of inhabitancy or settlement of the poor of different states, throughout the United States.

20. That Congress erect no company with exclusive advantages of commerce.

21. That when two members, shall move, or call for the yeas and nays on any question, they shall be entered on the journal of the houses respectively.

Done in Convention at Newport, in the county of Newport, in the State of Rhode Island and Providence Plantations, the 29th day of May, in the year of our Lord, one thousand seven hundred and ninety, and the fourteenth year of the independence of the United States of America.

By order of the Convention: signed,

DANIEL OWEN, *President.*

Attest, DANIEL UPDIKE, *Secretary.*

BIBLIOGRAPHY.

Acts of the Commissioners of the United Colonies of New England. See Plymouth Colony Records, vols. ix and x.

Acts and Laws of His Majesty's Colony of Rhode Island and Providence Plantations. Boston, 1719.

Acts and Laws of His Majesty's Colony of Rhode Island and Providence Plantations. Boston, 1719. Re-printed and edited by Sidney S. Rider. Providence.

Acts and Laws of His Majesty's Colony of Rhode Island and Providence Plantations in America. Newport, 1730.

Acts and Laws of His Majesty's Colony of Rhode Island and Providence Plantations in New England, in America. Newport, 1744-5.

[Acts and Laws of Rhode Island.] Supplement to the Digest of Laws of 1730. First Part. Probably published 1732.

Acts and Laws of His Majesty's Colony of Rhode Island and Providence Plantations in New England, in America. Newport, 1745.

Acts and Laws of His Majesty's Colony of Rhode Island and Providence Plantations in New England, in America, from Anno 1745 to Anno 1752. Newport, 1752.

Acts and Laws of the English Colony of Rhode Island and Providence Plantations in New England, in America. Newport, 1767.

Acts and Resolves of the General Assembly of Rhode Island. Original MS. Volumes in State Archives, Providence.

American Archives, Fourth Series. A Documentary History of the English Colonies in North America, from the King's Message to Parliament of March 7, 1774, to the Declaration of Independence by the United States. Edited by M. St. Clair Clarke and Peter Force. 6 vols. Washington. 1837.

American Museum, The. Edited by Matthew Carey. 12 vols. Philadelphia, 1787-92.

American State Papers. Documents Legislative and Executive of the Congress of the United States, from the First Session of the First, to the Second of the Twenty-second Congress inclusive. Edited by Walter Lowrie and M. St. Clair Clarke. 1st Series, 21 vols.; 2d Series, 17 vols. Washington, 1832-61.

Ames, Fisher, Works of. Edited by Seth Ames. 2 vols. Boston, 1854.

Annals of Congress. The Debates and Proceedings in the Congress of the United States. 42 vols. 1789-1824. Washington, 1834-56.

Arnold, Samuel Greene. History of the State of Rhode Island and Providence Plantations. 2 vols. New York, 1859-78.

Bacon, Matthew. A New Abridgment of the Law. 5 vols. Fourth Edition. London, 1778.

Bancroft, George. History of the Formation of the Constitution of the United States of America. 2 vols. New York, 1882.

Bancroft, George. History of the United States. 5 vols. New York, 1883.

Boston Gazette.

Bradford, Alden. History of Massachusetts, 1764–1820. 3 vols. Boston, 1822.

Brown, Moses. Private Papers of. (MS.) 18 vols. (In library of Rhode Island Historical Society.)

Coxe, Brinton. An Essay on Judicial Power and Unconstitutional Legislation. Philadelphia, 1893.

Documents Relating to the Colonial History of New York. Edited by E. B. O'Callaghan. Albany, 1856–81.

[Elliot's Debates.] The Debates in the several State Conventions on the adoption of the Federal Constitution, with Journal of the Federal Convention, etc. 4 vols. Washington, 1836. 5 vols. Philadelphia, 1891.

[Force's Tracts.] Tracts and Other Papers Relating Principally to the Origin, Settlement and Progress of the Colonies in North America. Edited by Peter Force. 4 vols. Washington, 1836–46.

Foster, Theodore. Correspondence of. (MS.) 4 vols. (In library of Rhode Island Historical Society.)

Franklin, Benjamin. Complete Works of. Edited by John Bigelow. 10 vols. New York and London, 1887–8.

Gammell, William. Life of Samuel Ward.

Greene, George W. Life of Nathaniel Greene, Major-General in the army of the Revolution. 3 vols. New York, 1871.

Hamilton, Alexander. Works of. Edited by H. C. Lodge. 9 vols. New York, 1885–6.

[Hazard, State Papers.] Historical Collections, consisting of State Papers and other Authentic Documents, intended as material for an History of the United States of America. Edited by E. Hazard. 2 vols. Philadelphia, 1792.

Henning, W. W. The Statutes at Large; being a collection of all the laws of Virginia, from the first session of the legislature in 1619. Edited by W. W. Henning. 13 vols. Richmond, 1823.

Hopkins, Stephen. A true Representation of the Plan formed at Albany for uniting all the British Northern Colonies, in order to their common Safety and Defense, etc. Providence, 1755.

Jameson, John A. A Treatise on Constitutional Conventions. Chicago, 1887.

Journal of the American Congress, 1774–1782. 4 vols. Washington, 1823.

Laws of the State of North Carolina. 2 vols. Raleigh, 1821.

Maclay, William. Journal of, United States Senator from Pennsylvania, 1789–1791. Edited by Edgar S. Maclay. New York, 1890.

Madison, James. Papers of. Edited by H. D. Gilpin. 3 vols. Mobile, 1842.

Madison, James.   Letters and other Writings of.   Edited by II. D. Gilpin.   4 vols.
   Philadelphia, 1867.
McMaster, J. B.   History of the People of the United States from the Revolution
   to the Civil War.   5 vols.   New York, 1886——.
Magazine of American History.   29 vols.   New York, 1877–1893.
Massachusetts Colonial Records, 1628–1686.   Edited by N. B. Shurtleff.   5 vols.
   Boston, 1853–4.
Massachusetts Historical Society's Collections.
Narragansett Club Publications.   6 vols.   Providence, 1861–74.
[New York Colonial Documents.]   See Documents Relating to the Colonial His-
   tory of New York.
Papers Relating to the Adoption of the Constitution of the United States.   MS.
   folio, containing Votes taken in the Towns with reference to adoption of the
   Constitution; Instructions to the Representatives in the General Assembly
   respecting Representation, Paper Money and the new Constitution; Papers
   Relating to the Ratifying of the Constitutions of other States; Returns from
   the Several Towns to the Convention: Instructions from the Towns to Delegates in the Convention, to vote for and against the new Constitution;
   Minutes of the Convention for the Adoption of the Constitution; Miscellane-
   ous Papers relating to the Constitution.   1 vol.   MS.   Rhode Island Archives.   Providence.
Pennsylvania Archives, selected and arranged from Original Documents in the
   office of the Secretary of the Commonwealth, by Samuel Hazard, 1664–
   1790.   First Series.   12 vols.   Philadelphia, 1852–6.
Philolethes.   A Short Reply to Mr. Stephen Hopkins' Vindication and false Re-
   flections against the Governor and Council of the Colony of Rhode Island,
   etc.   Rhode Island, 1755.
[Plymouth Colony Records.]   Records of the Colony of New Plymouth in New
   England.   Edited by N. B. Shurtleff.   12 vols.   Boston, 1855–61.
Providence Gazette.
Providence Town Meeting Records.   10 MS. vols. in office of the City Clerk,
   Providence, R. I.   1692–1832.
Rhode Island Archives.   MS. collection of Letters to and from the Executive of
   the Colony and State.   Acts of the two houses of the General Assembly, and
   originals of other public documents.   Vols. preserved at the State House,
   Providence.
Rhode Island Historical Society's Manuscripts,   9 vols. and Index.
Rhode Island Historical Society's Publications.   Old series, 9 vols.   1827–97.
   New Series, 5 vols.   1893——.
Rhode Island Historical Tracts.   Edited by Sidney S. Rider.   24 vols.   Provi-
   dence, 1877——.
Rhode Island Reports.   Reports of Cases Argued and Determined in the Supreme
   Court of Rhode Island.   17 vols.   Boston and Providence, 1847–93.
Schedules and Acts and Resolves of the General Assembly.   Forming together a
   complete series, 1748-.   80 vols.

Secret Journals of the Acts and Proceedings of Congress, from the first meeting thereof to the dissolution of the Confederation by the adoption of the Constitution of the United States. 4 vols. Boston, 1821.

Staples, W. R. Rhode Island in the Continental Congress, with the Journal of the Convention that adopted the Constitution, 1765–1790. Prepared by William R. Staples. Edited by R. A. Guild. Providence, 1870.

Staples, W. R. Annals of the Town of Providence from its First Settlement to the Organization of the City Government in June, 1832. Providence, 1843.

Statutes of the Realm. Printed by Command of His Majesty, George the Third, in Pursuance of an Address of the House of Commons of Great Britain. 11 vols. London, 1810–1828.

Sparks, Jared. Diplomatic Correspondence of the American Revolution. Edited by Jared Sparks. 12 vols. Boston. 1829–30.

United States Chronicle, Political, Commercial and Historical. Providence, 1784–1804.

United States Reports. Reports of Cases Heard and Determined before the Supreme Court of the United States.

Updike, Wilkins. History of the Episcopal Church in Narragansett, Rhode Island, including a history of other Episcopal Churches in the State, with an Appendix containing a reprint of a work now extremely rare, entitled "America Dissected," by the Rev. J. McSparran, D. D. Newport, 1847.

Updike, Wilkins. Memoirs of the Rhode Island Bar. Boston, 1842.

Varnum, James M. The Case of Trevett against Weeden. On Information and Complaint for Refusing Paper Bills in Payment for Butcher's Meat in Market at Par with Specie. Tried before the Honorable Superior Court in the County of Newport, September Term, 1786. Providence, 1787.

Virginia State Papers. Calendar of, and Other Manuscripts. Edited by W. P. Palmer. 9 vols. Richmond, 1875–.

Washington, George. Writings of. Edited by W. C. Ford. 14 vols. New York and London, 1889–93.

Weeden, W. B. Economic and Social History of New England, 1620–1789. 2 vols. Boston and New York, 1891.

Winthrop, John. History of New England, 1630–1649. Edited by James Savage. 2 vols. Boston, 1853.

VITA.

FRANK GREENE BATES was born at Shawomet in the town of Warwick, Rhode Island His preparatory education was acquired in the English and Classical school (formerly Mowry and Goff's) at Providence, R. I. He entered Cornell University, and graduated in 1891 with the degree of Bachelor of Letters. He taught for a year at Billerica, Mass. After a short course at the Boston University Law School, he returned to Cornell University in September, 1893, for graduate work in history. In 1894 he was appointed examiner in American History there, and in the following year was elected Fellow in American History. During the year 1896–7, he was University Fellow in American History at Columbia University. While at Columbia he was under the instruction of Professors Osgood, Burgess, Dunning, Robinson and Goodnow, and was a member of the seminar in American Colonial History. He is a member of the American Historical Association, and has read papers before various historical societies. In June, 1897, Mr. Bates was elected Instructor in History and Political Science in Alfred University. In June, 1898, he was promoted to the rank of Assistant Professor in the same institution.